# Just Do This
# One Thing For Me

# Just Do This
# One Thing For Me

 by Laura Zimmermann

 a novel

 Dutton Books

**DUTTON BOOKS**

An imprint of Penguin Random House LLC, New York

First published in the United States of America by Dutton Books,
an imprint of Penguin Random House LLC, 2023

Visit us online at penguinrandomhouse.com.

Library of Congress Cataloging-in-Publication Data is available.

Printed in the United States of America

ISBN 9780593530337

1st Printing

LSCH
Design by Anna Booth
Text set in Legacy Serif ITC Pro

# Just Do This One Thing For Me

**Heads up, Reader:**

The main character of this book is not a fan of surprises, mostly because she likes to be in control.

Some readers are wary of surprises, too, mostly so that they are not caught off guard by topics to which they are sensitive.

If this is you, know that this story includes neglectful parents, unexpected death of a parent, grieving, and uncertainty about child custody.

# PROLOGUE

The last time I saw my mother, I mean *saw* saw her, in real life, she asked for a favor. Our interactions almost always included her asking for a favor and me saying yes, so for that to close out our relationship is some kind of poetry.

"Come on. I just need you to do this one thing for me, Drew." She should have worn a sensor that played it automatically as soon as I came within range, like those Halloween skeletons that threaten you when you come up for candy.

Somehow, she always seemed to believe it really was just one thing. As though I hadn't already done "one thing" for her an hour before, a hundred the week before, a hundred thousand in the years before that. Either she never remembered that I'd been doing one thing at a time for her since I was old enough to push the button on the knock-off Keurig (★★★★★, even a kindergartener can do it), or she was hoping that I wouldn't.

The last one was big, even for her. Neither of us could have known how big. That that one thing would change everything.

# Part One

# CHAPTER ONE

S o apparently you need a passport just to go to Mexico?!"

"It's a whole separate country," Carna said, peeling the top off one of my yogurts. Goodbye, mixed berry. It was a lost cause; if I wrote my name on the things I bought, everything besides the Easy Mac and frozen pizzas would have a DKH on it. Any fruit, vegetable, or vitamin my siblings consumed was because of me. Why I should feel nutritionally responsible for a fifteen-year-old who would rather bite off my actual head than make her own sandwich was unclear, but I seemed to be doing a pretty good job because she went for the low-sugar yogurt instead of Cocoa Puffs about half the time. "With an actual border. In some places there's a wall."

Mom scowled. Mexico's status as an independent nation was not news to her, but it was an inconvenience. Its stubborn insistence on not allowing people in with just a Wisconsin driver's license and good intentions might jeopardize what sounded like the best thing (three children not excluded) that ever happened to Heidi Hill.

What was important about Mexico's national sovereignty? By the unlikely and never-before-mentioned grace of god, a miracle had happened. A goddamn miracle: Justin Timberlake was playing a show on Monday night.

Did Justin know that he'd been Heidi's top celebrity crush since high school? Not likely. Did Justin know that they shared a birthday, even if she sometimes lied about the year? Or that when they turned thirty she'd had both of their names on her cake? Doubtful. Did Justin know that Heidi's friend Lisa-in-Phoenix was Facebook friends with a guy who worked for the event planning company and had the power to score passes for "really not that much if you think about what you're getting"? Now how would Justin know any of that?

But god/Oprah/the universe must have known, because JT wasn't even touring and, still, there was to be a concert. On New Year's Eve, even—the only actually fun holiday, according to Heidi. The surprise offer had suddenly popped into Lisa-in-Phoenix's inbox, which set off a mad flurry of last-minute planning and favor-asking.

Unfortunately, G/O/U were great at surprises but not so good at geography, because they'd booked Mom's miracle in the aforementioned sovereign republic of Mexico. And they must have been too immortal and invincible to bother researching state department rules and regulations because—

"Now I'm going to have to drive down to Chicago to get a passport. They can't do the rush ones in Madison."

"You can't just walk in and pick up a passport." I assumed so, anyway. There would be a process. And rules. Some kind of protocol to foil terrorists and domestic criminals fleeing prosecution and middle-aged fangirls who decide to leave the country at the drop of a DM as though they didn't have three minor children at home.

"I'm going to drive down tonight and be there when they open tomorrow. They said they can do it same day if you pay more and it's an emergency."

Lock glided into the kitchen. "Who's having a 'mergency?" he asked, unconcerned about whatever emergency we were talking about.

He was very chill for an eight-year-old, witness to a lifetime of Heidi starting fires and me putting them out. Lachlan was oblivious to stress.

He took a bag of Doritos from the cupboard. I plucked the bag out of his hands and replaced it with a clementine, nodding to the clock. We had a pact that we wouldn't start on chips until after noon over winter break, and there was still fifty minutes to fill with stuff that wasn't crap.

"Mom. If she doesn't get to see Justin Timberlake in Mexico, she's going to die," Carna said.

"You're going to drag Lock to Chicago?" I asked. It was almost three hours from Larch Leap, plus hours standing around some government office for rush travel documents. I took back Lock's clementine to puncture the peel with my thumbnail. He liked peeling, but couldn't quite start them without squashing them. Heidi looked at me blankly. "Carn and I are going to Malcolm's, remember?" Malcolm was our dad, but not our brother's, something the man pointed out testily any time we mentioned the kid.

"We can skip it!" Carna blurted.

"No, we can't." Makeup Christmas was one of a handful of annual in-person visits to our dad's. I'm pretty sure he wasn't any more excited about us coming up to the cabin than we were about going, but he kept careful track of the boxes on the custody agreement he and Heidi had printed off the internet instead of hiring real lawyers. I could blame him for being a subpar father and generally an asshole of a person, but I couldn't blame him for dotting all his *i*'s when it came to Heidi. Give that woman an inch and she'll take your truck.

(I mean that literally. Right before I turned sixteen, Malcolm was late on a couple of checks, and it ended with me getting a dumpy old mini-pickup he used to haul small loads of junk or deer carcasses.

They used to call those trucks "toys," but *toys* implies something fun instead of something unreliable, inefficient, and embarrassing. It worked out fine for him, though, because the reason he was short on cash in the first place was that he'd bought a brand-new F-250. We missed the day he christened it with deer guts.)

"You should take Lock with you," Mom said. "It'll be fun. You can bring skates."

I glared at her over Lock's head. Every part of that was a bad idea.

1. We should not take Lock with us. Malcolm didn't like children generally (which made him a real winner as a substitute teacher and a father), but he hated that kid in particular. It had nothing to do with Lachlan, who was actually pretty great for a second grader. Malcolm regarded our brother as a disease Heidi had picked up after they split.

2. It would not be fun. Mostly because of 1. Also because Lock was eight, and we were asking him to come to a makeup Christmas at which Carna and I would receive presents, and he would not. They would be terrible, unwanted presents we would immediately try to sell on eBay, but technically speaking they would be presents, and any present is better than no present when you are eight. If I gave my dad a year's notice, ten thousand dollars, and physically carried him into the toy aisle at Target, he would not wrap up a Super Ball to make the kid feel welcome. He would probably accuse him of stealing used charcoal briquets to drop into his own stocking.

3. We *could* bring skates, and we might even get Malcolm to plow a mini-rink on the lake, but it was still a bad idea. Carn and I played hockey until we got to high school, and fighting it out on the ice was one of the healthier forms of interaction between us. Lachlan, however, was the combination of fearless and clumsy that guaranteed a concussion or a broken something, and I'd rather be closer than thirty-five miles from a decent hospital when it happened. Or at least a hospital that didn't sponsor middle-school tackle and treat head injuries with a raw pork chop and Bayer aspirin. Besides, it was supposed to drop well below zero, and with the windchill you could get frostbite in minutes. No to skates.

No to the whole plan. But Heidi wasn't looking at me. She was smiling at my brother like she'd suggested an indoor waterpark in the Wisconsin Dells, and he had the moony, hopeful look that said he'd love me forever. Now if I said no, I'd look like I was rejecting him, and the one thing I always tried hardest to protect him from— even harder than from an all-Frito-Lay diet—was the idea that he was unwanted.

My mother's ability to skip straight to checkmate was something I did not inherit. I got stuck thinking through all the steps—the practical, reasonable, safe, legal steps—which gave her an unfair advantage.

"Fine," I said, trapped. "We'll take him. Where are your keys?" She looked confused. "You said I could take your car?"

"Yeah, but that was before I knew I needed it."

"It's supposed to snow tomorrow night. You know how the roads are up there."

"I don't want it to get all muddy."

"It's a literal Range Rover. It's super bougie if it's not muddy."

She shrugged. "Your dad hates it when I have nicer things than him."

One of Heidi's most annoying qualities is her immunity to shame. "Can you get Lock's stuff together?" I finally said to Carn.

"Eww, boy-ee," Carna said. When we're not actively fighting, she can be an ally, even though she's sure our team was assigned by birth rather than merit. Otherwise, she would have made it onto a better squad. "Let's pack you some layers, bud. It's cold on the Lesser Starling Chain of Lakes, and Mr. Malcolm does not believe in wasting propane on your little extremities." Lachlan giggled at *extremities*.

"He's going to be pissed when we show up with Lock," I said to Heidi, who was poking a fork into the **Sens-a-Toast toaster (★★★★★, toasts evenly)** slot to get her waffle. She'd managed to return the fancy **Breville (★★★★★, fits bagels, too)** to Kohl's without a receipt, so we were stuck with the off-brand one that seemed destined to electrocute somebody. I leaned over and pushed the little circle to pop the waffle into safe-grab territory before she killed herself and had to miss Justin Timberlake. She's never been that careful, my mom.

"It'll be fine. He's always pissed. At least you'll know why this time," she said, eating the Eggo like a giant cookie.

"It's kind of an unwritten rule. He doesn't invite Stephanya and we don't bring Lachlan."

"*Stephanya*," she said with a gag. "She just posted the ugliest painting. I'm not sure if it was supposed to be Malcolm or a bear wearing a flannel shirt." I should have known that Heidi would follow Malcolm's fiancée with one of her fake Instagram accounts. "Let me find it—"

"I hope Dad doesn't make Lock sleep out in the deer stand." While I complained, I rinsed out the yogurt container that Carna had left on the table and put Lock's peel in the compost pail I kept under the sink.

"Carna's slept up there."

"That's because Carna was mad. Not because Mal was. And not when it was fifteen below."

"I was kiiiidding. It's going to be fine." She watched me refill the water for the coffee maker. "Oh yeah—I need you back by noon on Saturday to take me to the airport." I slapped the reservoir down on the counter so hard it cracked.

"I'm supposed to drive all the way back from Starling and then an hour each way to the airport?"

"It's like fifty minutes."

"It's not." I was beginning to think a bit of a break from her would be worth the hassle. "And you'll be back Tuesday?"

"No . . ." she said hesitantly.

"Wednesday?"

She shrugged her shoulders. "There was a special deal if you went Saturday to Saturday."

"You're going to be gone for a week?" Any other almost-forty-year-old JT groupie who decided to ditch their kids last minute to bring some SexyBack to Wisconsin would return the next day, at least, like she had when she drove to Minnesota to see his Super Bowl halftime show. But Saturday to Saturday? And who does she assume will take care of everybody in the meantime? It's Gonna Be Me.

"I'm going to say I have a travel blog and see if they'll upgrade my room." She scrolled through her phone, calculating potential discounts and freebies.

"That's a really long time to be gone," I said.

Some shade of recognition dawned on her face. "Hmm, you're right. Seven nights is a lot . . . of changes of clothes. I'm going to need the bigger bag." She glanced out the window at the storage shed in the backyard, where we kept the suitcases. "Is it super cold out?" Probably,

Mother. We live in Wisconsin and it's December. It has a tendency to get nippy. "Are those your boots by the door?" She looked at me hopefully. That's a hard no, Heidi Hill. Get your own fucking suitcase.

But that's about as far as my taking a stand ever went. I would do everything else. I'd make sure there was real food in the house. I'd drive my siblings wherever they needed to go. I'd wake up Carna when school resumed. I'd make sure Lachlan peed before he went to bed and that the liners of his boots dried overnight if they were still wet from recess. I'd salt the driveway so the UPS driver wouldn't wipe out when she delivered boxes of free products traded for Heidi's 5-star reviews, and then I'd keep track of them until we needed to ship those same things out again to buyers on eBay. I'd do everything that needed doing, as I always did. And she would go see Justin Timberlake in Mexico.

"Fine. What should I do with Lachlan on New Year's?" I sighed.

"None of you ever do anything anyway." She managed to make it sound judgmental. Like our failure to party—on New Year's or any other Eve—was a disappointment to her. "Why don't you have people over here? Dard's got friends, right? Are they all as loud as him?" The people I'd inherited from Darden when we'd started dating the fall of junior year should have counted as my friends, too, but Heidi still considered them all part of the boyfriend package. "I don't care if people drink as long as they don't burn the house down." Not. The. Point. Of course she wouldn't care. I'd care.

The point was that in a healthy family, the parents wouldn't assume that the kids, the house, holidays, fresh produce, gas in the snowblower, safe toasters, rules about drinking, the DS-11 passport application form, etc. were my responsibility. "I'll leave you money," she added. "If I don't forget."

"I'll remind you."

"Send me one of your little bills." She meant Venmo requests for the things I picked up for the house. It was the only way to keep track of what she owed me. (Financially. There was no app to track what she owed me emotionally, socially, or developmentally.) It would be much more efficient if I just took over her bank accounts directly. We practically wouldn't need her at all.

"You know you're not going to be able to pick up and leave whenever you feel like it next year," I scolded. Everyone else's parents were obsessed with their babies going to college. My mom was obsessed with Justin Timberlake.

"Huh? Why not?"

My head practically burst into flames.

"Kidding! Oh my god, Drew, your face!" She put a hand on my shoulder and laughed hysterically. "But you're totally right," she said, calming down. "This really might be my last chance. 'Cause I'd never leave Lock overnight with your sister." She was trying flatter me, as though I wasn't familiar with her momnipulation. "And I mean Mexico? When it's so fricking cold here?! How perfect is that?" She dropped her jaw and opened her eyes wide, like a super excited emoji. I was the emoji with a completely straight line for a mouth. Or maybe the one without a mouth at all.

"Perfect for you," I mumbled. I closed my eyes and exhaled deeply, surprised at myself for still being surprised by her. For a second, she almost looked like she felt guilty, and I wonder now if in that second I could have simply said no, and nothing at all would have changed. If none of us would have.

But it passed, like it always did. And then she smiled, tilted her head, and said, "Come on. I just need you to do this one thing for me, Drew."

# CHAPTER TWO

The thing about being raised ("raised") by someone like Heidi Hill is that you *could* end up with a very slippery relationship with the rules ("rules"). Like my sister.

But I am a born rule follower, a truth teller, a doer of homework, and a dotter and crosser of all letters and symbols and punctuation that require dots and crosses. And I don't dot them with hearts or open circles. Just dots, like they are supposed to be dotted.

I meet deadlines. I set alarms. I make lists. I check them. Twice. I never cheat on anything (or anyone). I don't round corners. I don't round up. If it was only twenty-one hours since I'd had a fever, I would insist on waiting three more before going back to school, even if there was a class party that day.

Case in point, fourth grade:

"Aren't you getting on the bus?"

"I can't go until 10:07. That's when I checked yesterday and I didn't have a fever anymore. You have to drive me at 10:07."

"It's fricking freezing out. I don't want to wrap up the baby. Just stay home if you don't want to go."

"It's the Valentine's party!" I held up my sack of valentines: hearts, cut out of Post-it notes, each stuck to a Tootsie Pop. Heidi had not gotten any even though I'd put them on the list, because she hadn't remembered to take my list. So I'd improvised. I'd written each name in my best writing, double-checked everyone's spelling, and added what I thought was an appropriate sticker—dinosaurs for the dinosaur boys, soccer balls for the soccer girls, pencils or books for the ones I wasn't sure about. "Britelle's mom is organizing the party."

Heidi gagged. She gagged whenever Brenda Olziewski or any of the other do-everything mothers came up.

"Either get on the bus now or bring them in tomorrow."

"Tomorrow?! No one saves valentines for the next day."

"Then you'd better get moving."

"It won't be twenty-four hours till 10:07."

"Maybe your fever was already gone at 10:02 but you didn't take your temperature until 10:07. Or maybe it was 9:41. Did you think about that?"

I hadn't, but I didn't think you were supposed to guess about something as important as a fever. The policy was twenty-four hours.

"If she's not going, I'm not going," piped in a perfectly healthy Carna.

I might have gotten over the valentine exchange, but the idea that Carna would miss a day of school for nothing was just too much for me. I tied my scarf around my face to cover my germs during the bus ride, then hid in the school bathroom until ten, checking my head with my arm in case it got hot before I reported to class.

That's what kind of person I am. Or was, until I couldn't be anymore.

Before New Year's Eve, no one would have thought I was capable of doing anything besides exactly what I was supposed to do. And no one, including me, thought I was any good at lying. But maybe it was there in my genes all along, dormant, because once I got started, I caught on quickly.

# CHAPTER THREE

Carna thought we should tell Malcolm we were bringing Lachlan so he'd freak out and disinvite us. I thought we shouldn't, for that same reason. Once we got on the road, though, we didn't argue about it anymore, because the kid perched right between us playing selections from the *Trolls* soundtrack interspersed with old *NSYNC through the **MeJamz Personal Speaker (★★★★, sounds like you're at a club)** he got for Christmas, cranked all the way to hear over the noise of the truck. He inherited Heidi's musical taste.

"I like Mom's car better," he said.

"Pretend we're on an adventure," I said.

Malcolm's new deer sled, which wasn't wrapped except for a red ribbon tied to the rope, bobbed in the bed of the truck next to 150 pounds of bagged sand to keep us from spinning out on the ice. (Malcolm taught me that, so I can't really say he hasn't been a great father.) Our bags were back there, too, except for Lock's, which had two cans of Pringles and some dried apple slices (my addition) for the road.

It's two and a half hours to Malcolm's on a clear winter day. It's longer in the snow and even longer in summer because of the lake and cabin traffic. Lachlan loved the drive. He got both of his sisters at once, which was rare. He also had very unrealistic expectations about how much fun we'd have once we got there. (My prediction was zero fun or less-than-zero fun. His was ALL THE FUN.)

He had been misled about the cabin in Starling. The summer before, we'd gone up with Heidi and stayed for a few days while Mal drove to Montana for his father's funeral. We never knew that grandpa, and Malcolm hadn't had much to do with him in years, but he needed to "settle some things," which meant make sure that his stepmother didn't try to claim the property in Starling. Mal and Heidi had been getting along pretty well then, and he offered us the place while he was away. It wasn't really a favor—after some weekday break-ins around the lake he was paranoid about leaving it unattended—but it was a free cabin on a nice lake in a hot July.

We fished off the dock and messed around in the woods and ca-noed through the narrow passages from one lake to the next. Carn taught Lock how to cannonball off the tip of a canoe, and I trained him to be as patient as a Jedi with marshmallow roasting. We climbed up the deer stand because lunch tastes better up there. We found at least four different kinds of poop, all of which Lock thoroughly docu-mented on my phone—photos and, inexplicably, video. ("We call it *scat* when it's from an animal," I'd explained. "You want to make a scatapult and fling it into the lake?!" Carna had said.) We promised he could sleep outside, knowing he'd give up by eleven, when the dark amplifies the sounds of foxes into the sounds of monsters, and try to crawl in with Carn in the little bedroom, or fit himself onto the couch with me.

To be clear, all that was me, Carna, and Lock.

Mom spent the week lying on the dock playing Animal Cross-ing or driving the side-by-side to the 12-Point Grille and Buckshot Room (she likes to make sure she's still on the leaderboard of their an-cient *Ms. Pac-Man*) or searching through Malcolm's mail to calculate whether she should ask him for more child support (and concluding, "Man, your dad is broke. I don't know why he doesn't sell this place. People from Chicago pay buttloads to build up here.").

Northern Wisconsin lake country is not the same during the winter, though, especially when it's unseasonably cold even for a cold season. And Malcolm's cabin, which might feel rustic and welcoming if you let yourself in with the key hidden under the chainsawed bear sculpture and ignore the random piles of junk, can be a claustrophobic chamber of mildew and festering orneriness when he is actually there. The one good thing about winter is that the half-hour drive to the town bar shrinks to only fifteen minutes when you take a shortcut across the frozen lake.

The whole way up I tried to warn Lachlan that it wouldn't be like last time: "It's winter, so it's more of a quiet, inside time," I said, emphasizing *quiet*. "Remember, we're not going to take down the deer head and pose with it this time." "If you get hungry, don't say you're starving unless you want to learn about the Donner Party. I'll find you something." But Lachlan was deliriously excited to see if the winter poops looked any different from the summer poops, and if they flung farther when they were frozen.

"Does your guyses' dad like Justin Timberlake as much as Mom does?" he asked as we pulled off the gravel road onto Malcolm's long drive.

"Ummm, let's not mention where Mom's going, okay?" I said, stealing a glance at Carna.

"Why not?" Lachlan was no stranger to "let's not mention," and quite good at it, but it didn't squelch his curiosity. How to answer, though? Well, for starters, because if Malcolm thinks Heidi has more money than him he might rethink his child support. Also, because it made her look really irresponsible. And she was, but part of maintaining the uneasy peace was not giving either of them extra things to yell at each other about. And mostly, because I didn't want anyone to inform the boy that it's bad parenting to ditch a kid with teenagers and your cranky ex for a last-minute vacay. I wanted him to think we were a normal family till he was at least a little older.

"Because he would be jealous," Carna filled in when I didn't answer. "Malcolm would feel so sad that he didn't get to go." Carna was a natural liar. "What if we tell him that you came up with us because you wanted to see what the lake looked like when it was frozen?"

"I *do* want to see what the lake looks like when it's frozen!"

"Perfect. Then Drew doesn't even have to lie."

# CHAPTER FOUR

As soon as we parked, Lock was over my lap and out the door. The air was bracing, but he ran straight past the house to the edge of the lake. I plodded after, pulling my hat down till it reached the top of my jacket, but the wind found its way to my neck anyway.

"There are so many!" He stood on a log looking at the ice-fishing houses with wide eyes, like he had discovered a secret hobbit village that appeared only when the world froze. The fog of his breath confirmed the magic. "Which one is Mr. Malcolm's?"

"The ugly one that's not next to the other ones," I said, peeling off my mittens to zip up his jacket.

"It's like a little town," he whispered.

"Pretty sad town," I mumbled, pulling his hood over his head.

But I didn't mean it. Carna and I both loved the ice house from the time we first saw it. Malcolm had built it himself, like most things. And like most things Mal built, it was functional, not cute. But that made us love it more. It sat on smooth wooden runners that made it easy to pull on and off the ice. It was accidentally cozy, with a built-in bunk for naps if the fish weren't biting, and shelves for books, tackle, and airtight containers of jerky. No generator or satellite TV like some had, but there was a small portable propane heater and solar lights, and a stock of rechargeable batteries for other devices. Over the winters he experimented till he'd found the ideal place on the lake, pulling it behind the truck the first day the ice measured thick enough. He angled it to catch morning sun through the lone window, if there was any sun to be had.

I used to go out alone and pretend it was my own tiny house. I'd draw pictures or rearrange the shelves and imagine the day I'd have a place all to myself, where I could decide not to answer the door if my family came knocking, and the only messes would be mine, if I ever made any messes. It never lasted long because I was too afraid to fire up the heater.

Carna, though, could stay out for hours. She never minded the cold like I did. She didn't even mind Malcolm when they were out there, because as long as the focus was on fishing, it wasn't on criticizing each other. Once I came to get them because I'd made the three of us dinner—spaghetti with meatballs from a big bag in the freezer—and when Carna pulled in the lines, I saw there was nothing on them. No bait, no lure. Malcolm probably thought they were just unlucky.

Lock looked up at me expectantly.

"Maybe we can go out tomorrow," I said. "It's way too cold today."

"I'm not cold!"

"I am. And what if my nose gets frostbite and I can't smell you anymore? Hey, wait . . . maybe we should stay out for a while." I turned him toward the house, where Stephanya was outside shaking out a handful of paintbrushes. She waved, mimed being cold, and ducked inside.

We weren't the only ones with a surprise plus one.

THE UPSIDE OF THE STEPH SURPRISE was that it diffused the rage about Lock. What would have been a full-blown profanity-ridden rant about Heidi turned into a prickly, simmering annoyance. He didn't want to blow up in front of Stephanya, who had a perpetual hippie vibe that even Carna couldn't provoke her out of.

The downside was that the already-small cabin shrank considerably when Steph moved in. Her stuff completely took over the little bedroom: easels, bins, stacks of canvases, lights, arrays of brushes, drop cloths, and piles of fresh boxes with BE YOUR BESTU printed on them. That left the couch and a worn recliner in the main room for me, Carn, and Lachlan.

She'd moved in November, but Mal hadn't mentioned it. Her landlord sold her building to developers who hoped they could Property Brothers downtown Starling into something charming and expensive. They hadn't succeeded yet, but the lakes were clean and deep, and every year a few more old family cabins were replaced by sprawling log homes like the Petersons' next door, with European appliances and outdoor pizza ovens that only got used on the weekends. In the meantime, though, Steph needed a place to live, and Malcolm's only roommates were taxidermied.

Steph had decorated a patchy little pine that Malcolm dragged in with arty god's eyes and wood circles hanging from twine. She'd laid little spruce bundles on all the flat surfaces, and arranged some birch branches in a tall pot. Those things plus a dozen pillar candles made it more Christmassy than it had ever been. I recognized the candles' labels from last year's holiday gifts. Stephanya had been a Scentavo Originals distributor before the company declared bankruptcy and stuck all the reps with shelves of unsold merchandise. Forest, pumpkin spice, and vanilla mist were aglow at once, and the combination smelled like a T. J. Maxx.

Heidi's house wasn't exactly a Christmas wonderland anyway. We had a pre-lit **artificial tree (★★★★★, your family will think it's real)**, plus a near-endless paper chain that Lock worked on for weeks, and a small collection of tomtes that had been Grandma Sharon's. That was everything. Nothing like the explosion of reindeer and baby Jesuses that Darden's family put on display. The McMurrays even used different towels starting at Thanksgiving. Decorating, holiday-themed or otherwise, was about as worth the time to Heidi as PTA meetings, book clubs, or a job.

What we lacked in wreaths and cookie-scented hand soap, though, Heidi made up for in gifts. By Halloween, retailers start shipping like mad to reviewers in the hope that 5-star product ratings will help their **off-brand AirPods (★★★★★, sound great and don't fall out unless you sneeze)** and ab rollers ("Show me the model number, Carna. I think I forgot to post that one") capture some Christmas market share. The best stuff she resold online, but there was plenty left over, like a Toys for Tots drop site. All of Lock's things were wrapped carefully by me, even the Hula-Hoop and the egg chair. Mine and Carn's were usually in the shipping boxes they arrived in, with gift tags taped on top of the address labels. (Wrapping was also not Heidi's thing.)

The gift array at Malcolm's was comparatively spare: two identical gift bags, plus the box for Lachlan I had snagged from the sell pile at home and slipped under the tree. Malcolm usually got us something like a subscription to a jerky-of-the-month club, or maybe a few new lures. (Once I opened a small box and was weirdly touched that he'd picked out a pair of ugly mismatched earrings for me, but it turned out they were for bass fishing.) Since Steph had been in the picture, the gifts were less survivalist but somehow worse. Those bags probably held a personalized watercolor or the last of the candles. I hoped she wasn't already down to balsam or bergamot.

As we settled in, Mal eyed Lachlan like a well-fed German shepherd eyeing a bunny: not hungry, but likely to devour it for sport. While I set the table, carried in wood, and got a tour of Steph's latest paintings, Carn and Lock shot bits of trail mix out the window with a slingshot Malcolm used to keep squirrels out of the bird feeder. Lock giggled nonstop, which made Malcolm's scalp visibly sweat. I hoped the squirrels would appreciate the irony of a buffet of peanuts and raisins being delivered by the same weapon meant to chap their furry little asses, but they mostly seemed unreflective about their change of fortune. The cold bored through the open window until Stephanya finally said, "Can you close that for a bit? I'm freezing my nips off."

Dinner was pheasant jambalaya with venison andouille, or as Heidi would have called it, Stuff Malcolm Shot. A lot of hunters are foodies when it comes to preparing the game they've killed or caught, even if they'll happily eat gas-station hot dogs the rest of the time. Mal's freezer was stocked with the bounty of his expeditions, wrapped in butcher paper and ziplocks with masking-tape dates. And also with Tombstone pizzas. The jambalaya was delicious, and the store-bought dinner rolls that Lock ate instead weren't bad either.

Conversation was left to Stephanya and me—Mal was busy scowling and chomping, Carn eye-rolling and mumbling occasional rhetorical jabs, and Lock nearly falling asleep from boredom. All I had to do was prompt Steph with an occasional question and she'd be off: art fairs, travels, plantar fasciitis, or, especially and effusively, BestU Wellness Supplements, which she was now the sole distributor of for the upper half of Wisconsin and which Carna should please stop referring to as vitamins.

"I had been having pain, well, not pain exactly, but kind of, like, tightness? In my ankles?"

"Tight ankles. Yeah, that's a real thing," grumbled Carna.

"Carna," I said, low and serious, as though warning Carna would mean anything from me. Malcolm forked a sunchoke like he was killing a garter snake.

"And a lot of people said to take glucosamine. But you know me, I like things that are naturally derived"—Carna mimed smoking a joint, but thankfully Lock was absorbed in buttering both sides of a roll, and Mal was absorbed in watching him do it, so they both missed it—"so I did a little research and found out about BestU. It's not even about the supplements—it's about really listening to what someone needs and finding the right fit. I mean, it could be something like ginger or cinnamon or maybe it's krill oil or, I don't know, throwing away your BPA water bottles. We sell really good water bottles, by the way." I tried to look as interested as a person could look about water bottles. "I like that I can be learning all the time, and then sharing what I learn with people."

Carna was about to say something but I interrupted. "I'm sure you're really good at that."

Steph nodded in agreement. "A company like Goop has some pretty good stuff, too," she added, "but I like that BestU has a direct person-to-person connection." She had overdosed on BestU bullshit supplements. Would it be better or worse someday when she joined an actual religious cult?

"Oh my god, you are literally the Gwyneth Paltrow of Wisconsin," Carna said, and Malcolm slammed his hand on the table with a "Forchrissakescarna." Being mean to Stephanya was never about Stephanya, because it slid off her like krill oil, but it was one of Carna's favorite ways of inflaming Malcolm.

By the time we got to trading gifts, we were not surprised that our matching bags held the starter collection of the TeenDream Beauty and Wellness nutritional supplement not-vitamin line. I said I was really excited to try it out, and I pinched Carna's leg under a blanket until she said, "Cool. Thanks." Lock opened a golf ball stamper we'd need to remember to give five stars on pro shop sports outlet dot com. He somehow believed Malcolm and Stephanya had picked it out for him and was polite enough to be flattered by their thoughtfulness. I'd taught him that.

Malcolm thanked us for the deer sled we'd brought him (gotten in exchange for a 5-star **pulled a 10 pointer a quarter mile solo** review for a hunting website), but told us that he'd already bought a cart with rough terrain wheels to haul heavy dead things out of the woods, so we should take it back.

Heidi had also sent along a bottle of brandy, which was easily the most appreciated gift of the night and which was quickly dwindling.

I felt a little bad we didn't have anything for Stephanya, but she was enjoying the brandy, mixed with Sprite and a couple of maraschino cherries. "How come they take out the pits but leave these stupid stems?" she said into her glass.

"Because they're full of glucosamine," Mal said, taking the bright red stem from her and swallowing it.

"And probably red dye number cancer," Steph added, sounding conflicted.

"Yum."

"I gotta stop eating these things," she said, eating another cherry. "I tried to make my own ones from scratch but I guess the cancer just tastes better." They both got a little funnier when they were buzzed; maybe Heidi had been looking out for us in her own way.

Lock had crashed on a camping mattress in Steph's studio, and Carn was either pretending to be or really was asleep in a chair. The rest of us were in various states of drowsy, and I was dying for them to go to bed so I could unfold the couch, when Stephanya's brother called.

Steph's brother was one of those guys who worked very hard at finding ways not to work very hard. Kind of like my mother, except she was successful at it. Not everybody could pull it off. Sometimes you ended up working harder than if you'd just given in to working. And that was Kevin.

He called to ask if one of them could drive over and give him a jump because his car wouldn't start in the cold. "He's at work now?" Mal asked, annoyed.

"One of his side jobs," she said. When Dad just sat there, she nudged, "Like one he does after hours? Like a *side job*?"

There was a long pause, and then Mal finally grunted, "Fine." Steph and I eyed him carefully. There's some flexibility about blood alcohol content for drivers around the Lesser Starling Chain of Lakes, especially in the dead of winter when your chances of seeing another car are small, but there are still trees and ditches to drive into, and he wasn't at his sharpest post-brandy. Steph was practically shit-faced.

"I'll drive"—I sighed and plucked the keys out of his hand—"but I'm staying in the truck." At seventeen, I'd already been the most responsible adult in my family for years. I pulled on my Sorels and hat, and we took the F-250 and the jumper cables into the subzero night to rescue Kevin.

That favor turned into the thing that allowed Carna, Lachlan, and me to make it past the February thaw. Because that's when I found out where Kevin's side job was: Northern Lights Funeral Home and Crematorium.

# CHAPTER FIVE

By Saturday morning, there were twelve inches of new snow on the ground in Starling. It would add an hour to our drive back to Larch and a half hour to the airport from home, assuming we didn't slide into a ditch and freeze to death, plus now we needed to build in time for a stop at Cabela's to return the stupid deer sled.

I was up at five with Malcolm to clear the long drive. It looked bad enough that I might have considered staying in Starling an extra day, except that I got no response from Heidi asking her if she could get someone else to take her to the airport. Malcolm said repeatedly, "Once you hit the highway it will be fine," which was his way of saying GTFO of my house already. It would have been a hundred times better if we'd had the Range Rover. Or parents that bothered to worry about three kids driving in a snowstorm in a rear-wheel-drive rust bucket ten years older than I was.

By the time we left, Malcolm was mad at me for Lachlan shooting a hole in the screen door with a close-range peanut. Stephanya was mad at me for not agreeing to host a Facebook Live info session to crack into what her regional rep assured her was a very hot youth market for supplements. Carna was mad at me for not letting her drive without a permit or for driving too slow or for being a self-important bitch or some combination of those things. Lachlan was mad at the new speaker for dying already (still gets five stars; that's how it works) and then at me for not finding a satisfying solution while driving (slowly, like a self-important bitch).

And I was mad at Heidi for constantly putting me in situations where everyone was mad at me when all I was trying to do was save them from themselves.

CABELA'S WAS WALL-TO-WALL forty-year-old guys who'd braved the snow to cash in Christmas gift cards for rounds of ammunition and Gore-Tex. Carn and I do fine in that crowd because we've been around them our whole lives. I know a lot of girls who are the same. They can rig a line faster than they can braid their hair and learned to hunt as a rite of passage before they realized how pointless and cold it is. But there's always somebody who assumes we're there for the fudge shop or ski pants, and Carna goes full Artemis on them.

That day it was a couple in line, a man and a woman, who had probably come up from Madison. I took Lock to find golf balls to stamp his initials on and left Carn in line to try to return Malcolm's gift without a receipt. (It's not worth selling really big things online because the shipping is too much.) The guy was exchanging a new blaze-orange vest for a bigger one and the Missus had found a jumbo box of hand warmers and some marshmallow sticks to buy. Carna (according to Carna) was patiently waiting, playing a game on her phone, when the guy said, "You know, if you're looking for something for sledding, that's not it."

It's what you expect: a guy assuming he is being of great help when he has no idea who he's talking to or whether she wants his help. I ignore it, but Carna can't. It's one of the reasons why a lot of people don't like Carna—she can't just let people suck without commenting on it. It probably doesn't say much for me that I can.

What made things worse at Cabela's was that the wife kind of tee-heed, Carna told me, and then tried to explain to her where the toboggans and snow toys were kept. It felt like the woman was mansplaining, and that annoyed Carna more than the man mansplaining.

"Thanks, I know the difference," she claims she said, but my guess is it was less polite than that. The helpful shoppers seemed to interpret this as a signal that she was too embarrassed to admit she was wrong and pressed on about what a deer sled is for.

Lock and I got back with a half pound of fudge and a half dozen golf balls just as Carna was saying loudly, "I know what it's for. I want to exchange this one because once I saw your dumbasses I knew I'd need something bigger."

I stepped between them and forced a smile, because you never know who's actually carrying in Cabela's and that lady looked like she wanted to blow Carna's head off. The clerk at the register called, "I can help who's next," and Orange Vest and Hand Warmer stalked to the register. Carna yelled after them, "I'm going to need a fucking MOOSE sled. Do you know where they keep those?"

The store wouldn't take it back without a receipt.

When we got home at 11:55, still with no word from Heidi about whether her flight was delayed, neighbors up and down the street were snowblowing or shoveling their driveways. Ours looked like an untouched blanket as I pulled in. We were in terrible moods, except Lock, who was eager to stamp a golf ball for Mom to bring for Justin Timberlake. "I don't think there's time for that, bud," I said, checking the clock. "Mom and I are in a big hurry. Maybe make one with Carna, though." But Carna dropped the deer sled in the middle of the floor, retreated to her room, and shut the door. "Can you bring that out to the shed?" I yelled at the same time Lock bounded by saying, "Mom, you *have* to see this thing!" But neither of them responded.

Heidi was gone. She must have found someone else to take her without letting me know. She'd even left early because of the snow, which I might have been proud of her for if I wasn't so pissed. There was no note, no promised cash, no goodbye. Just the soft, insistent click of the blinds in front of the sliding-glass door, which she hadn't even bothered to close all the way. It was freezing in there. I slammed it shut and locked it.

She had posted a picture of herself outside the passport office the day before, holding up her little blue book. "So long, suckahs!!!" it said, with sunshine, sunglasses, and blinking cocktail stickers. It felt like we were the suckahs she was talking about. Us and the fools at State who had given her a passport. My mother could get away with murder if she wanted to. Among the comments on her post was one from Lisa-in-Phoenix that said "SO bummed to miss this! Have a" and then an emoji that was probably supposed to mean "blast" but read as "explosion."

Lisa, the source of the tickets, wasn't even going. She included a string of sad and red-faced emojis and #workinggirl and #sucks2bme.

Nothing my mother ever did was surprising, and yet, somehow I was surprised each time. Typical can still be profoundly disappointing.

The house was dull and quiet, filled with the flat gray not-quite light we get so much that time of year. It wasn't dark enough to turn the lights on, but with Christmas over, the sun was falling into the depression that would keep it under colorless clouds until March.

"Hey, buddy." I plucked the hat off Lock's head when he slumped back into the kitchen. His hair floated up with it, and he smoothed it back with both hands. I remembered how I'd felt when I was his age and she blew me off, and wished there was a way to fill in the holes. "She was really worried about missing the plane."

"Planes can't wait for one person," he said, making excuses for her.

"Right. Do you need some lunch?"

"I'm full from fudge samples."

"Do you want to try out the stamper?"

"Maybe later," he said. "I think I want to draw in my room."

"Sounds good." I patted his head. He was processing Heidi, even though he didn't know that's what he was doing. "I've got to shovel the driveway, but show me what you make later. Hey, maybe you can draw all the scats we saw and I'll guess which ones they are?"

He looked over his shoulder, cheeks alight and the smallest grin. "I hope I don't run out of BROWN!"

"Or GREEN," I said, cringing. He'd loved the mossy-looking ones left behind by the geese before they fled south. He laughed and trotted to his room, on a mission now.

Oh, little boy. If only poop could always be the answer.

# CHAPTER SIX

W hy isn't your mom picking up?"

I had sent Aunt Krystal to voice mail twice, but she kept hanging up and retrying. Carn straight-up blocked her without even pausing her show. Lock was in bed, and I was stressing over writing a tactful reminder to the school guidance counselor that I was going to be submitting my application soon and it would be great if she remembered to do my recommendation. How do you gently nag someone to write a glowing letter about you?

Krystal was never gentle about nagging when she needed something. She persisted regardless of whether it made you hate her. "Is she mad at me?"

"She's on her way to Mexico." Long pause.

"Are you fucking with me right now?"

"I'm not fucking with you. She's on a plane. Or maybe landed." I checked the time.

"Jesus, so she already knew? And she just took off?"

Hmm. This was interesting. "Knew what?" Long pause. "Aunt Krystal? What did my mom know?" Long pause. Carna looked up.

"What's she going to Mexico for?" she finally asked, sounding suspicious.

"Lisa got her tickets to a New Year's thing with Justin Timber-lake."

"Wait, are you fucking with me?"

"I am still not fucking with you. Unless Mom was fucking with us, which is possible. She can be a fuckerer."

"Well, I need to talk to her."

"Well, she's in Mexico, so—"

"God damn it. She just *happens* to be leaving the country today?"

"That's where JT *happened* to be playing." Long pause. "Lisa got her the tickets because she knew someone. Maybe she can get you in, too."

"I fucking wish." Super long pause.

"You can keep trying her, but I don't know if she'll have service down there. I don't think our plan works in other countries." **(WISCELL Family Pak, ★★★★★, just as good as Verizon but half the price.)** "It's pretty low-rent."

She made an exasperated noise. "Okay, Drew. Here's the thing. I need to drop off the grid for a little bit, too, so there's some stuff you and Carna should, ah, be aware of till Hi gets everything figured out."

Something to know about Aunt Krystal: Even my mother thought she was too much trouble, and my mother ate trouble like Brenda Olziewski ate Tic Tacs. Whatever technically illegal things Mom did, she did under the radar. Whatever blatantly illegal things Aunt Krys did, she did holding one of those giant Dish Network saucers over her head. She gets away with a lot on her own—she's thirty-six, white, and female, which is like 100 percent DEET repellent for your criminal record—but if she's really stuck, she calls Heidi. Mom's been her alibi for boyfriends and police officers, provided employer references and doctor's notes, and once backed her own car into Krystal's front bumper so there'd be a viable reason for the dent besides that my aunt smashed into a guy's garage after he broke up with her.

The trouble Krystal had gotten into this time quickly turned into trouble for us. She tried to fill a prescription for my grandmother. You're not supposed to fill someone else's prescription, but that's not the important part. The prescription was for medical marijuana, but that's not the important part. It was written by some University of the Tropics Med School certificate holder whose entire function in life was to write BS prescriptions for weed, but that's not the important part either. There was some confusion at the dispensary about the patient's current address and Medicare coverage, and that is the important part.

That part is important because Grandma Sharon died when I was in eighth grade, a fact that no one had mentioned to the government agencies who care about that information, for example, Medicare or the Social Security Administration. The SSA sends old people checks. When you hear someone say that their grandmother or great-uncle or the cat lady next door is "on Social Security," it means that an agency of the government is sending (or really, auto-depositing) a few hundred dollars out of the jillions of dollars they paid in taxes when they were younger. It's meant to support senior citizens or people with disabilities that make it hard to work. *Living* senior citizens or people with disabilities. It's not supposed to supplement the other unreported and dodgily acquired income of their families after they die.

It's technically fraud—well, not just technically—and Mom had been guilty of it since Grandma Sharon died. I knew because when I started filling out FAFSA forms, I found out a lot about our family finances on both sides—and then stopped filling out FAFSA forms. Mom assured me she'd be in a better position to help out with tuition if she wasn't in jail.

The arrangement might have gone unnoticed until Grandma's one hundred fortieth birthday, except when the dispensary couldn't verify coverage or an address to get Grandma the weed muffins Aunt Krystal heard were both low-fat and provided a nice, mellow buzz, it tipped off some bored office worker who started a chain of inquiries that led to an investigation into the whereabouts and existential status of Sharon Alberta Hill.

Some of that we pieced together later. At this point all we knew was that Aunt Krystal had tipped a snowball over a cliff and it turned into a full-blown avalanche headed toward our house. "If anybody calls and asks about Ma—Grandma—say that she lives with you guys."

"WHAT?"

"Those Social Security people are such losers. This girl I knew was on disability because she has fibromyalgia super bad sometimes but someone reported her working at a restaurant and they canceled it! They took away her disability money!" Aunt Krystal had a tendency to thread irrelevant stories about strangers into important information, which was sometimes how she got away with things—by distracting you from whatever shit sandwich she was serving until you accidentally ate it.

"Are they going to want proof that Grandma Sharon's here?" Carna, who I'd forgotten was listening, laughed out loud.

"I don't know. Maybe. Do you have proof?"

"Um . . . what?"

"When did Heidi say she was coming back?"

"In a week."

"When next week?"

"No, I mean a week. Like next Saturday."

"She left for a week?" I imagined her look of surprise. Even my aunt, who had a history of releasing impulse-adopted pets into the wild when she found them inconvenient, seemed to think it was a long time to leave the kids alone. "Whatever. If anybody calls or shows up, even if they say they're old friends or something, say she's, I don't know, at a hair appointment."

If I couldn't even tell my fourth-grade teacher that I'd been fever-free for an extra couple of hours, there was no way I was going to tell anybody that my dead grandmother was out getting her hair done. "Won't they just send a letter or something?"

"Yeah, Drew, they're going to send a letter. 'Dear Mrs. Hill, Are you still alive? Please return the enclosed RSVP if you are not dead. And if you are dead, tell your daughter she's fucked.'"

"It's that big a deal?"

"Uh, yeah, it's a big deal. Plus Heidi doesn't really want them looking at her finances, if you know what I mean"—I did—"so maybe she can say she didn't realize the money was still being deposited and give it back."

Ignorance would be a hard sell. Heidi used Grandma's debit card, her name for the senior discount, and I was pretty sure Grandma had voted absentee in the last election. "My mom will figure it out," I said and believed it. She couldn't figure out dinner or childcare or parenting, but with a little light fraud, identity borrowing, and a touch of emotional blackmail, she'd gotten away with worse. Heidi could handle a couple of government inquiries. "Hopefully nothing will come up until she's back."

I've replayed that conversation many times, and this last part always creeps me out. If I mentioned it to Krystal, she'd probably say, "You know I've always been a little psychic." ("Psych-*o*," the rest of us would correct.) Carna just thinks I rewrote a memory, and maybe that's true. It was around the time my grip on real life started to get slipperier. It doesn't matter either way, though, because I can hear Krystal's reply in my head, clearly, every time.

"Hopefully nothing will come up until she's back," I say.

"*If* she comes back," she replies.

# CHAPTER SEVEN

Sunday morning I was on the opening shift at Badger State Bagels, the first one in besides the baker, who comes at four to start up the giant boiling vats and never shows their face out front. Audrey Kidder was already behind the counter at the Roasted Badger, the coffee place connected to the bagel shop by an open archway. The coffee workers and the bagel workers traded drinks for carbs and quarters for dollars and complaints about the customers who were confused about why they couldn't order both things from the same person. ("The bagelry was originally set up under a franchise license and so any revenue . . . ," I would explain. "Yeah, it's dumb," Audrey would say.)

Audrey was one of Darden's crowd officially, but we were the only two high schoolers I knew who could manage an early shift and among the few who lasted in their jobs more than a couple of months. I liked her best out of everyone who came with the Boyfriend Package, Basic Social Life Edition.

She wandered over to my side after she'd dispatched a plain black coffee to my freshman English teacher, who had peered through the archway with no recognition as I waved. Good thing I hadn't asked her for a recommendation.

"What's it like having the house to yourself?" Audrey asked, pulling herself up on my counter.

"The house to myself sounds like heaven. Carna and my little brother are home, too." I counted twenty quarters into the till. "How do you know that, anyway? Did Darden tell you?"

"No—your mom. She stopped by Friday on her way back from getting her passport. I didn't know you could get one so fast."

"Rules don't really apply to my mother."

"She's lucky she drove back before the snow got so crazy."

"She is always very lucky."

"She said they asked what was the reason she needed to expedite her passport application—"

"And she said because Justin Timberlake is the greatest performer who ever lived—"

"Wait—she didn't tell you this? She said one of her children had a brain tumor and she was trying to meet Justin to ask him to do a Make-A-Wish." Audrey laughed.

"Which kid?"

"Oh. She didn't say."

Definitely me.

*I just need you to do this one little thing for me, Drew. It's a brain tumor.*

"So they felt sorry for her and gave her a passport?"

"She said the guy just looked at his screen and was like, 'Sooo, last-minute travel.'"

"The passport office doesn't care about my fake brain tumor? That's cold." Audrey kept laughing.

"Your mom is so funny." To my friends, my mom was young and fun and the good kind of crazy. The parents didn't see her like that, but their judgment bugged me just as much. I wished her nonconformity didn't dominate so much of my life.

"Hilarious." I nudged Audrey off the counter as a customer came in. She rearranged the row of day-olds while I took the order, and then stood next to me at the fresh baskets while I collected an assortment.

"It must have been pretty late when she was here."

"Yeah. She was super tired after all that driving. She wanted some caffeine so she could stay up and pack. Brandon made her his special latte on the house. Extra large. He's like, 'If you like it, maybe we'll feature it, so let me know what you think.' I think he's got a crush on her." Of course Heidi got a free coffee out of that story. Of course the stupid manager had a crush on her. She'd probably get JT to Make-A-Wish me. You almost had to admire the woman.

"Oh yeah, and she picked up your check."

Or not.

**A CAR WITH ILLINOIS LICENSE PLATES** sat in our driveway, taking up most of what I'd shoveled, and leaving me to park along the street. A trim man in a lightweight down jacket stood on the step talking to Carna through the storm door. Despite the frigid temperature, he wasn't wearing a hat or gloves. His gel had frozen in place like the molded plastic hair on man-Barbies. He was probably selling Jesus or solar panels.

The second he spotted me, he threw out a rapid-fire "Oh, hello there. I was hoping to catch Heidi Hill. Maybe you know where I could find her?" Carn was mouthing *He wants Mom*, or maybe *Ewoks Mob*, behind the fogging glass. Her face was tense. This was not an ordinary proselytizer.

"I've been at work since six." Buying time.

"I told you already, Mom took Grandma to Lands' End to see if there was anything good on sale. She likes how their slacks fit." Carna was even more condescending than usual, as though the man had no short-term memory. Now we were on the same fictional page, and the page was from a catalog with comfortable slacks. "You know, it's dangerous to be out there without a hat. You're going to get frostbite," she added, pointing to her ear.

It was brutally cold. I would have taken Heidi's car that morning if mine wasn't blocking the garage. It has a remote start so you can warm it up before you even leave the house. Mine takes the whole ride to heat up and then just blows straight in your face while your feet freeze.

But the guy was determined. Seven degrees outside, underdressed on the front step while a fifteen-year-old girl in pajamas at noon lectured him about windchill. I looked down at the bare fingers gripping his leather portfolio, and wondered if they were usually that purple.

He made a curt introduction and handed me a business card. K. David Barth—or K-Darth, as Carna dubbed him later—was an investigator for the regional branch of the Office of the Inspector General of the Social Security Administration and, even though we'd only just met him, clearly a dick.

Uh-oh. "And you're sure your grandmother was with your mother? Today? This morning?" He addressed it to me, the nice working girl, assuming I was a better source than the bristly lazy one in the doorway.

"Unless my mother brought a container of ashes along in her suitcase, no," I wanted to say.

"Mom wanted to get Grandma a cardigan," I blurted instead. "She gets chilly." If they weren't already red from the cold, my cheeks would have flushed. Carna raised her eyebrows, surprised. I had added a cardigan to her slacks, all on my own. I, Drew, had lied to an authority figure. I pressed a mittened hand to my face, which would crack in pieces if I stayed outside another minute.

He said to make sure Grandma or Heidi called him ASAP. I

promised to pass on the info, though the fact that I hadn't gotten so much as a read receipt from her since she'd left made me skeptical that she'd respond. If her Out of Office applied to children, it definitely applied to quasi-federal agents.

"Thanks for stopping by," I said as he closed his portfolio and turned to leave. I tried to match Carna's sarcastic tone, but it came out like I was sincerely grateful for his visit. I am naturally unintimidating.

Just as we were about to be rid of our visitor, though, Lock popped into the door frame draped in one of Carna's old T-shirts, no pants, and a pair of fuzzy Pikachu slippers. "Did you bring the cinnaminis?"

K-Darth's eyes lit up like my brother was an actual Pikachu with a hundred-dollar bill in its mouth. "Hey there, buddy! Does your grandma live here?" he said.

"I got them!" I practically shouted, pushing through the door in front of Lock.

"She's with Mom," Lock said. Echoing someone else's lies was basic etiquette training in our house, like please and thank you, but it was still a cheap shot to ask a second grader. The man frowned, annoyed, and we watched him drive away in a billow of exhaust.

Carna said, "That's not a good sign."

"What's not a good sign?" asked Lock, breathing onto the glass and drawing a snowman in the condensation.

"Where are your pants?" I asked. He didn't respond, just traced some stick arms onto Frosty. "Lock." Nothing. "Lachlan Randall." Nothing. "Poopface." Slight smile that meant he was listening. "Pants. I'm serious. You can't come to the door in your underwear. You don't know who it's going to be."

"Yeah, what if it's some creeper who likes to see kids in their underwear?" added Carna.

"*God*, Carn" I said. Lock was unfazed.

I snapped the elastic waistband, and he grabbed the bag of mini-bagels and ran. There would be a trail of cinnamon sugar from the front door to his **egg chair (★★★★★, fun to spin around in)**, and from the egg to wherever he finally ran out of bagels. It was too cold for ants, so the only one trailing the mess would be me, with a **Swooper (★★★★★, cleans up like a Swiffer but cheaper)**.

We were on the fourth day of a Heidilessness we thought was temporary, at the beginning of a problem we thought she would come back and solve—a problem we thought was *the* problem. Door-to-door pedophiles posing as federal employees or spilled sugar or the Social Security Administration's resident Sith Lord? Manageable. Everything was still, at least by our definition, pretty normal.

# CHAPTER EIGHT

The next morning I was reassuring Carna that Darden and I had only invited a few people over, all of whom were pretty laid back. Lock had been invited to sleep at his friend Liam's house, with proper parental supervision and, if it wasn't too cold out, sparklers to light on the deck at midnight Greenwich Mean Time. ("Do you think that would be okay with your mom, as long as I'm watching them carefully?" Liam's mother asked. Mom would have let them launch a missile at real midnight.) Carna couldn't use babysitting martyrdom as an excuse for having nothing to do on New Year's Eve.

"You can hang out with us," I said. "We're just going to be watching stuff."

"I don't want to hang out with Darden's douchey friends."

"They're my douchey friends, too," I said, not sure who I was defending.

"Sure."

I didn't know what she wanted me to do. Make different friends? Find her her own douchey friends? Get rid of everybody else so she could sigh disapprovingly at me when I tried to make conversation like every other night?

Our unproductive exchange was interrupted by K-Darth repeatedly ringing the doorbell like he was calling a slow elevator. "I didn't get a call back, so I thought I'd stop by," as though Larch Leap was simply on the path between whatever dimensions of hell he traveled. He dodged his head left and right, like a boxer, as though someone or something behind me would confirm whatever suspicions he had. My grandmother's corpse on display like Kim Jong-il?

"Sorry. Grandma's not home."

"Darn it. How 'bout your mother?" More head weaving. It had gotten even colder, and this time K-Darth had come wearing an ear warmer that flattened his ears to his skull, making his head look like a sperm swimming through a health video.

"She's not here either."

"So was your mother really shopping yesterday, or is she out of town?"

I crinkled my nose at him. He knew something.

"Look, I'm going to be honest with you," he went on, "and the best thing you can do is be honest with me."

My heart skipped. I was good at being honest, but honest was *not* the best thing to be at the moment. The best thing was to make stuff up, and Carna was usually better at that.

"I've been tasked with looking into some pretty serious questions about some pretty serious stuff. Now, maybe it's just a misunderstanding. Maybe it's something more serious. But until I can get some answers, things are going to get more and more serious."

"Seriously?" Carna slid up beside me like a sarcastic guardian angel. Her ability to raise an adult man's blood pressure with one word had been perfected on Malcolm.

"This is not a joke. It's ser—" The last part trailed off. He caught himself too late.

"Nice headband. I see you took my advice about covering your ears," she said before I hit her in the stomach with my elbow.

"I'll tell my mom that it's important," I told him politely. "It's been a crazy week."

"And how's her Spanish coming?"

"Spanish?" I repeated nervously. She could order any flavor margarita and ask where the baño is. I taught her those, plus *alergia a las avellanas*, which means "hazelnut allergy," before we left for Mal's. "She doesn't speak Spanish."

"You're really going to keep this up?" K-Darth half smiled, like he was a master detective and I was a silly amateur liar he could crack like a knuckle.

It's true that I was an amateur, but since I didn't know what I was supposed to be lying about, he couldn't actually crack me. As far as I knew, the only thing the Office of the Inspector General wanted to know was if my grandmother was living her best life with their $1,062 a month deposit or if she was dead, tied up in a hole, or otherwise no longer in need of financial support. Heidi's tourist-bar Spanish didn't seem relevant. "Keep what up?"

K-Darth glanced at Carna, but it was hard for anybody to withstand Carna's glare. If he thought Wisconsin winter was cold, he did not know my sister. He turned back to me.

"Look, I know that she got a rush passport and had a plane ticket booked from Madison to Chicago to Mexico City"—I squeezed my teeth tight to try to keep my face from moving, but there wasn't anything I could do about my stomach, which suddenly felt very shaky. It wasn't a crime to fly to Mexico to see Justin Timberlake, but we had been trying to keep the fact that she'd left a bunch of minors on their own for a week on the down low—"which was canceled when the airport closed after the snowstorm."

Wait.

The airport what now?

WHAT?!?!

"So did she fly straight out of O'Hare or Milwaukee?" The Madison airport *shut down* and she didn't tell me? At least she didn't make me drive her to Milwaukee. Or to Mexico. "What I'm asking is if she crossed a border some other way, or if she's still around and avoiding me?"

I clenched my jaw so hard all the major arteries to my brain burst and my entire head blushed. The left corner of K-Darth's mouth lifted again.

I had a tumble of questions, none of which I could ask.

How did he know about the passport and the flight? Was she was on some kind of watch list? We knew about the Social Security stuff and a little light tax fraud, but was she an actual terrorist, too? And if she was trying to flee the country, why would she fly to Mexico when she could drive to Canada in six or seven hours? Was Justin part of the escape plan? And most important, if she hadn't made it to Mexico, where the hell was she and why hadn't she answered my Venmo request asking for money for Carna's contacts?

Darth leered at me, a cocky "gotcha" that might have been more intimidating if he wasn't earless. Still, I stood there opening and closing my mouth like a fish on the dock.

"She canceled," Carna interjected. "It worked out for the best anyway because she doesn't like leaving Grammy."

*Grammy?*

"It totally sucks for her," Carna went on.

Darth narrowed his eyes, suspicious.

"Missing Justin Timberlake? The whole reason she was going to Mexico? You didn't see that on Facebook when you saw the stuff about getting a passport and everything?"

She spoke with impatient confidence. The ball in my chest loosened. Of course Darth was tracking her not-private social media, not checking her against a terrorist no-fly list.

Or maybe she was also on a no-fly list.

"I don't give out any specifics about my investigative methodologies."

"Sure," said Carna. "Obviously." Her tone was pure condescension, like his "investigative methodologies" were as highly classified as a family chili recipe. She smiled at him insincerely.

It reminded me that, somewhere in there, Carna had a real smile. A great one. Or at least she used to. More cheeks than mouth, but you could feel it, because her face would just kind of shine. Everyone thought so. I wonder if Carn knew it, too, and that's why she hardly ever used it: because she hardly ever thought anyone deserved it.

K-Darth got the yearbook version. The lie. All mouth, no cheeks, no shine.

He let out a breath that sounded like a growl. "So where is she if not in Mexico? Please don't tell me she's with your grandmother buying slacks and cardigans."

Carna slow-blinked him, and I couldn't tell if she was thinking of an answer or thinking about shooting him in the ear warmer with her crossbow.

"Hopefully *winning*!" I said, clapping my hands. The two of them jumped. "Oh no!" I gasped. "Did I just get them in trouble? Is Grammy not allowed to gamble?"

"Damn it, Drew," said Carna, shaking her head. Her mouth was flat, but her cheeks were on the rise. "Can't you keep anything a secret?"

"Look, I swear she hardly spends anything," I said to Darth. "She just likes the machines."

Whether or not he bought it, there wasn't much K-Darth could do with the two of us standing there telling him about the time our grandmother won a hundred and forty dollars on her first nickel and then divided it into our college savings accounts (the first part did happen, the second didn't because we didn't have college savings accounts). I'm sure he wasn't supposed to be talking to us anyway, since we were minors and not (yet) suspected of anything. He handed each of us another business card, and said to make sure Heidi got hold of him soon.

"You mean Grandma Sharon, right?" said Carna.

"Sure," he said with a smirk.

He chucked the earmuffs into the passenger seat as he slid into the car. It was a Honda Accord, not even four-wheel drive, which meant he lived somewhere the streets got plowed before you got up in the morning. Chicago probably. A good long drive to listen to true-crime podcasts and wonder why they never made one about the brilliant minds that cracked cases of Social Security overpayment.

"Fucknutter," mumbled Carna. She started to close the door, but he tapped his horn.

"Oh, say?" he called from the driveway. "Which casino was it?" Carn looked to me, eyebrows raised. "Ho-Chunk or Potawatomi?"

Did it matter? Was it a trick? Was he going to show up to look for them? I leaned out the storm door and called unsteadily, "I'm not sure?" He grinned kind of smugly. His window started to rise. I was annoyed that he had the nerve to doubt a perfectly good alibi. "The one with the good buffet," I yelled, louder. "Grammy loves the crab legs."

# CHAPTER NINE

You think she just Ubered to Chicago and flew from there?"

"That would be really expensive," Carna said, locking the door. "She probably found someone else dumb enough to drive her."

I ignored the implication. "I don't know. It seems like she'd mention it." Carna headed for the kitchen, and I followed her. "Have you heard anything from her at all?"

"No, but I haven't tried," she said, opening the fridge. She scanned it and took out one of Lock's juice pouches. "Crab legs, Drew? Really?"

"He bought it, didn't he?" I said, unsure.

"You know your voice wobbles when you lie."

"I'll work on that," I snapped.

"Just be aware of it," she said, exasperated. "You usually give off this very uptight vibe, so you could actually be really convincing if you work on your delivery."

"Wow, Carna, that's wonderful advice and I'll be sure to take it to heart."

"Better," she said.

"You know, I'm not sure if Heidi's even getting messages down there. I turned on her read receipts but she might have realized it and turned them off again."

"Yeah, I think she probably turned *us* off for the week."

"If that's true, it's unacceptable. We need her to deal with the Social Security thing."

"It's 'unacceptable'?" Carna sucked up the last of the fruit punch and smirked.

"Well, it's shitty."

"Welcome to the family, Drew." She dropped the empty pouch on the counter. "It's probably just the dodgy cell service. You'll probably get all her replies at once telling you to stop asking her for things while she's on vacation."

"*I* should stop asking *her* for things?"

"Maybe she's ignoring you so you don't start nagging her about sunblock or parasites or Benadryl or something."

I glared at her.

She groaned. "Just see if you can tell her what's going on without actually saying what's going on. In case he can hack texts or something."

"You think he can see our texts?"

"Maybe." She seemed unconcerned. "Eww, you're not sending anything gross to Darden, are you?"

"What would I even write? 'Aunt Krystal wants the recipe for our ead-day andma-gray's special uffins-may'?"

"You'll figure it out." She shrugged, walking out of the kitchen. "It's only a few more days, and then it's her problem. Chill out, Drew."

# CHAPTER TEN

If Heidi and Carna weren't going to freak out about Darth, I decided I wouldn't either.

I sat down in front of my computer and logged into the University of Wisconsin's portal. I reread my application, wishing for the hundredth time there was something phenomenal to say about myself—I write poetry in three languages, I rowed Greta Thunberg to shore, I discovered Atlantis—instead of a truthful essay about being a hard worker who really wanted to go to the University of Wisconsin-Madison.

It had been my plan since eighth grade, when we went on a field trip to the capitol and had lunch on campus, a stop intended to get middle schoolers thinking about college. It worked: the buildings; the crowd of students; the autonomy; the chance to do something amazing and different; and that huge, beautiful lake. It was perfect. I never even thought about going anywhere else.

The application wasn't due yet, but I'd finished most of it weeks before. The main reason I hadn't submitted it right away was that I'd been hoping I'd do better on the ACT on the retake. I didn't, but the scores were good enough to be in the range for in-state students. Something about Heidi ditching me and the New Year about to begin, though, made it seem like the perfect time to send it. I held my breath and hit submit.

The application was in, the first giant step into my future, a future with new people, high expectations, and no last-minute babysitting.

Heidi was right: New Year's Eve was a fun holiday. I started to text her, but remembered she wasn't responding. I considered telling Carna, but she wouldn't care. I savored it myself, just for a minute, before I got back to work.

I moved from room to room, shutting the door to Lachlan's tornado, sweeping Carna's contact solution into a drawer in the bathroom. My own room was irrelevantly neat in the basement, where no one would see it. I liked that I had utter control of the space, although sometimes the distance between me and everyone else felt vast.

I moved Heidi's junk (Tooth Whitening Accelerator Lamp, ★★★★★, my teeth shine like cultured pearls; Beaded Allergy Alert Bracelet, ★★★★★, gift from my daughter, almost pretty enough to wear) into her room and stacked the unopened mail on the dining room table, which was her office. Our house functioned well as a shipping and receiving center, but it wasn't exactly homey. It didn't have the kind of personality—grumpy as it was—of Malcolm's cabin or the obsessive, treacly fussiness of Darden's. The house had been my grandmother's before it was ours, but it wasn't the house Heidi had grown up in. Sharon had moved in during Heidi's freshman year at Eau Claire, the same year my grandfather dropped dead of a stroke just before he could divorce her for a woman in his curling league. She buried him and unburied a whole lot of debt he had hidden at the same time, which took the edge off any grief. She had to sell the bigger house and all the nice things in it, and was too humiliated to want to make this one feel like home. And then Heidi and Mal took it over, and then just Heidi, and it still looked like a place we'd rented and never quite settled in. The only things on the walls were things Carna or I had hung. Still, the house was mostly clean, thanks to me.

When I got back from dropping off Lock, the deer sled was still in the middle of the living room. It was the one thing Carna was supposed to clean up. She'd helped Lock fill it with old blocks, cans of soda, and taped-down Chipotle straws to make a giant maze for his Hexbugs. They'd spent hours making videos that Lock was sure would go "biral" before he forgot about it and moved on to trying to stamp things with the golf ball stamper (Super Balls, eggs).

"Carna!" I yelled, pulling up straw barriers and cans. "Can you take this thing out to the shed before people get here?"

"What's your deal with Douche-Mac?" was her answer. She stood over me watching me disassemble the maze. "Are you planning to be together in college?"

That was definitely not the plan. We hadn't talked about it, but I was going to Madison and he was applying to D3 schools where he hoped he could play hockey. Since there was no overlap, I assumed we assumed the same thing. As soon as Carna said it, though, I had this pang like I might have to explain it to him.

I realize that sounds cold. I liked Darden—I really did. More at first, maybe. But after more than a year together, he felt like another person who wanted more attention than I could give. If there was a movie he was excited about, I was supposed to wait to see it with him. If there was an assembly, he'd want to sit together, even if that meant giving up a spot by the exit. If he brought in his skates to be sharpened, he FaceTimed me so we could wait together, even though I wasn't stuck and bored at the skate shop. There wasn't anything exactly *wrong*—when we broke up, I would look like the bad guy—even if there also wasn't anything exactly right. Other people might have appreciated the attention. I just wasn't interested in so much of it.

But I wasn't going to give Carna the satisfaction of knowing how unexcited I felt about Douche-Mac. (That was his own fault. He was the one who made a "D-Mac" account on SoundCloud.) I said, "I'm not planning on marrying him, if that's what you're asking. It doesn't mean I can't go out with him now." *It doesn't, right?* I thought to myself. Was I supposed to have an exit strategy?

When people started arriving, Carna disappeared to Heidi's room. It had a new **Sankio 50-inch HDTV (★★★★, the picture is so realistic)** that made everything look slightly pink and a **king-sized mattress (★★★★, excellent back support)** that collapsed in the middle.

The whole plan for the night was drink a little, eat a lot, watch stuff. Six of us; seven if you counted Carna. We didn't do those giant rager parties you see in movies. I don't know anybody who does. It must be an East Coast thing.

Even on New Year's Eve. Especially on New Year's Eve. No one can ever think of anything to do at midnight besides watch the people standing in Times Square watch the ball drop on TV. And because we live in the Central time zone, we don't even watch them watching live. By the time we see people see the ball drop, those people have gone home or gone to a bar or whatever it is Times Square people do.

Connor Amundson showed up with eleven of a twelve-pack of Leinie's from his dad's garage fridge; Taylor Minn, a big bottle of pre-mixed strawberry margaritas and a half bottle of vodka; Audrey, two bottles of red wine, which she must have known the hockey players wouldn't drink. Logan came late with the Absolut Citron his brother had given him for Christmas. And Dard had no alcohol, because his parents paid attention to everything, but had a ten-gallon bag of popcorn, because his parents paid attention to everything. I imagined his mom stopping him on the way out. "Oh boy! You kids will need some snacks!"

Somewhere right between the McMurrays and my family is what you're looking for in parents.

I had gotten chips, guac, queso, frozen pizzas, candy, noisemakers, and a party pack of sparkly 2019 tiaras, but everyone looked to Darden like he was hosting the party. I was just housing the party. Or non-party. Only Audrey hung out in the kitchen while I tried to pound loose some ice. Audrey found two wineglasses and opened one of her bottles, and it seemed like such a nice thing to do I pretended the wine didn't taste like my tongue was dying.

"How's Mexico?"

"Hot, I think," I said. I wasn't about to tell anybody we hadn't heard from Heidi in days.

Audrey laughed. "Compared to here, Iowa is hot. Did your mom hook up with Justin Timberlake yet?"

I stabbed into the ice maker with a knife and a big chunk broke free. Audrey grabbed a rogue cube and plopped it in her wineglass, and another in mine. The chapped edges of her lips were stained like a friendly vampire.

"I will let you know the second I hear." Even I could forgive her if hooking up with JT was the reason she was ghosting us.

Dard popped in and reached around me to put the margarita bottle in the freezer. "Taylor said to put this in the freezer so it will get slushy."

"That seems seasonally inappropriate," I said.

"Or seasonally very appropriate," countered Audrey, "depending on how you think of it."

I handed Dard the ice I'd freed. "Thanks, babe," he said, leaning in for a quick kiss, as though a bowl of ice cubes was a romantic gesture. I smiled obligingly. He kept standing there.

"Yeah?" I asked.

"They want to watch a Jordan Peele movie—if that's okay with you? What's the password again?"

"Same as everything. Oh-one-three-one-eight-one?" I whispered when he looked blank. Heidi's cybersecurity was weak, but so, apparently, was Darden's capacity for numbers. He repeated it loudly, like he was making an important announcement, so he'd remember all the way to the adjacent room. I cringed.

Dard was always loud. It didn't matter if he was telling a secret or watching a Blackhawks game. Maybe it was a lifetime of shouting through a helmet or over the emotive chaotic togetherness of an overly communicative family or maybe it was just that big people have big lungs. Everyone in his house must have heard him say, "Do you want me to, you know, use my mouth?" through a closed door and under a blanket, because after that his mother always tried to keep us out of his room with an endless buffet of snacks and inane questions. Darden McMurray: Good intentions. Soft emotions. Overdeveloped vocal cords.

Audrey laughed and shook her head. Her history with Dard was longer than mine, and her future would be, too; their moms had graduated together, six years before mine. "I'm not going to feel bad if you don't like that," she said, nodding at my wineglass. It wasn't that I didn't like it; it was more that I felt like I was at work. When I didn't say anything, she took the glass from my hand and dumped it in hers. "And same thing goes for him," she whispered, pointing the empty glass in Dard's direction. She hopped off the counter and carried a tray of snacks one-armed into the living room.

# CHAPTER ELEVEN

Carna loves scary movies, and especially smart, weird ones, maybe because she's scary, smart, and weird, so I again invited her to hang with us. It was half because I wasn't sure she liked being alone as much as she said she did, and half because sometimes I felt outnumbered with Dard's friends. Carn was all mine, at least. And maybe she'd like the movie more than she hated us.

She said, "No, but will you bring me something to eat?"

Darden had saved a spot on the couch for me. I would have rather sat between Audrey and Taylor on the floor, sharing a box of Cheez-Its, but since we were the only ones there who were a couple, everyone expected I'd want to be next to him. (Plus he was a baby about scary movies.) He smelled like hockey and Head & Shoulders.

About twenty minutes in, Carna came in quietly, holding a pillow and a bag of pretzels. It was dumb that that mattered, but even then, even though she had made it clear in a million ways how disappointing I was, I felt more of an allegiance to her than to any of the others—including my supposed boyfriend, who was rubbing his giant thumb back and forth over my hand in a super annoying way. I was happy to see her.

Logan was sprawled on the floor with his head on a Nerf football and hadn't noticed Carn standing right above him. As the floor creaked, he jerked up, twisted around, and yelled, "Fuck! God. Fuck! Where the fuck did you come from?"

Connor threw his head back laughing so hard he hit the wall, Taylor spit-taked vodka Coke, and Dard accidentally squashed the hand he was trying to sexily caress.

"OW!" Connor and I yelped.

"Logan just peed," said Darden.

"Logan just got a boner," said Taylor. Carna looked mortified. Connor paused the movie so everyone could speculate on what might have happened in Logan's pants, the top theory being that his dick was actually hiding between his butt cheeks because it was so scared, a theory put forth by Logan himself. Then came endless jokes about hot dogs, bratwurst, kielbasa, and other wieners.

"Oh my god," said Audrey finally. "Literally NO ONE cares about your genitals, Logan. Can we just watch the movie?"

"Ouch!" said Logan, then looked down at his lap. "It's okay, li'l buddy."

More howls.

I smiled up at Carna, hoping she'd appreciate how harmless they all were. Connor got up to get another beer and motioned for her to take his spot on the couch. "You can sit there, little sister."

She said, just to me, "I forgot to put that thing away in the shed."

"Leave it!" I called after her, but she was already through the living room with the deer sled in one hand and the pillow in the other. "It doesn't matter. Carn! Do it tomorrow! It's a million below!"

Someone restarted the movie, and everyone resettled. She'd retreat straight back into Mom's room as soon as she returned. Part of me wished I could go with her.

# CHAPTER TWELVE

**CARNA**

get out here

          **ME**

          why

**CARNA**

just come out

          **ME**

        just come in

It was unreasonable, but still. Maybe she wanted to hang out with us but she was embarrassed, and I should go out and talk to her.

**CARNA**

GET OUT HERE

On second thought, maybe she just wanted me to come out so she could tell me in person that everyone in the house was an asshole.

I ignored it. She called. An actual call. I declined.

**CARNA**

it's an emergency

The shed door was probably frozen shut.

                                                                **ME**

                                                        no it's not

Another call. Declined.

Again. What was she doing? Decline.

Again. Maybe something's the matter? The matter is I tried to include her, everyone was perfectly nice, and now she's being a jerk. Decline. I slid my phone between the cushions.

A long time passed. Was she really stubborn enough to stand out there and get frostbite?

A few minutes later I heard the door from the kitchen to the back slide open and shut, and felt the vibration of another text though the couch. I didn't budge. I could be stubborn, too.

Carna came to the edge of the living room, still in her jacket and boots, cheeks bright red. You could feel the cold come off her from across the room.

"I need you out there," she said.

She didn't just look cold. She looked scared. And I found my-self glued in place, processing, because Carna never looked scared. "What's—"

"*NOW.*" She growled it and left. Everyone giggled or oohed.

I pushed out of the tangle of Darden's arm and bolted after her, furious and embarrassed.

A million tiny blades of cold cut through the open door to the backyard. My first thought was to lock it and let her freeze out there, but I was too pissed to be satisfied with the simple loss of her fingers or the tip of her nose. I grabbed the first jacket and boots I found—Dard's—and followed in her footsteps through the snow. The moonlight was enough to see the outline of the sled where she'd dropped it outside.

I was going to kill her.

"What the hell, Carn?" I started before I was even at the threshold to the shed. "Why do I have—"

Carn stood in Lock's old baby pool. All I could see in the glow of her phone was that her eyes were wet. I couldn't remember my sister crying. Ever. Not when she hooked her own finger baiting a line. Not when a neighbor's dog decimated the warren of baby rabbits we had discovered at Mal's. Not when her closest/only friend in school got adopted by some theater kids and left her behind. Ever. My rage evaporated, and in that second, I would have cleared every one of those people out of the house—told them to fuck off forever—if she would just sit with me and we could cry together, because whatever could break the heart of Carna Krause Hill would surely shatter mine. I stepped toward the little pool and kicked something that sounded like a paper cup.

And then my eyes dropped to the circle of light Carna aimed at the floor.

There was something there that hadn't been before. Something in the way of simply stowing the deer sled, cranking up the thermostat, and watching people in New York count down on replay. An unmoving thing. A thing that didn't belong here.

A thing that belonged with Justin Timberlake being selfish and spontaneous and fun.

She was shining the light on Heidi.

# CHAPTER THIRTEEN

I dropped to my knees to start CPR.

"There weren't any tracks," Carna said vaguely.

I started compressions, even though it was like pressing into concrete. Health class dummies felt more like real people.

Carna pulled me back by the shoulders, softly first, then a shove. "Drew! No! I said there weren't any tracks when I came out."

I fell to my butt and looked up at her.

"The snow was Friday night. She's been here the whole time."

There's a plus and a minus to having your sister twenty minutes ahead of you when it comes to finding your mother dead and frozen in a storage shed.

The plus was that she'd already done the obligatory breath-checking, pulse-checking, and wake-up-can-you-hear-me? cheek-slapping before I got there, though the results should have been obvious just looking at her.

The minus was that Carn wasn't very patient about giving me time to process what she'd already processed. She could at least have given me a heads-up before luring me to the shed:

"Hey, if you want me to put this sled away, I'm going to need help moving some stuff. Like Mom, for example." "Mom's in a better place.

And I don't mean a Justin Timberlake concert." "Bad news: Mom is stone-cold dead. Emphasis on the cold." But all I'd gotten was *get out here* via text.

I'm not saying I wasn't freaked out—then, and for a long time after, and really, maybe I will spend the rest of my life half freaked out—but so much has happened that I can't just go back and relive it without all the other stuff I know now. And I don't want to.

I really don't want to.

What does it matter if we screamed or cried or ripped our hair out or hyperventilated? If we fell to our knees and tried to shake Heidi by the shoulders, if we dropped her immediately because she felt more like a frozen bag of potting soil than a person? If we were so sure we were dreaming that we bit off a piece of our cheek trying to wake up? Or if we didn't, and we just stood there like calculating, unfeeling robot monsters?

It doesn't. That was then, before the identity thefts and the pyramid schemes, the tiny fictions and the great big lies, the digging and the covering and the goodbye-ing. If there's one thing my family has in common, it's believing that what you feel matters way less than what you do. That's true for Carna and for Malcolm. It was true for Heidi. It's always been true for me. The jury might be out on Lock. And I don't know which way I hope he lands.

While I was still reeling, Carna was thinking out loud. "She must have come out to get the suitcase before she started packing," she said, shining the light over to the **zebra-striped hardside (★★★★,** **finally found a suitcase that isn't boring)** sitting on the floor next to her. "Do you think she had a heart attack? Mal's got high blood pressure, but I didn't think she did."

I reached in the pockets of Darden's coat and found no phone. "Have you called yet? Did you call?"

"Remember when that English teacher collapsed at school? They said that was an aneurysm. And she was only thirty-seven, too."

"Give me your phone." I grabbed the phone from her, the beam of the light trailing over Mom's still face and resting on the rose-gold down puff of her jacket. I turned the light off, then back on. It was hard to know which was worse: seeing or not seeing.

My fingers were so cold that the touch screen barely registered them. It took multiple tries to get to the dial screen.

"Who are you calling?" Carn said.

It was a startlingly stupid question, the kind that is so stupid that you wonder if you're the stupid one for not understanding why someone would ask it. "911?" The 9 took, and I breathed on the tip of my finger to warm it up enough for the 1s.

She grabbed her phone back and erased my progress. "Why?"

"Because we found a dead body? And it's MOM'S?" I snatched the phone away.

"Right. A body. An ambulance can't do anything once you're dead." She stared at me, the glow from the top of the phone softer than the harsh flashlight below, but enough to see that she was as certain as I was, or maybe more. "Let's first figure out what to do."

Her eyes had cleared but the lashes were still wet. They'd freeze solid if we stayed out there much longer. I took her phone back. "I'm going to call."

If you don't live in a place where it can be far enough below zero that you can freeze a pair of wet jeans so solid they'll stand up in the snow (or freeze a human body so solid that it fails to decompose after three days), you might not realize how hard extreme temperatures are on batteries.

The red depleted icon glowed for a half second, and then Carna's phone died. Too. The only light was a murky square of moon inside the door. I reached again into Dard's empty (except for a puck, a bagel loyalty card, and a quarter) pocket, where there was still no phone. "Damn."

Wind whirred through the vents in the roof and the doors swayed on their hinges. Malcolm would have eventually finished wiring the shed and put in a motion light if Heidi hadn't sent him to the lake for good. Neither of us spooks easily, but anything dead is at least a little disturbing. What seems gentle and harmless alive loses those qualities when their eyes are stuck open: Deer. Rabbits. Ducks. What you were already unsure about definitely doesn't get any better: Coyotes. Fish. Mothers.

"Let's go in. My phone's in the house," I said. On our way out, I knocked into the cup again and sent it skittering out the door. In the faint light, I recognized the design: a poorly drawn mammal holding a mug of coffee over the words "The Roasted Badger: Keeping Wisconsin Ornery Since 2003." I'd always hated that slogan, and now I always would.

# CHAPTER FOURTEEN

D on't be mad." Dard stood just inside the door to the house blocking me, feet apart, knees in, chest wide, like a goalie.

Unless it was a whole bunch more dead people he was blocking me from, I was not going to be mad. I tried to step around him, but he maneuvered in front again, still talking. "It was an accident. Audrey is cleaning it up."

Someone spilled a beer. Or kicked over the dump-truck load of popcorn his mom sent along. Or broke one of those wineglasses that had seemed so nice an hour ago. I deked, but slipped in his giant boots. He caught me by the elbow and boosted me up. "It's totally going to be fine. I promise." I jerked my elbow back. Why did guys think they could make such ridiculous promises? It was definitely not going to be fine.

Usually, I would be moving into crisis management mode at "don't be mad," identifying the problem, assessing the problem, addressing the problem, checking the problem off the list of problems, and moving on to the next problem. My modus operandi. But I was already in crisis mode, and whatever Darden thought was a crisis could not possibly be a crisis, and he was annoying me. I stepped out of his boots and kicked them into the door.

"Darden, I really don't fucking care right now." He winced. Mc-Murrays didn't like the f-word.

Audrey walked in carrying a dustpan in one hand. "Oh god, Drew. Taylor is so, so sorry."

I heard Carna slide the patio door open and shut behind me. She was carrying the coffee cup. "Did you tell them?" she hissed.

"Did you tell them?" is a rookie move, one neither of us would make now. We were spared, though: Logan poked his head into the kitchen and said, "Does one of you have a clean shirt Taylor can wear? She's rinsing hers out in the bathtub."

Dard, dustpan, so, so sorry, and bathtub shirt? The thing (dead mom) you would think would crowd out any other thought moved over just an inch, enough so that instead of saying, "Hold up everybody because my mom who you all thought was so cool and spontaneous is now *very* cool and spontaneously dead," I said automatically, "What happened?"

Audrey looked at Dard and back at me. "Taylor threw up a little, well, kind of a lot, and then when she ran to the bathroom, she knocked into that little round table and—" I followed Audrey's eyes down to her hand. Not the dustpan hand. The other hand. The hand holding a lidless pewter container shaped like a cookie jar with a cross etched on one side. (Classic Pewter Urn, size large, ★★★★★, can be personalized with the name of your loved one.)

"Jesus," I said.

"You guys spilled Grandma?" said Carna.

That's the moment that interrupted what was clearly the right thing to do: Call authorities. Report tragedy. Put lives of three minors in hands of anyone but me.

But suddenly it was obvious that the first thing I needed to do was not call the ambulance (police, fire department, non-murder death responders, whoever), but get these dumbasses out of our house. If this was the worst night of our lives, I didn't need any of them livestreaming it, which at least two of them definitely would have.

Heidi could wait a bit. (She could technically wait until the temperature got above freezing.) The drunk idiots who had spilled my grandmother could not. I have always been excellent at prioritizing.

"Let me see." I held out my hand. Audrey reluctantly handed over the urn. "How'd the lid come off?" It was always screwed on tight, because whenever Lachlan picked it up, I'd say, "Make sure the top's on tight" before he used it on the edge of a blanket fort or traced the bottom for a good circle or shook it like bartenders shook cocktails on TV.

They stared at me like a bunch of guilty campers who ate all the marshmallows before the fire was lit. "Connor wanted to see what was in there," said Darden sheepishly. Connor, whose giant pickle-jar-loosening hands had freed Grandma Sharon, was nowhere in sight, probably wandering around opening drawers like a curious oaf seeing what other treasures or cremains he might find. "I guess he didn't put it back on tight."

On top of everything else, Carna was right: These guys *were* douchey. "I guess not," I sighed, exasperated.

"The part on the table was easy to sweep back in," Audrey said. "It was harder to get off the carpet, but I think I got most of it. I don't know why it's still so empty, though." She peered over the edge with me, where the chalky sand that used to be my mother's mother filled only half the urn. She sounded sincerely apologetic, even though she wasn't the peeker, the puker, or the spiller. Audrey wasn't an asshole. She was the one who was cleaning things up. Usually, that was me. Maybe she could help haul Heidi out of the shed.

I shook my head. "It's fine. They sent a large but she was only a hundred ten pounds when she died, so it should have been a medium."

"They come in sizes?" Audrey said, then looked guilty for asking.

I screwed the lid back on Grandma Sharon, as tight as I could. She shouldn't have been out in the open anyway, since she was supposed to be enjoying crab legs at the casino. I could imagine Darth hunched over bits of spilled crumbs with a magnifying glass, trying to determine if they were human or Frosted Mini-Wheat.

Logan said again, "So do you maybe have a shirt for Taylor?"

"Carna, grab something from my room." She hurried out without calling me a wannabe boss bitch or telling me to get it myself, which should have been a flaming red warning to anybody who knew us that something more was wrong.

In the living room, Audrey and Darden scrubbed a puke spot on the couch. Connor was cleaning up popcorn, which had also spilled, by eating it off the floor. They'd switched from the movie to the NBC broadcast from Times Square. The singer was wearing body glitter instead of a good wool base layer and a wind shell. People are so impractical.

I went to check on Taylor. Somewhere between taking off her puke shirt and putting on my clean one, Taylor and Logan had both been inspired to stand shirtless in front of the mirror comparing biceps.

Carna yanked me hard into Mom's room. "As soon as I can get them out of here, I'll call," I said.

"I told you not to invite them."

I glared.

"I found Mom's phone out there," she said. It sat on the **MiCharge Cordless Charging Pad (★★★★★, works as fast as a cord)** next to the bed.

"The cord will work faster. That thing takes forever."

"It won't turn on even with the cord. It's completely dead." We both winced at the word, although what else you could say about a battery? Utterly depleted? Without charge?

(Could you say those things about a person? Was that better than dead? "I'm sorry to tell you she is utterly depleted." "You mean she passed away?" "I prefer to say she can no longer hold a charge.")

"I'll get mine. I think it's in the living room."

"Drew, you need to think about this first."

No one has ever accused me of *not* thinking about something first. I am a planner. A list maker. A pros and cons-er. My family complains I think too much.

And right then I was thinking that Carna was pissing me off. "I need to think about what first?"

She checked the hallway and shut the door softly. "You call, and they send an ambulance, probably, then police, too, once they realize she's dead. Or the police come first and then the ambulance."

"I don't care what order they come in."

"But think about it. We know whatever happened happened Friday night. Right? Because of the snow? So she got back from the passport place and came home to pack—"

"Oh, are we doing a timeline now? Don't forget the part where she stopped to steal my paycheck and flirt with Audrey's manager." I lifted up the Roasted Badger cup, which Carna had set next to the charger. It said *Drew's Mom \*\*Special\*\** in Brandon's scrawl.

"Yes, we're making a timeline. The timeline is the point. Think! What happened *today*? Remember? We told the guy that she was on her way to the casino? *You* said they were going to get crab legs. This morning?"

"*Crrraaappp.*"

"Nobody's going to buy that she got back from Ho-Chunk this afternoon and froze that fast. It's going to be a little hard to explain why we claimed she was here this morning. And they're *definitely* gonna wanna know where Grandma is."

I wanted to puke on top of Taylor's puke. "Actually, I looked it up and I think Potawatomi is the one with crab legs," I mumbled.

This is why I don't lie. Because you think you're solving one problem but really you're creating another. It's like doing a maze in pen where maybe—maybe—your wrong turn makes a quick loop and lets you back onto the right path, but maybe it sends you all the way to a dead end with no way to double back. Making up a story without knowing how you'll solve all the problems you've created is really risky.

Correction: It's why I didn't used to lie.

We needed to get back on track. It was all fixable. We hadn't actually done anything wrong. Or not *very* wrong. "Okay, what if we just wait till the morning, and then when they come we'll say we thought she was just staying at the casino for New Year's?"

"I still don't think she'd freeze that fast." Carna said, wrinkling her nose.

"*Fine*. Tomorrow night, then. It's *cold*. But shit. That still leaves the grandma problem."

"Maybe the next day," said Carn. "So we have time to figure stuff out."

"We can't just leave a body in our backyard," I said.

"It's not in the *open*."

A sudden, concerted countdown started with seven out in the living room. I waited till after the "Happy New Year" shrieks to continue.

"We just have to act normal for now," I said more to myself than Carna. "So whichever day we call, we can act surprised. We don't want it to seem like we've been hiding something."

Carna nodded. "If we were, though, we wouldn't call 911. We'd bury her or something."

"What?"

"Dad's place would be perfect if the ground wasn't frozen."

"WHY WERE YOU ALREADY THINKING ABOUT THAT?"

*BAM!* The door banged open against the hamper. I'm sure we both looked guilty as hell. Audrey's bubbly face dropped when she saw how serious we looked. "What's wrong?"

The real answer was "virtually every single thing you can imagine," but before I opened my mouth, Taylor, fresh as an all-done-puking daisy in my new Wisconsin T-shirt, popped beside her, full of conspiratorial excitement. "Come on, guys! We're trying to find your mom!"

# CHAPTER FIFTEEN

ogan had found a livestream of the New Year's concert in Mexico City. The camera was trained on JT and his dancers, but every time it panned the crowd, everyone leaned in to search for Heidi. The potential brush with international fame had them riveted to the screen like they were searching for Waldo in a souvenir sombrero.

I looked to Carna, mortified. She gave me the slightest yeah-this-is-messed-up shrug, and pretended to watch the screen.

"Text her and ask if she's on the left or right side of the stage," Audrey suggested.

"I don't think she'll answer," I said.

"Is that that guy from *Grey's Anatomy*?" asked Logan.

"You watch *Grey's Anatomy*?" Audrey asked.

I tried to think through the next day (or two, if I listened to Carna), but something felt off. Not just the part about Heidi being out in the shed. Obviously, that was very off. But there was something else that my mind kept circling but not quite landing on.

Everyone but Connor had switched to Coke or Lock's Capri Suns after Taylor threw up, which meant they'd be sober enough to send home soon. Not sitting on Darden's lap would make it easier to think.

We'd stick with the story about Heidi being home, but we'd have to cop to lying about our grandma. There was no good way around that. We could blame all that on Heidi, though; it's not like they could charge her. Krystal would probably blame a lot of her own things on Heidi, too, once she came back aboveground, which wasn't really fair. But those parts weren't the hard part.

It clicked into place like the reels of a slot machine, if the payout was quarters that blew up in your face. The next days weren't the problem. Not even the next months, which would be hard no matter what. The problem was the next years. Nine or ten of them. The problem was Lachlan.

Excuse me, Darden's parents, but *fffuuuuuccccckkkkkk*.

"THERE!" Taylor yelled, and no one jumped higher than Carna and me. "In the pink sombrero!" She pointed insistently at the bottom corner of the screen, before the video panned back to the stage. Darden nearly tipped me off his lap trying to catch a fleeting glimpse of Heidi.

"Yeah, that was totally her," confirmed Logan, even though he'd never met my mother.

Everyone agreed, rewriting what they saw to include what they wanted to see. Everyone wanted so badly for it to be true. Maybe me most of all.

"Did you see her?" Audrey asked, when Carna and I had said nothing. Carna raised her eyebrows at me.

I swallowed hard. "Yeah," I said, making sure my voice didn't wobble. "That was her hat."

If we could make them see Heidi on TV, what else could we make people believe?

# CHAPTER SIXTEEN

If you waded through the piles of clothes and balls and stuffed monkeys and Marvel guys that covered the floor of my brother's room, and then pushed aside the Happy Meal figures and stacks of Fly Guys and Big Nates on his dresser, you would find a framed photo of an Internet-perfect man in his late twenties, wearing camo fatigues and smiling in the sun. Lachlan's father. Captain Chad West.

Captain West was killed in Afghanistan. He was heroic and handsome, kind and honest and a very fast runner. He had always dreamed of serving his country, and he did so bravely. He was good at Legos and liked Cartoon Network. He got lots of army guy awards because he was the best one. He danced like Justin Timberlake and burped the alphabet. He and Heidi were going to get married if only he wasn't killed saving children and their pets in a school.

What else are you going to tell a kid?

That you hooked up with an orthodontist, who was such a tool that he offered to pay you as a part-time employee for the next eighteen years instead of giving you child support because he could run it through the business and his wife wouldn't find out? That you knew what a tool he was anyway, so you were glad not to share custody, but you were such a good negotiator that you also arranged for the full health plan plus a discount on braces for your firstborn, even if that meant he was going to tighten those wires like a vise?

That is a much worse story. The fictional Captain Chad West is sad, but no sadder than the true-life orthodontist. The fake late Captain West loved Lachlan more than anything; the real living orthodontist hadn't even bothered to meet him.

Heidi had added details over time, depending on Lock's questions (not many) or other inspirations. For example, Captain West was only Lieutenant West until Carna googled army ranks and we promoted him.

But if you're eight and your mom is dead, you can't live with a made-up dad whether he was made-up dead or made-up alive, no matter how terrific he was. Either you find yourself sprung on some shitbag tooth jockey and his wife (who doesn't know you exist) or the State of Wisconsin scrapes the bottom of your extended family barrel and comes up with an aunt too lazy to drive to Colorado or Illinois like a normal person to buy her own weed pastries.

"I bet they'll let you move in with a friend to finish senior year," Carna said when everyone had gone. "I mean, I don't know *who*." Rude. "Audrey seems all right. And then you go to college. They'll try to send me to Starling, which completely sucks an entire ass. But bright side there's a lake at Mal's, so I can drown myself if I need to."

Carna living with Mal and Stephanya in Starling would be a disaster for all of them, a hellscape of anger and argument that might push Steph to trade in her lavender oil for pepper spray. Still, it was nothing compared to the black hole that Lock would fall into as soon as anyone found out there were no adults in our house. It didn't matter that I was ten times more responsible than Heidi. What mattered was that I was seventeen.

"How could you put us in this situation?" I said to no one.

# CHAPTER SEVENTEEN

HAPPY NEW YEAR!!! OPEN 8–2

→ WHO'S DOWN TO BREW ←

JANUARY SPECIAL!!! TRY OUR MILF LATTE!!!

The Roasted Badger must have wanted to make sure the Instagram story was up before its hungover customers were, but it was probably only me seeing it in the tiny hours before dawn.

I'd been scrolling mindlessly, trying to distract myself from existential anxiety while I waited for Carna to come down to brainstorm our way out of an impossible mess. The post was obnoxiously chipper, like someone had discovered stickers and exclamation points and wanted to use them all at once. It was the description of the manager's new special that grabbed me: espresso, oat milk, and real Nutella, with whipped cream and toast sprinkles on top. It sounded delicious. Excellent work, Brandon. Heidi would have loved you for it, if only it hadn't killed her.

In sixth grade, Will Schatz brought me a small Christmas box of Ferrero Rochers, which, to his credit, are the fanciest-looking chocolates you can get at Walmart. The crush wasn't mutual, which is why

I felt too guilty to eat any. Heidi didn't feel guilty, though. She ate them all.

Fifteen minutes later her face was splotchy and her tongue was swollen, and even she thought it was bad enough to call the nurse line.

That was how we found out she was allergic to hazelnuts. As in, the main ingredient in Nutella.

The clinic said allergies can appear out of nowhere in adults, but it was more likely she just hadn't had a lot of exposure to hazelnuts, because my grandma said later, "Oh yeah, that used to happen to you every once in a while, but I never figured out what it was. I thought maybe fruit." Grandma Sharon was where Heidi got her top-notch parenting.

Since it had taken her whole life to have such a serious reaction, and even then, she was fine after a double dose of Benadryl, Heidi more or less ignored the whole nut thing. Even Lisa paid more attention. The last time she'd visited from Phoenix they'd come back from lunch with a leftover salad, sprinkled with goat cheese and toasted hazelnuts. "Here. You can have this. I wouldn't let your mom eat it."

"I was going to pick them off," Heidi complained. And then, "I hate salad anyway."

I threw it away rather than have it in the house, and made sure Lachlan got tested by a nurse, instead of her homegrown method of trial-and-anaphylaxis.

"Guess what?" I tossed the empty cup to Carna as she came in. "It wasn't an aneurysm. It was a latte."

# CHAPTER EIGHTEEN

<u>OPTION A: CALL POLICE ASAP</u>
*drew* ⟹ *stay with friend til uw*
*carna* ⟹ *drag to starling hellhole—die of boredom + stephanya*
*lachlan* ⟹ *surprise family reunion at mansion w/assholes*

<u>Cons:</u>

- *orthodontist = dursley family dynamic*
- *starling = duck dynasty family dynamic*
- *lock loses mom (fake) dad us school faith in justin timberlake etc*
- *carn gets arrested for burning down starling house*
- *those people don't want lock*
- *those people don't want carna*
- *lock ends up an orthodontist*

<u>Pros:</u>

- *ortho = $$$$*
- <u>*legal!*</u>
- *lock lives with responsible(?) adults in mansion*
- ~~*get rich from supplements pyramid scheme*~~
- ~~*free retainers 4 life*~~

OPTION B: CALL POLICE BUT LEAVE OUT ORTHODONTIST

*drew* $\Rightarrow$ *friend til uw*

*carna* $\Rightarrow$ *bestU headquarters and mutually assured destruction*

*lachlan* $\Rightarrow$ *aunt krystal or home alone kid when she forgets he exists*

Cons:

- *most of above plus . . .*
- *krystal = sooooo irresponsible*
- *krystal = hates children*
- *krystal = steals from children*
- ~~*krystal = eats children*~~
- *lock ends up a small-time criminal*

Pros:

- *krystal less evil than orthodontist (maybe?)*
- *legal (pretty much)*
- *krystal move in here ~~until she burns down house through negligence~~*
- *see lock whenever*
- ~~*lock probably natural at crime*~~

OPTION C: DON'T DO ANYTHING STUPID
TIL WE FIGURE STUFF OUT

*drew* $\Rightarrow$ *home*

*carna* $\Rightarrow$ *home*

*lachlan* $\Rightarrow$ *home*

Pros:

- *home!*
- *together*
- *life goes on*
- *masters/mistresses of own destiny*

Cons:

- *illegal*
- *insane*
- *IMPOSSIBLE*

"That whiteboard is earning its stars. *Helps with organizing. Comes with markers.*"

"JESUS!" I whirled around and tripped over my own feet, scrambling backward like a panicked crab.

"Not quite."

My supposed-to-be-dead mother was stretched across a **papasan chair (★★★★★, great for girl talk with your bestie!!!)**, examining a photo cube that Darden gave me for some month anniversary. She wore a white tank and jeans that had self-conscious rips in all the places the manufacturer ripped them. Long feather earrings brushed her shoulders. And on her head, a hot-pink sombrero.

"I didn't know you'd be able to hear me," she said, mildly surprised. Like how you'd feel if you learned that Justin Timberlake thought that JC Chasez was the best singer in *NSYNC.

"Yeah, I can hear you," I stuttered.

"Wait—can you see me, too?" Heidi twisted from side to side, a feather catching in her hair.

She had to be a hallucination, but she didn't look like a hallucination. She looked solid. But wasn't that the whole thing with hallucinations? "Yeah. Can you see *me*?"

"Of course I can see you, but I thought I'd be like a spirit or a voice or something. *Wooo-ooo*," she put in Halloweenily.

I stood up and took a step closer. "Are you . . . you *are* dead, right?"

Heidi laughed. "*Now* you're asking? Maybe you should have thought of that before you left me out there. It's like forty below." I must have looked concerned, because she added, "Duh. Obviously. I'm super dead."

"So if you're dead, who am I talking to? Am I just talking to myself?" I didn't believe in ghosts, but whenever I talked to myself, it was to-do lists or Spanish vocabulary words, and then it was only me that answered back. And never any visuals. This didn't feel like talking to myself.

Heidi made a noncommittal shrug. "How do I look? Normal? Or like a zombie?" She rolled her eyes up and hung her mouth open zombie-style.

I dug the **Beauty Mate Lighted Two-Sided Magnifying Mirror with USB (★★★★★, can see every blackhead)** from a box of junk that never sold and was headed to Goodwill. She looked in one side, then the other. I leaned in to see my own giant eye and an empty papasan chair. I should go back and update the review. **Does not work on dead people. And why would a mirror need a USB port?**

"Does this mean you're a vampire?"

"Nah."

"That's too bad," I said sympathetically. She'd always had a thing for Robert Pattinson.

"Right?!"

I sat down on the edge of my bed. "Honestly, you look exactly the same."

"Any thinner?" It was impossible to miss the excited lilt. She always wanted to be skinnier than Krystal.

"No, just the same."

"Figures." She crossed her legs under her, the tattooed ring of flames around her ankle tucking beneath. Heidi and Lisa-in-Phoenix got them right after the members of *NSYNC did. She was sulking now, either because she was dead or because she wasn't a skinny vampire.

When other people claim a spirit is communicating with them, it's a voice saying they'll be okay, they are loved, forgiven, etc. Last-minute bits of wisdom. Advice to cherish. Encouraging words or bible verses. This was not that. This was a dull, non-vampire, non-zombie version of my mother acting no more philosophical or profound than she ever had in real life. This was Heidi examining her nails, pushing back the cuticles with her thumbnail, probably thinking about asking me for a favor.

If you had told me that one day my mother would come back to haunt me, this was exactly what I would have expected.

I was tempted to wake up Carna, who had finally crashed after several hours arguing that we could probably cover up Heidi's death forever, or at least until I turned eighteen in the spring and could be everybody's legal guardian. She reasoned that the two of us (meaning me) already did almost everything anyway, so who would even notice? And in the fall I'd simply arrange my schedule at Madison to drive down for class a few days a week. Carna's Plan C was too stupid to even go on the board, but I like three columns and the first two were not exactly winners, so I hadn't erased it when she'd written it up there. She'd eventually gone to bed pissed at how stubborn and unimaginative I was (also selfish and a rule follower and my breath smelled like garbage and so on). Obviously I should have gone to bed, too, because now I was talking to a dead person.

If I had lost my mind, though, I didn't want Carna to know until I'd found it again. And if somehow I hadn't, maybe Heidi would visit Carna, too, and we could talk about it then.

"What happened?" I asked.

AfterHeidi nibbled on a hangnail. "Exactly what you think happened." It was obvious that she had nothing more to say on the subject.

"Jeez. Sorry," I said.

She lifted her hand to push her hair back and felt the hat. She took it off and looked at it curiously. "Me too. I just wish I had made it to Mexico before."

"That's your big regret?"

"Don't start, Drew." She scratched the pin-dot scar where a nose ring once was, a habit she had never been able to break. It had been rebellious when she was in her twenties, but when all the women she called the "yoga bitches" started getting them for their fortieth birthdays, she let the hole close.

"Look, you kind of left us with a mess." It was an understatement, like "I've noticed a slight change in the polar ice caps" or "Malcolm seems somewhat laissez-faire about parenting."

"Yeah, all that stuff with Grandma is kind of a cluster," she laughed. Actually laughed. "It was working fine until my sister decided she needed muffins. Typical Krystal." She looked amused. She had never taken anything as seriously as I had—and maybe that's why she had gotten away with it. It was me who made sure that the beeping batteries in the smoke detectors got replaced. It was me who carefully picked through Carna's scalp night after night when the sixth grade couldn't quell its lice outbreak. It was me who didn't think it was cute that Lock started preschool still calling himself "Walkwin He-yew" and made her take him to a speech therapist. Nothing seemed to worry Heidi Hill, even less now that she was dead.

"I know you're just in my head right now, but you're still pissing me off."

"Am I?" She arched an eyebrow. I didn't know if the question was about pissing me off or being just in my head.

"I don't care about Social Security or your taxes or any of that. You can't get in trouble now. But what about Lachlan? Did you not plan for anything? Is there a will somewhere?"

"Psh. Lawyers."

"Well, there's no way he's going to the orthodontist. That douchebag didn't want him before, he's not getting him now."

"Plus remember how he used to crank on your wires? I never saw anybody finish braces in twelve months."

"I was also very good about my bands."

"Obviously. But he's a total dick. And maybe a sadist."

"But then what? Krystal? Krystal would last one weekend before she tried to find an elementary boarding school."

"Remember when she stole all your Polly Pockets because she thought they were the kind that were worth something?" I did. I also remembered that Heidi had done the same thing with a bunch of Pokémon packs.

"And I don't know what to do about Carn either. Can you imagine her at Mal's? I know she hates everybody here, too, but she'll go nuts in Starling. Plus Stephanya's moved in, so there's not even any space for her."

"Not with those paintings of loons and beaver dams and all those smelly candles." Mind Mom gagged.

"If Carna moves up there, she'll end up some kind of prepper. She'll find a cave and stockpile weapons and beans."

Heidi mimed paranoid rifle holding, checking over both shoulders.

"You really left us with no options."

She crossed her arms and tilted her head at me, one feather earring dangling low. What kind of poltergeist accessorizes like that, but doesn't impart any otherworldly wisdom at all?

"No options?" she asked.

I followed her gaze to the whiteboard, where Carna's third column had a lot of white space and no actual detail. I shook my head hard. "That is only up there because I didn't have anything to put in that spot. It's not a real option."

"You sure?" She fake-pouted a little, but she was clearly amused. "Come on," she said, and I knew what was coming next. "I just need you to do this one thing for me, Drew."

Heidi was as bad a mother dead as she was alive. And I was just as much a sucker.

# CHAPTER NINETEEN

never thought my mother was very smart, because she didn't do great in school, she dropped out of college, and she never had a job that seemed like a real job. I thought those were the things that measured how smart you were. Sanna Tempe's mom? Chiropractor. Super smart. Britelle Olziewski's mom? Stayed home, but graduated from Grinnell and organized everything in the school district. Medium smart. Mine? Internet reviewer, Social Security scammer, orthodontist blackmailer, piece-it-together type. You get by with what your genes give you.

Now I understand how smart she had to be. For one, she was an absolute virtuoso of dishonesty, and you can't lie so smoothly, so well, for so long if you're not at least some kind of smart. She pulled money out of nowhere. She solved her sister's problems and managed to keep her mother out of trouble when her husband died with eighty thousand dollars in credit card debt. She wasn't exactly on top of school or medical appointments or emotional and behavioral growth, but she did keep Lock out of a Snow White–level stepmother situation. Plus she got us employer-sponsored health care without an actual employer.

She was decent to people who had had a hard time, and a wolf around those who only thought they had. I can think of times she took advantage of people (me, for example, all the time), but I can't think of a time someone took advantage of her. So no: not a 3.9 GPA or an impressive resume or a letter about education funding published in the *Wisconsin State Journal*. But you have to be smart to keep all those balls in the air, the plates spinning, the secret things secret, the ducks in their proper rows.

And that's how I know that I'm actually really damn smart, too.

No matter what the admissions department thinks.

# Part Two

# CHAPTER TWENTY

The weirdest part was how normal everything seemed at first. Life should change more if your mother drops dead. We all went back to school. I worked my regular shifts. I packed a sandwich for Lock if school was serving French toast stix. (It's bread and syrup. Buddy the Elf is the lunch lady at Larch Leap Elementary.) Carna complained about everything and didn't do anything. Darden's hockey season was in full swing, so I only had to text that I missed him too once or twice a night and he was taken care of. Even the persistent, high-pitched ring of anxiety wasn't entirely new. Just louder.

It was pretty much how we'd already operated. We had known she wasn't going to be there for a little while and then she just kept not being there.

I hadn't agreed to Carna's Plan C. I was biding time until I could come up with a Plan D. What did another day or two matter, I thought every day or two. It hadn't gotten warmer than eight degrees, with the nights dropping below that, so Heidi was more or less Han Solo out there. Part of me knew that every day we were making it harder to turn back, but still, we kept going.

"Any response from K-Darth?"

"Nothing."

"Man, he is really shitty at his job." Carna sat on the edge of a chair to turn a **NüWül Sock (★★★★★, genetically modified sheep are a game changer)** right side out. "Do you think he gave up that easily?"

All we'd done was send one email from Heidi that said the kids had forgotten to give her the messages (which killed me, because I would never *not* deliver a message promptly), and asked how she or Grandma could be of help. We cc'd Sharon Hill at a Gmail address Carna registered five minutes before. And then nothing. No response via email or mail or his own earmuffed spermy-headed in-person self. Maybe that's all it took. I'd noticed a couple of slow, unfamiliar cars, but there was a house for sale on the block. Once people discovered how sad a row of 1960s houses looked compared with the bright new development where the orthodontist lived, they moved on.

"If not, I hope he's watching Grandma's Amazon account." I hit "buy now" on a Victoria Houston mystery. Sharon also bought herself a pair of heated slippers. They had excellent reviews, which might have convinced my grandma but didn't fool me; someone like Heidi was writing those reviews. See, Darth? My grandmother is alive and well and ordering grandmother things online. If we could satisfy him that the mysterious case of Sharon Hill was a false alarm, it would give us time to figure the rest out.

I shut the cover of the laptop and stood up. "Okay, let's go."

It was getting dark. Lock needed to be picked up from school in a half hour. As far as he knew, Mom was still in Mexico trying to take a selfie with Justin. Second graders don't keep track of time or parents very well. Sometimes ten minutes is ten hours, and sometimes a week is a day. We'd been on "Is Mom coming back today?" "Not yet, bud! A few more days!" for two weeks. Sooner or later he'd need an explanation for her absence, but that was part of the Plan D I hadn't come up with yet.

"This is pretty much the worst thing you've ever made me do," Carna complained, scratching her ankles viciously as she laced up her boots.

"I'm not *making* you." But I was; I could do a lot of things alone, but not this. "You're going to get a rash from those socks," I said, leading the way through the sliding door.

"I might be allergic to NüShēēp."

The shed looked like it always looked, if you didn't count the corpse: a mess of boxes; small appliances and home goods no one had bought; camping gear Malcolm left behind; a mini picnic table Lachlan had used once for an unsuccessful lemonade stand; unused yard tools. And now Heidi, who, thanks to the subfreezing temperatures, looked pretty much the same as always, too.

"Grab that blue tarp and those bungees," I said, lining the deer sled up next to the body.

Carna and I held opposite corners of the tarp, like we were folding a sheet, and laid it across the sled. She took hold of Heidi's ankles while I reached under her shoulders. We'd cleared tree limbs out of Malcolm's drive like this, when Malcolm or the wind took them down. Now we lifted Heidi together, just as efficiently, and set her on top of the tarp. I held my breath; Carna did, too. I don't know why. She wasn't heavy.

It was a good fit. One end of the sled angled up under her head, like she was watching TV in bed. We wrapped the tarp over her and crisscrossed bungees on top, securing the hooks to the sides. Carn snapped a cord, lightly, to make sure it was secure.

Now if Darth, Lock, someone hoping to steal the lawnmower, or anyone else happened to look in the shed, what they'd see was a roof rake, a **SalonMe Inflatable Bonnet Hair Dryer Attachment (★★★★★, everyone assumes I had a blowout)**, and a sled that appeared to be preloaded with provisions for the Iditarod.

I don't mean to suggest that it was easy to wrap our momsicle in a tarp and bungee her into a hunting sled. We were just being practical, more task than trauma. We weren't "over" it. We probably never will be, entirely. Besides, the AfterHeidi who showed up to harass me felt more like the real her. A body, at some point, is just more stuff.

Carna stood up and cocked her head. "It's much less creepy than walking in here and seeing her face."

It was. I bit the thumb of my mitten, thinking. "We'll just have to take her out again when we're ready to report her missing."

Carna cringed. "The hell?"

"If she's all packaged up in our sled, it's going to look like we murdered her." It didn't seem that much grosser to unwrap her than to wrap her up in the first place, as long as she stayed frozen.

The last time I'd been at Darden's, his mom set a gallon pail of ice cream on the deck and said, "Best part of winter: outdoor freezer space!" I bet that was still outside, too.

All our research said that as long as it stayed cold, we had time. It was only the beginning of January. It was only the beginning.

"Get used to it, Carn. This is our life now."

# CHAPTER TWENTY-ONE

don't even get a blanket?"

I ignored her and kept typing. She played with the buttons on my **Panometric Projection Alarm Clock with Bluetooth (★★★★★, displays the time on the ceiling so you know whether to wake up).** Even with her hand in front of the projector, the digital readout on the ceiling said 11:55.

She laughed to herself and unzipped her jacket. "Thanks for not blowing off Lisa, by the way. I don't want her to hate me." I said nothing, trying to focus on the free response section of my world history practice test. It wasn't enough to know the material; you had to feed it back to them exactly like they wanted it but still make it sound like it was your idea. "Even though she should have come with me to Mexico."

I looked at her. "You didn't actually go to Mexico."

"Oh good! I almost thought you couldn't hear me this time!"

I went back to my screen and got half a thesis sentence written before the screen blacked. Heidi appeared in a FaceTime window. It was the third time that week that she'd shown up in my room.

"I really need to do this, so if you're bored and want to chat, maybe you could haunt Lisa this time."

"Hah! I can't haunt her! She doesn't even know I'm dead!"

Keeping up with the flow of messages from Lisa-in-Phoenix was another part-time job. The whole time Heidi's phone was unconscious she'd bombarded it with messages that started out wishing Heidi a great trip, then moved to why she was ignoring her, then guessed Heidi was mad at her for not coming along, and finally, in a burst of empowerment, remembered that she hadn't even been thanked for scoring those tickets in the first place, which seemed typical and self-centered. I would usually agree with the last part but it seemed unfair given the circumstances.

Carna wanted to fire back a solid *fuck off* to save us having to deal with her, but I felt too guilty. They'd been friends since high school and it seemed harsh to end it that way. We settled on "sorry! didn't want to tell you i had to miss it after you got me those amazing tix!" The story was that after the first flight got canceled, she tried to re-book, and then she thought her phone got stolen but it was really just lost. Lisa, to her credit, sent back lots of gasping and sad emoji faces and promises they'd go to Mexico together SOON.

I wanted to write back "I shouldn't because I'm the single parent of three children and I can't keep expecting Drew to do everything for me," but Carna wouldn't let me.

Instead there were some Single Ladies dance GIFs, agreement that it was going to be amazing, and a heads-up that it probably couldn't happen for a while because things were crazy with some legal stuff and the kids. That part was actually true, as well as a good excuse to not respond every time Lisa sent a screenshot of someone on Bumble or a video of dogs doing dog things or a meme about chocolate, which was often.

Lisa would definitely appreciate an otherworldly visitation from Heidi more than me.

I switched back to the Google Drive window, but a second later, YouTube opened with Mom's face in the thumbnail. She reached over the frame of the video and full-screened herself. I put my hands in my lap and sighed. "WHAT?"

"Jeez, you really need to work on being more welcoming."

"I really need to work on getting on some antipsychotics."

She laughed harder at that than she should have. "Drew-el! I don't know why you're getting so stressed out about everything. It's all fine." I gaped at her and she amended herself. "I mean, it's not *great*, but it's fine." She looked up where a ceiling would be if poltergeist mothers have ceilings and rocked her head back and forth. "Coupla things to work out."

No shit there were a coupla things to work out. Which coupla did she mean? "Such as?"

She leaned farther into the screen like she was letting me in on a secret. "The big thing right now is that you're getting behind on product reviews."

"REVIEWS? I don't care about product reviews."

"You *should*. If you're going to keep this up awhile."

"I'm not going to do your stupid reviews. I don't have time." I motioned to the open book next to my keyboard. Every teacher must have realized over break that they hadn't plotted out the quarter correctly, because suddenly it seemed like they'd doubled assignments. Even Lachlan was bringing home more worksheets. (Carna ran hot and cold on homework, mostly cold.)

"Look, if you don't start reviewing, you'll run out of things to sell, and if you don't start selling, you're going to run out of money," she chirped. It was more parental than she usually sounded, which was extra annoying. "Also, you haven't posted to Heiding_In_The_ Kitchen since before Christmas, and I was working so hard to build up followers. I was almost at a thousand. At twenty-five thousand, you can start doing affiliate sale stuff."

"*I* haven't posted?"

On the screen, she raised her eyebrows and threw up her hands. "Well, I can't do it."

"How am I supposed to do any of that stuff?"

"Everything's on my computer."

"Well, where's your computer? We looked but we can't find it. Hello?" The screen froze. I riveted the space bar. "What am I supposed to do? Hello?"

"I'm hungry." I whipped around to see Lock, then back to my computer where my unfinished free response window awaited up to eighty more words. I slammed the top shut and glanced around to make sure Mom wasn't lurking. No Heidi. Just Lachlan, my real-life brother staring at me from the door. The Wisconsin T-shirt (which somehow came back from Taylor straight to him) hung to his thighs over outgrown Paw Patrol pajama bottoms. He looked too small and too big at the same time.

"Why are you up, bud?"

"'Cause I'm hungry."

"Why are you so hungry?"

"Because my stomach is empty?"

I put out my hand to lead him back upstairs. He lifted both of his to my neck, and I found myself lifting him up, cold ankles wrapped around my waist and warm cheek pressed to my neck. Too small and too big at the same time.

"I think you should just go back to sleep."

"I think I should have a healthy snack." He's either unconsciously adorable or really knows how to manipulate me. World history homework and budget crises would have to wait. I carried him up the stairs and sat him on the kitchen counter.

He slurped Honey Nut Cheerios and milk from a coffee mug while I stood in front of him. "Let's not make this a habit, okay?"

"Hey, what am I missing in here?" Carn shuffled in to refill her water bottle. She peered over the edge of the mug and he laughed guiltily. "Mmmm. Midnight snack." She pulled out another mug for herself and offered one to me, which I declined.

Carna turned to Lock and said, "Drew is such a midnight-snack pooper." She filled her cup. "She must not know they taste better after midnight." Lock looked back and forth between us, beaming and giggling at Carna's cartoonish nom-nom sounds.

He scooped up a spoonful and held it out for me, milk dripping from the bowl of the spoon onto the floor. The little Os danced in the spoon, soggy and spitty and waiting. We should all be in bed. It was a terrible habit to be encouraging. I wasn't even hungry.

But they were right.

**Lachlan's Cheerios, ★★★★★, best after midnight.**

# CHAPTER TWENTY-TWO

Hey," I said super casually. "Next time my mom comes in, don't mention the thing about spilling my grandma's dog's ashes, okay?" I didn't look up, just kept wiping down the bagel bins. "My grandma would totally flip out if she found out."

"Your grandma's *dog*?" Audrey said.

"Yeah, remember? On New Year's? Taylor knocked over the—"

"I remember about the ashes, I just thought you said it was your . . ." She suddenly looked embarrassed. "I was confused, I guess."

"Oh, did you think it was *our* dog?"

"No, I thought it was . . . never mind."

"Yeah, Grandma lives with us some of the time, so she keeps a lot of her stuff there. Oh, I think you have a customer."

# CHAPTER TWENTY-THREE

Does your sister, like, hate guys?" Logan was still trying to figure out Carna a couple of weeks after New Year's.

"Pretty much," I said, not looking up. It was too cold to leave for lunch, so we were all smushed into one table in the cafeteria. I was rewriting my formulas sheet for statistics because Lock had gotten something sticky on it. Stats was supposed to be easier than pre-calc while still showing colleges that you were serious, but it was killing me. It was statistically unlikely that my B minus in statistics was worth more than Darden's A plus in Keyboarding Essentials.

"So what's her *deal*?" Logan continued. Not in a judgy voice. More fascinated, maybe.

Darden was practically sitting on top of me, dripping buffalo sauce out of the wrap his mom had made. I tugged my paper closer. I didn't want to have to make a third version of my notes. "She hates girls, too, if that's what you're asking."

"Carna pretty much hates everybody," added Dard happily. A big squirt of orange escaped his sandwich and obliterated my standard deviation formula. I folded the math notes into a square and took out a new page. Carna wouldn't even need the formulas sheet. She'd just *know*.

"Why?" Logan went on. It was actually possible he was interested in her. That happened sometimes, an unsuspecting student would sidle up, think they could break through her crusty exterior to find him or herself a real sweet girl under there, that kind of thing.

"Hard to say," I mumbled.

"I don't think she hates everybody," Audrey piped in. "She might just hate everybody here." She looked pointedly at Logan. It wasn't exactly a great defense, but it wasn't exactly wrong. I glanced a silent thanks toward her, and then she managed to change the subject altogether. "Which prompt did everybody pick for that *Twelfth Night* essay?"

I didn't weigh in on the mix of answers and oh-yeah-when's-that-dues.

Dard leaned in and barked into my ear, "What do you wanna do Saturday?" He thought he was whispering.

"I can't Saturday. I've got to hang with Lock."

"Saturday night, though. Remember we said Saturday night for sure because last weekend you had to cancel?"

"I don't know how late it's going to be."

"I could come over. I have an old air hockey I could bring for him. My mom keeps saying I should get it out of the house."

Yeah, except that I need to keep Lachlan as far away from you as possible so when you ask if Heidi's on a date, he doesn't say only if her date's in Canada, which is where he thinks she is now. Dard looked hopeful and accommodating, though, and if the reasons to avoid him weren't so good (dead body, living life of lies, schoolwork), I'd have felt bad for avoiding him.

People started scooping up trays and books to head to whatever magic the next bell might hold for them. "I guess you could come over after he's in bed," I finally said. "Like ten." He looked very satisfied.

"Wait, so what's up Saturday? We going to Drew and Carna's?" Logan asked on the way out. I heaved out a sigh. The last thing I needed was Carna shooting Logan in the face; then I'd have to keep two bodies in the shed.

"Not you, bro," Dard said, shoving his shoulder. He winked at me.

# CHAPTER TWENTY-FOUR

Just give it to me." I held a hand out.

"I'd do it myself," she said, "except I don't want to."

We had found Heidi's laptop. My truck didn't start that morning because Lachlan had left on an overhead light when he went out to get the missing Drax that I had told him not to carry to school in the first place. We could jump it later, but I'd have to sit with my foot on the pedal for a half hour to recharge the battery, and there wasn't time for that. I didn't want to leave Heidi's car in back of the building for my whole shift because it might draw attention, so a half-awake, totally annoyed, and not-at-all-licensed Carna drove me to work at 5:45 a.m. in Heidi's Range Rover while Lock and the rescued Guardian slept.

Right in front of the bagel shop, the dumbest, fattest raccoon ambled out between two cars like it owned the place. Carna might have just hit it and put an end to its dumb, lazy existence, but her reflexes were too quick. She stopped short, saving the ungrateful animal and causing a slim **Xi-Book ProTech Series 7 Personal Compute Station (★★★★★, love the touch ID)** to slide out from under the driver's seat.

We'd been able to access some of Heidi's accounts using her usual Timberlake-centric passwords on my computer or her phone, but this laptop was the holy grail. If there were additional accounts, overdue reviews, documents, treasure maps, memoirs-in-progress, a will specifying that in case of death the children were authorized to raise themselves, etc., we needed her hard drive, bookmarks, and search history.

By the time I got home, Carn had it charged, but the Xi-Book didn't want a password. It required a fingerprint.

"Good luck," Carna called from the door.

I was still wearing my bagel shop polo under my jacket, which was probably a violation of some public health code.

"Heyyy, Mom," I said, squatting next to the deer sled. "I need to borrow your finger for a quick sec." It had warmed up to almost twenty, still cold enough to suspend decomposition, but warm enough to feel pricks of nervous sweat in my armpits. "Please don't answer me," I mumbled.

I unleashed the bungees and peeled back the tarp on her right side, where her arm was bent up at a slight angle. Her palm faced outward, like she was about to share a crazy story. I flipped the computer upside down and positioned the sensor over the pad of her index finger, rocking it back and forth to get it to register.

Touch ID Error

Try Again

I held her hand steady and pressed her finger more firmly into the sensor. It thought for a few seconds and then:

Touch ID Error

Try Again

Too cold? I was going to have a heart attack. Leaning in, I breathed over her fingertips, trying to thaw enough skin to trigger the sensor. Dard did the same thing to my hands when he touched them; maybe I felt dead to him, too.

Touch ID Error

Try Again

The battery was already dying—depleting—in the cold, as was my nerve. But we couldn't exactly bring the laptop and the finger into the Geek Squad to diagnose the error. It had worked before. It had to work now.

I pictured Heidi at the table, talking to Facebook while she scrolled. "We all know you're proud of yourself. You don't have to post your gross hashtag-plant-based dinner every day." "Sorry about the cancer, but I'm not GoFunding your random coworker." "Jesus Christ. Drew, come look at this. This baby looks like a clam."

The computer was working as recently as Heidi was. I rewound my memory further. There she was, jamming a fork into the Keurig (really, the MyBrew K-Cup Deluxe Koffee Kafe) to press the last drops from the pod into her mug. She carried the cup to the table, flipped up the top, asked me to call in sick to take Carna for new contacts while she was gone . . . and reached across the keyboard to open it.

Right. She was a lefty.

I stepped over to her other side. That arm was pinned partly underneath, which meant I had to tip her whole body onto its side to get to the pad of her finger. I told myself I was rolling a snowman.

The home screen sprang to life: Heidi and Lisa taking a selfie with Lance Bass in LA. Props to the **touch ID (★★★★★, it even works with dead hands).**

"See ya later," I said, suspecting it was true.

# CHAPTER TWENTY-FIVE

Remember how you told me to check to see if Heidi had other seller profiles and email accounts and stuff?"

Carna slid along behind me as I sprinkled a path of ice melt from the front door down the dark driveway. Lachlan had finally gone to bed. I wished I could, too, but FedEx had left a note that said they wouldn't deliver if we didn't do something about the ice. Maybe K-Darth would come and wipe out, hit his head, and forget what he was investigating us for, but we still hadn't seen or heard from him. Probably moved on to someone else's dead grandma.

"She did."

"Anything important? Or just a lot of Bed Bath and Beyond coupons?"

"Both. There are two people from eBay who paid for things that never got sent. They're mad. And some companies asking for links to our ratings and offering more stuff to review." So that's what Heidi had been talking about. "Do you want to five-star a laminator? That's one of the things. You could laminate all your to-do lists."

I dumped the last of my ice-melting pellets over her boots. "Where's the stuff the eBay people bought?"

"I found it. A paper shredder and a set of Eiffel Tower glasses. I told them we'd ship them tomorrow. They still need reviews, though."

"Tomorrow?" I kicked my boots off at the door, wondering when I'd have time to bring in packages to ship and concluding it was just after I cloned myself and before my shift at the bagel shop. In the meantime, I needed to read two chapters of *La Calaca Alegre*, do twelve pages of World History notes, check the application portal to see whether Ms. Flynn had turned in my rec and transcripts yet, and now, apparently, find something nice to say about paper shredders and novelty tumblers. "Can you please write those reviews?"

"I'll label the packages," Carna offered instead. It was something, at least.

Reviews intimidated me. Heidi had tried to get me to do them before, but I could never think of what to say, especially if we hadn't tried the things we were reviewing.

I found the product page on Mom's computer. French-Themed Glass Tumblers, Set of Six.

**★★★★★, Holds up to 16 ounces each**

"You sure you don't want to measure them to make sure you don't misrepresent the volume?" said Carn, picking up the Arc de Triomphe from beside me and rolling it in a piece of thin foam.

Backspace-backspace-backspace.

Carna was smart. She could have aced any subject she wanted to, but what she really cared about was what she did with her hands. The only time she and Malcolm could stand each other was when they were replacing rotten decking on the dock or wiring a fence to keep the deer out of the tomatoes. She didn't draw or paint. She built things that were useful or things that pretended to be useful—she would fly through Lock's Lego sets before he even had the minifigures sorted.

### ★★★★★, Decorated with French theme and holds up to 16 ounces each

"That's literally the product description." She cut two slits in a long bit of cardboard, then cut another to match. Unsatisfied with the quality of the original packaging, she was constructing her own.

It was a big part of what made school such a bore for her. She could do the work—most of the time easily—but doing the work never resulted in anything she thought was *necessary*. She was only in first or second grade when she'd gotten a worksheet back marked with a perfect score and a smiley face, and was incensed. "If he already knew the answers, why did he ask?" I believe she thought the teacher had really needed the help.

### ★★★★★, You can drink anything out of them

Oh my god. I was getting worse. "Who looks at reviews for glasses? They're just glasses."

"Algorithm." Carn shrugged, taping a flap.

If Carna could build or fix something, though, the prize was the doing. While I fretted over flattering six ugly tumblers, she packed them securely enough to survive a drop from the Eiffel Tower. She'd used extra cardboard to build a double-walled frame with a snug compartment for each glass. Notched bracing secured it from sliding, like a tiny hotel with private rooms for its fragile occupants. It was elegant and elegantly overkill. They would have arrived just fine buried in bubble wrap, which is all Heidi would have done.

"Next time I'm doing the boxes," I said, deleting everything I'd typed for the tenth time.

"You suck at boxes." She leaned over my blank comment box. "Say why you liked drinking out of them."

"But I didn't actually drink out of them."

"Oh god, Drew. You are so . . . Drew." Carna huffed. "Just say whatever you think someone who likes this kind of shit would want to hear."

I tried to imagine a person excited about tumblers that said MAGNIFIQUE! Not a French person. It would be someone who would have special drinkware for special occasions. The kind of person who had special towels just for Christmas. What would Darden's mom say about these glasses?

★★★★★, They make me feel like I'm in Paris

Carna looked over my shoulder. "There you go," she said. Her tape wheel screeched over a box flap.

"Wait." I added an exclamation point. **Paris!**

"Very enthusiastic," Carna said. It still seemed vague.

★★★★★, They make me feel like I'm in Paris! Bought these to use when I made—

"What's something French? French food, I mean."

"French toast?" she tried.

I frowned.

"Crepes?"

I searched on my phone and *voilà*.

when I made Ina Garten's beef bourguignon—

"What is that?"
I slid my phone to her while I typed.

and everyone commented how cute my theme was! I would buy an Italy set, too, for lasagna night.

Carna looked at me skeptically.

"Too much?" I asked.

"A little."

I deleted the part about the lasagna and posted.

"Très bien," said Carna, dropping my phone back in front of me.

"Mercy buckets," I yawned hard. "Hey, could you drop these things off after school tomorrow?"

She narrowed her eyes. "Like at the post office?"

"Yeah, or FedEx? Since you told the buyers they'd ship tomorrow. I'm really busy and if we don't send them tracking numbers, they're going to flag our seller profile."

She squinted at me. "You mean, like, drive there?" I nodded. It was probably a bad idea, but I didn't have time and didn't want to have to refund the buyers. "Can I drive Mom's car?" she asked.

"Just don't make it obvious. And don't get pulled over."

She almost looked like she was going to hug me. "I will be the most cautious driver in Larch Leap. I'll drive twenty miles per hour the whole time."

"No, then you'll just look high. Just be careful. And seriously, don't get pulled over."

Carna put a new label on the box for the **paper shredder (★★★★★,**

**turns sensitive documents into confetti; can't be too careful about iden-
tity theft)** and got up to go.

"Are you staying up?"

"I want to get through a few more before bed," I said, checking the list of unreads in Heidi's mailbox. It was so late, but it wouldn't be hard to say something positive about an aquarium. I liked fish. I navigated to the Everything Aquatic! website.

She hovered over me a minute like she wanted to say something.

"Good night," she finally said.

"Yeah," I answered, finding the model number of the tank to review.

She paused one more time on the way out. "Actually, that recipe sounds good. We should have that sometime." I assumed that meant I should make it. "All the reviews have five stars."

I snorted.

# CHAPTER TWENTY-SIX

The Google Doc was a masterpiece.

It tracked items expected, received, reviewed, posted for resale, sold, and shipped. I reviewed under a dozen names, sold under a half-dozen different ones, and used multiple seller sites. Entries were color-coded and cross-tabbed, so if you were curious about what products "Holly Heidkamp" had received in exchange for her honest and unbiased review, you could pull up that information, or if you needed to see how much "Midwest Kitchen Overstock Warehouse Supply Co." was asking for a new-in-box egg cooker, you could find that as well. I stopped reviewing anything we couldn't sell for more than fifteen dollars and looked for lightweight or compact things so we could make money on the shipping, too.

Payments routed through a variety of Venmo and PayPal accounts, or sometimes the Chinese version of those platforms when we could pull it off, which connected to Lock's Larch Leap Community Bank savings account. We figured no one would actually audit a child, and if Darth was monitoring Heidi's accounts, at least that part might be under the radar.

I laid out a budget for the month. Income included reselling everything we got for free "in exchange for our honest and unbiased

[5-star] reviews," Heidi's pretend job as a part-time bookkeeper at the orthodontist's office, Social Security deposits for a dead woman, child support from an absent father, and legitimate paychecks from my real shifts at the real bagel shop.

Expenses included house payments, car payments, heat/water/ etc., credit cards, cable, and all the stuff you couldn't get free in exchange for an honest and unbiased [5-star] review. It just worked. If only we could keep the Social Security for another year, we could pay off the Range Rover. (It was not a coincidence that the monthly payment on Heidi's car was nearly the same as the monthly payment to our grandmother. In Heidi's mind, she had more or less traded Grandma for a luxury SUV.)

Everyone assumes rich people are the best at managing money, but how hard can it be to pay your bills when you get a five-thousand-dollar paycheck every two weeks and all you have to do for it is show up to work?

Carna did the boxing and unboxing, and occasionally even tested out the products we were supposed to be testing, mostly out of curiosity. (The only thing we ever gave one star was a stuffed narwhal that was supposed to double as a heating pad for children. The horn got so hot you could hardly touch it. ★☆☆☆☆, **Dangerous, irresponsible, and should be recalled. A child would be safer with an actual narwhal.** We didn't get any more free stuff from that distributor, but we had standards.)

Besides that, Carna's main job was driving things to UPS or FedEx. Her lack of a license wasn't ideal, but after all our time at Malcolm's (whose only requirement was whether you could see most of the way over the dash), she was better behind the wheel than most of the licensed drivers backing into each other in the school parking lot. I still wouldn't let Lock ride with her, though. She had strict instructions about speeding, although in that unending cold snap, you would have to be doing eighty in a thirty to get a cop out of their warm cruiser. She loved driving the Rover; those errands were the only things she'd do without complaining.

As Carna had predicted, we (mostly I) could manage almost everything without Heidi, even if it meant having no time for sleep, fun, or normal human relationships. But in addition to school, future planning, and the generally acknowledged challenges of adolescent development, I faced several obstacles my mother had not:

1. an active investigation by a government agency that felt strangely personal;
2. a nagging conscience when it came to stringing Lachlan along; and
3. a body in the backyard that would not stay frozen forever.

Any of these challenges—professional adult investigator, curious quasi-orphan, decompositionally delayed body—could have been overwhelming, but I buried myself in a well-organized spreadsheet and the logistical problems I could solve. As long as I didn't stop long to sleep, eat, or think too much, it started to feel like we could pull it all off.

# CHAPTER TWENTY-SEVEN

Lock was quiet at dinner, focused on rolling a meatball around the rim of his plate. Each time it fell, he'd start it up at twelve o'clock, determined to complete the loop without error.

I looked at Carna, who shrugged.

"What's up, Poophead?" I said. "You're quiet today."

The meatball fell off. He carefully put it back in its starting place.

"Did something happen at school?"

"We had music."

I glanced at Carna, who was as clueless as I was. "Did something happen in music?"

"We sang. And did shakers."

So far so good. He liked music, and shakers were extra fun. "So music was okay?"

"Music was good. Music is always good." The meatball made it all the way to the top spot. Instead of starting over, he took a second meatball and put it in the starting spot.

"Maybe we can get some shakers for home."

He looked up at me, then at Carna, then back at his plate. He seemed to be considering what to say. I looked again at Carna, who paused over her own spaghetti.

"I want to know where . . ." He was suddenly distracted by the new meatball. He leaned his face close, then picked it up to examine it.

"Where what, Lock?" I tried. If this was the moment he was finally going to demand to know where our mother was, I wasn't exactly ready for it, but at least we were all together. But he was very focused on that meatball.

"What is *this*?" he asked, holding it up toward me.

"A piece of oregano."

"Why?"

"I don't know. Because it makes it taste good?"

He licked the meatball in that spot and registered no reaction. Instead of putting it back for a lap around his plate, he took a tiny bite out of it, then a slightly bigger one.

Carn and I watched him stretch a three-bite meatball into nine or ten bites, until she cleared her throat to change the subject. "I need Mom's other Visa for the post office tomorrow. The one with the—"

"WHERE...," Lock interrupted loudly, and we froze. "WHERE... is the Mickey Mouse Club?"

"The . . . Mickey Mouse Club?"

He blinked at me, not willing to be put off.

"Buddy, what are you talking about?"

"Ms. Emily asked if any kids had a favorite song, and I said 'Can't Stop the Feeling'—"

"No kidding?" said Carna, who had suffered a record twelve plays in a row while they built a box fort and I was at work.

"—and she said can I sing it, so I singed it." He stopped himself, thought for a minute, and corrected. "Sanged it. And then she said did I know whose song it was and I said everybody knows that, except some kids didn't. So I got to tell about him. And *then* she said Justin Timberlake was on a *show* for singing when he was only a little older than us and it was at the Mickey Mouse Club."

Carna scratched her eyelid with one finger to cover up how hard
she was trying not to laugh.

"Is it by Sam's Club?" he asked.

"Um, no," I said, straight-faced. (I have a lot of practice taking
earnest boys seriously.) "It's not a place. It was a show. It's not on
anymore. But she's right; Justin Timberlake was on *The Mickey Mouse
Club*. So were a bunch of other people."

Lock frowned. "Are there other shows for kids who are good
singers?"

Carna stifled a laugh. I kicked her. "I'm not sure. I think you have
to live in LA or Orlando or somewhere like that. But you know what?
In middle school, they do a musical, and everyone can try out for it.
And sometimes the high school needs a younger kid to be in the show.
Darden's sister got to be in a high school musical when she was only
eleven."

Lock looked amazed, imaginary stage lights brightening his eyes.
"Did she sing?"

"And danced."

A slow smile spread across his face. "I'm good at singing," he declared, and tucked into his noodles.

"Yep," Carn said.

Future career sorted, his usual wiggle was coming back. "Ms.
Emily said so." He wrapped a single strand of spaghetti around the tip
of one finger and nibbled at it.

I looked at Carn and smiled. Crisis averted, or at least deferred.

"Mom thought so, too," he added.

I almost threw up in my meatballs.

# CHAPTER TWENTY-EIGHT

O h, hey," I said, stepping to the side to let Dard in. He was not supposed to be here, and yet, here he was. "Don't you have practice?"

"I'm skipping today." There was dramatic catch to his voice, exaggerated by how loud it was. I hoped that it was just that Netflix had taken *Miracle* off streaming, but I was pretty sure it was something I did. Or didn't. He pulled off his hat and rumpled his hair, looking like a giant, fragile child.

"You can do that?" I tried. "Won't Kopanieck freak out? Sectionals are coming up . . ." Please go to practice. I really don't have time for this.

"He knows that some things are more important than hockey practice, Drew." If only our school had one of those win-at-all-costs coaches instead of the I-support-the-emotional-needs-of-my-players type. "Can we talk?"

"Yeah, okay." I automatically checked the time on my phone. He winced.

He'd be a good boyfriend for somebody. He was nice. He was sensitive. He shared his feelings. (All of them. All the time.) He liked me and told me often. If I'd ever sent him a topless selfie, he would have wiped his entire phone rather than risk an accidental share.

But honestly, it was a bit draining. Darden was needy in a totally different way from Heidi or Lachlan or the rest of my family. They were logistical; he was emotional. Part of me wondered if Dard was what normal needs looked like, because most of my relationships were with children or very immature adults. (Even Stephanya didn't care about building a relationship—she only cared if I would buy enough supplements to get her to regional sales director status.)

It was one thing to check "after-school snack" off a list. It was another to take responsibility for periodic ego boosting and reassurance. Where does that go on a schedule?

He looked at me, chin low, eyes raised, both wounded and challenging like a character from a Lifetime movie. I wondered if he had rehearsed.

"What's up?" I said, trying to sound compassionate.

"I should be asking you what's up."

"Excuse me?" I said, unable to keep the edge out of it. *If I actually answered that question, it would blow your fucking mind.*

"I should be asking *you* what's up. I never see you anymore. It feels like you have time for everything else but me." I closed my eyes to keep them from rolling or shooting lasers.

"You're working all the time."

*Yeah, because some of us don't have parents who* . . . well, I guess I could just stop there.

"You never wear the earrings I got you for first Valentine's."

I automatically felt my lobes. I actually liked those earrings, but I hadn't seen them in a while.

"You haven't even come to a game since New Year's."

The last burned with indignation, probably fanned by his mother, who watched every minute of every period wearing a McMurray jersey and who had taught herself video editing so she could make

Darden-centric highlight reels to post. Of course the McMurrays would notice that I wasn't showing up to the ice. Of course they'd know their winger deserved better in a girlfriend. Of course they'd tell him so. "I *miss* you. Don't you miss me?"

I missed a lot of things. I missed getting more than five hours of sleep at night. I missed going to school without worrying that Heidi's phone would ring in the middle of Spanish because Lock accidentally stapled his fingers. I missed having my own Instagram account instead of a half dozen fake ones. I missed being happy when the extended forecast showed a late January thaw instead of panicking the shed would get above freezing. I missed knowing that my life was on the track I'd laid out.

And believe it or don't, I missed my mother.

But Darden? I guess I'd forgotten to miss him.

Whatever had linked us together in the first place had rusted through, and I'd known it for a while. But up until New Year's, dating Darden had been easier than not dating Darden. I had an identity at school, a place to sit at lunch, and someone to hook up with who didn't send me dick pics without asking. And he got a zero-drama girlfriend who knew how to skate, didn't complain if he had hockey every night, and kept his family in leftover bagels. The boxes were checked. Whether my social circle was really my first choice of social circle didn't matter, because the idea of floating around outside of one was worse. It was where Carna had been for the last few years and it didn't look good out there.

But holding out for graduation so no one got their feelings hurt didn't seem like it was going to work anymore. It was one thing to have no fucks left to give; I also had no room in my schedule, a dozen new false identities to maintain, and a woman wrapped in a tarp in my backyard.

I needed either to dump him or to get him to dump me.

"You're right. We should talk," I started.

"I'm so glad you're saying that, babe," he blurted, "because I think so, too. We have a lot of stuff to talk about."

I glanced down the hall at Carna's door. She would be listening to every word he said; it was impossible not to. I just hoped she'd be able to restrain herself from heckling him.

"Oh, sorry! I didn't mean to say *babe*! I know you don't like that."

Carna's voice in my head said: "No offense to pussies, but that kid is a pussy."

Just do it, I told myself. You'll probably be in jail when prom rolls around anyway. "Things have been really crazy lately."

It was not untrue.

He looked worried.

"Look, babe." I forced the "babe" because he looked so sad. "There's a lot going on"—I instantly regretted the "babe" because now he looked hopeful—"right now. Stuff you don't know. It's just not a great time for . . ."

His face, which had ticked from worry to hope, and back to worry, suddenly looked curious, like a dog noticing that his owner picked up the leash instead of her car keys. "Who's that?" he interrupted. I followed his gaze out the window to see K-Darth walking purposefully up the driveway. He stopped behind Darden's car to look at the license plate, dug a pen out of his inside pocket, and scribbled something on a pad.

Now? Seriously, now? The two most annoying guys in the state pick the same day for a visit?

Maybe that's unfair to K-Darth, since he was only doing his job.

Maybe it's unfair to Darden, since he was only being Darden.

Or maybe it's unfair to me, since I wasn't the one who chose the least interesting version of being a detective as a job or the one who needed constant reassurance about being sensitive and desirable.

"Do you know that guy?" Dard asked.

Possible explanations tumbled through my head: "That guy? Just an investigator looking into Social Security fraud. No biggie." "That guy? He sells solar panels." "Oh, him? He's an amateur ghost hunter, so if he asks about my grandmother, pretend she's alive. He's always looking for ghosts to hunt."

K-Darth rang and knocked at the same time, because that's the kind of asshole he was. It was such a stupid coincidence of timing. Maintaining different lies to different people simultaneously was advanced duplicity, and I wasn't sure I was up for it. What would Heidi do? Or Krystal? Finally, Darden said, "Aren't you going to get that?"

"I don't want anything to interrupt our conversation?" I tried to make it convincing.

"Oh. Gosh. Thanks. But, uh, he can see us."

K-Darth was staring at me through the window. He rang again without breaking eye contact. I started toward the door, then turned to put both of my hands on Darden's arms. "Can I trust you?"

"Of course! Always!" He looked so sincere.

"Remember how I said things had been kind of crazy? I'm going to need you to back up whatever I say to this guy, okay?"

"Okay."

"Like even if it sounds like, um, like not a hundred percent true."

"Wait, what?"

"Actually, just don't say anything. Not a word. Can you do that? Look like everything is normal and *don't talk*." He was looking over my shoulder at Darth's face in the window. "Is he looking at us?" He nodded. "Smile like I'm telling you something nice, like I just said I love you or something." He smiled painfully. I suppose I should have just said I loved him instead of telling him to pretend I did.

The bell rang again, and Carna stormed in, annoyed. "Can't somebody— Uh-oh. Shitcurds." She turned back around again.

"Yep," I mumbled, swinging the door open. "Oh no!" I gushed, propping open the storm door just enough so he could hear me. "You have the worst luck. They just left!" I tried a friendly, sympathetic frown.

"*Both* of them."

"If you'd only been here ten minutes ago . . ." He looked skeptical. I exaggerated a shrug.

"I suppose you don't know when your mother will be back." He didn't bother making it a question, just an exasperated statement.

"Nope. I'd say to wait in your car, but it'll probably be a while. Plus the neighbors will freak out if they see a strange guy sitting out in his car. The lady in the brown house—no, maybe it was the white house?—had this ex who kind of stalked her and . . . Holy crap, it's cold. Windchill, am I right?" I pulled one bare foot out of the door to massage my toes. "Do you want to leave a note?"

I'd gone with the classic Aunt Krystal: drown them with words, like a camper talking a black bear away from the tent. Make enough noise till they back off.

"Next time you should let us you're coming, you know? Like text or call or email or something," I went on.

"I was in the area, so—"

"And you don't have a phone with you?" I pulled my fingers into the ends of my sleeves and switched feet again. I would lose a toe to frostbite if this went on much longer.

Darth looked past me and focused on Dard, standing behind either protecting or stupefied, depending on what you thought of him. "Hello," he said. "We haven't met."

"Hi," replied Dard, then looked guilty because he wasn't supposed to speak.

K-Darth pulled off a glove with his teeth and fished a business card out of his inside pocket. He tried to hand it through the tiny opening in the door to Dard. "I'm—"

I snatched the card from his hand and said, "We're letting all the heat out! Drives my mom nuts!" It never had and never would, but it seemed the kind of thing people with mothers would say. "You should email. I think that's the best way to contact people."

"Do you live here, too?" Darth said to Darden.

"This is my boyfriend." I pulled on his arm and he inched closer. "We're just hanging out." Under other circumstances, I would have felt guilty about how pleased Dard looked that I was still calling him my boyfriend, but I didn't have the luxury of not confusing his expectations. The freshly reassured Dard waved awkwardly.

"Does your boyfriend have a name?"

I stared hate at Darth and he stared it back at me, the impossible tension of a face-off. I watched his lashes freeze. Then Dard broke in with "Darden McMurray. Sir." *Stay out of the circle before the puck drops, D-Mac.* He flinched and looked at me like a confused puppy: Oops. Was I supposed to wag at the man or not?

I forced a smile for both of them. "So I'll say you stopped by. Bye." Darth looked back and forth between me and Darden again before he turned to go, waving a hand over his shoulder. "There's black ice on the highway; try not to drive into a ditch," I yelled through the foggy glass, hoping he would drive into a ditch.

On the way down the driveway, he looked at Dard's car again, then up at the house. I wondered if you needed any kind of special warrant or permission to track down someone's granddaughter's boyfriend to ask him if she was dead.

I looked at Darden—sweet, loud, well-meaning Darden—who believed that relationships in high school were real, that our biggest problem was not having enough time to spend together, and that whatever was going on, we would get through it together.

It was not the right time to dump him.

# CHAPTER TWENTY-NINE

I wish you'd scheduled an appointment." Ms. Flynn peeled off her hat and threw it on top of a pile of papers. She sat in her chair without taking off her parka, and pried the lid from a Styrofoam soup container. "This is supposed to be my lunch break."

"I emailed you a couple of times, but I didn't hear back."

"Everybody is doing their applications right now. And there is only one of me for five hundred students." Wrong. There were four hundred thirty students, not five hundred, and only a quarter of them seniors, including a bunch who weren't applying to anything, but it didn't seem like the right time to point that out.

"That's why I gave you my stuff in November. Because I know you're busy."

She dipped a plastic spoon in the container, touched it to her lip, and frowned. Even if there were only two seniors and the other had enlisted and didn't need a rec, I'd still be sitting here watching her test her soup. Between coffee breaks, soup breaks, and sharing pro-life memes from her personal account, there was hardly enough time to complain about district budgeting in her six-hour day, let alone help students, which was her actual job. Renata Flynn sucked.

My bio teacher might have been a better choice for a recommendation. She didn't know me very well, but she seemed to appreciate that unlike everyone else, I never asked for an extension. But I'd been too intimidated by her—she seemed way too smart to be teaching in Larch—to ask. Or I could have asked my Spanish teacher, who sometimes came into the bagel shop with a "¡Buenos días, Drew! ¿Tienes semilla de amapola?" and left a two-dollar tip through the Square reader. But I hadn't wanted to draw attention to the fact that it was only Spanish III, or risk Madison being hung up on the fact that we didn't even have a native Spanish speaker for a teacher. ("Oh, look— another Olson teaching Español up in Bumfuck, Wisconsin.")

Besides, Flynn was the admissions whisperer. She knew someone at every Wisconsin school, and a lot in Minnesota and Michigan, too. If her name was on your rec, someone would read it, and usually, they'd let you in. There were medium-smart kids at University of Michigan and Lawrence who got there only because of her string pulling.

But there she was, not recommending anything. Not pulling any strings. Not, according to the portal, even submitting my transcript. Just sighing at her soup.

She stood up and maneuvered around me like I was as inconvenient physically as I was professionally. She set the soup in a small square microwave on a file cabinet. I recognized the model. The 5-star **ZenGen Compact Microwave heats fast and fits anywhere**. "That container's going to melt," I said.

"No, it won't," she chirped defensively, and turned the dial extra hard. We both watched through the door.

A happy ding announced her lunch was ready. She shuffled back to her desk, huffing as she went around me like I was turning left in the middle of a busy intersection. One edge of the bowl sagged, like it belonged in the Dalí poster pinned above Carna's dresser. I would have given the ZenGen five new stars just for backing me up. Ms. Flynn turned the melted part toward herself and sniffed.

"I was wondering when you might be able to turn in my transcript and recommendation. It's the last thing they need, and it has to be in by Tuesday."

"Where, again?"

"Madison? I sent you everything in the email." If I was my mother or my sister, I would have lost my shit, but I was me, and I needed her to submit my stuff more than I needed to rip her head off. "Twice," I mumbled to myself.

"Hmm. Madison's pretty competitive." She raised her eyebrows, looking into her bowl instead of at me.

"My GPA and test scores are in the range for in-state students." Why was I justifying myself? This was her job. If someone asked me for a bagel with honey-nut cream cheese, I wouldn't question whether honey-nut was too good for them. I'd just cheese the damn bagel.

She stirred the soup, thinking. The steam coming off it collected on her upper lip like sweat. I bet her face smelled like chicken. "You know your dad was a student teacher in this building." I had known that. I hadn't known it was relevant, but she said it like it was. She took a bite of soup and stifled a gasp. I hoped it burned her taste buds down to their roots. "I had just transferred from the Perch Lake district up in Door County. Your mom was here, too, of course, as a student."

*Oh god,* I thought. *She hates Heidi.*

She wasn't the only staff member who had been there since my parents' days, though most of them never mentioned it—not because they hadn't been memorable, but because I wasn't. "You've been here a long time."

She sneered a little. "I've seen whole families come through Larch.

Some good families." She blew on another bite of soup and changed her mind about it. "And, you know . . . others. Some just don't respect the system. And you hate to see them rewarded for that."

She might have sat across from my mother just like this, eating soup, and convinced herself that there were too many students in the school for her to be responsible if one of them happened to be dating a student teacher. She might have thought Malcolm was wrong to hook up with a student, but he was young, just finishing college, and young men can't be responsible for being young men. More likely, she blamed Heidi. More likely, Heidi was a bit of a slut. More likely, girls should know what and who is off-limits. And you hate to see someone rewarded for disrespecting the system.

True, Heidi disrespected most systems, but had her reward really been Malcolm?

"Your dad never did end up pursuing a career in education, did he? Just kind of threw that away." Forgetting that it was scalding, she popped the spoon in her mouth and swallowed hard. One eyelid fluttered.

My dad had thrown lots of things away over the last twenty years—job opportunities, mini-pickups, animal carcasses, goodwill, scrap lumber, us—not much of which he seemed to regret. A full-time job here, indoors, placating parents, not swearing in front of the school board, sitting in the staff lounge with Renata Flynn and her soup? Didn't seem like a huge loss.

"It turns out he doesn't like kids." I shrugged. "He still subs up in Starling, but it always confirms how much he doesn't like them. Us, I guess."

She sighed and motioned to the piles on her desk. "I'm swamped right now. I don't know when I'm going to get to it." She didn't look swamped. She looked like an old bag too lazy to transfer her lunch to a microwave-safe container.

How do you get this woman to do her job? Maybe if I looked depressed about the whole shitty-parent thing it would prompt her to put the stupid soup away and turn in a good recommendation **(Drew Hill, ★★★★★, unfortunate upbringing but a hard worker)**. Was I supposed to tear up or beg or something? I tried to remember how, but right then Britelle Olziewski popped in.

"Oh! Hi! I didn't know you were busy!"

"I'm not! Just trying to eat my lunch." Flynn smiled at her, neither of them acknowledging me. "What do you need?"

"Nothing! I just wanted to drop this off! It's a thank-you for all your help with my applications so last minute!" She set down an entire pie wrapped up in clear cellophane with a twine bow, and then crossed fingers on both hands and smiled so hard it wrinkled her nose.

I looked at the gift on the desk and back to Britelle.

She brought a pie.

A pie.

A PIE.

"Oh, Britelle, that certainly wasn't necessary!" But Flynn couldn't take her eyes off it, probably waiting for us to leave so she could pitch the soup and dive into the pecans. Along with the pie were two cards, one of which said "Ms. Flynn" and the other "Renata," in what I was sure was Britelle's mother's confident, easy hand.

Here are the two ways to get the attention of a school administrator:

1.  Have parents that write your whole life script for you (and write the script for the school, too, if they're really good). Teachers eat that shit up, like pie. Or:

2.  Be such a giant hot mess of a human they make a project
    out of you. They like feeling like saviors as much as they
    like pie.

Anything in the middle and you are an obstacle on the way to the
microwave.

Flynn's loving gaze finally moved up from the pie to meet my eyes.
She shifted uncomfortably. Even she would have a hard time justifying what I witnessed: "All your help so last minute."

"I'm . . . I'll . . . get it in, Drew," she said.

"I would really appreciate that," I forced myself to say.

I didn't fool myself that she was going to write the glowing or-
gasm of a tribute she would have written for Britelle, but I hoped
it didn't need to be. As long as it had Renata Flynn's name on it, it
should still do the trick.

# CHAPTER THIRTY

No one who knows us believes that Lock's dad is a dead war hero. Maybe people who don't know us don't believe it either. It doesn't matter what they think, as long as they don't mention it to Lock.

Lisa-in-Phoenix and Aunt Krystal know it's the orthodontist; everyone else has their own theory. People have asked about Malcolm, which proves how stupid people are about secrets. There's been speculation about guys in town; or a random hookup in Madison; or that time she left us with Grandma and stayed with Lisa-in-Phoenix for such a long time; or that the UPS truck is at our house *an awful lot*. The reasons they think Heidi must have a ton of unprotected sex with random men is that she never got married, didn't seem ashamed of not getting married, and didn't belong to any book clubs. Shocking behavior. Whoever they pick in the baby-daddy bracket, though, they agree that Lock must have been an "accident."

Nope. An accident is getting the wrong latte when no one is around with an EpiPen. My brother is not an accident.

Heidi was careless about a lot of things—I can whiteboard out an impressive list—but I can vouch, from *very* thorough conversations at *very* young ages, that reproductive health was not one of them. She was very on the ball about that. Or on the balls.

Before I knew what a penis looked like, she was making water balloons out of condoms to prove how strong they were. She put a box in the linen closet between the junior and regular tampons so we'd know where to find them. (I labeled the tampon boxes with my label maker; she Sharpied FREE CONDOMS with smiley Os.) She pushed birth control pills harder than certain people pushed nutritional supplements. "You can never be too careful." The absolute only thing Heidi Hill ever used those words about was birth control.

On the way out of the house for my third date with Darden, she told both of us that we should get a standing order for an RU-486 prescription, just in case, and she paid for Krystal's abortion when she was in a relationship with a creepy cop.

I remember when someone from her high school class posted about being blessed by their third "happy little accident," Heidi complained about how dumb she had to be.

"Oh, and you planned all of us so perfectly," I'd said. I was thirteen and judgy, pissed about having to babysit.

She looked at me, annoyed, and said, "Drew, I might not have known what I was getting into, but I knew I was getting into it."

The orthodontist didn't. But he was selfish, rich, and uninterested, with genes that promised success and good hair. That the douchebag didn't want to jeopardize his pretty marriage with news of an affair was not a surprise. That he was relieved when she suggested a purely transactional/stay-the-fuck-out-of-my-business solution was not a heartbreaker.

So, no, Lock was not a "mistake." I don't know why someone so meh about parenting would have wanted a third baby, but someday when I come clean to Lock, I won't be lying when I said she did.

# CHAPTER THIRTY-ONE

Carna considered herself entitled to unlimited lav passes as compensation for coming to school, but I only excused myself during class if it was really necessary, like when Heidi's phone kept buzzing in the **SAF-T Travel Belt (★★★★★, keeps my passport and other documents SAF)** I was wearing under my sweater.

My hand was up my shirt unzipping the belt when I walked into the first-floor girls' bathroom and found a guy in camo pants and an olive-green tee sitting on the counter playing *Fortnite*.

"Oh, hey!" he said, looking up with eager brown eyes. His cheekbones were hard but his smile softened them, dimples transforming the intimidating soldier to a razor model. His hair was dark, close-cropped but not buzz-cut. It had some curl to it, the kind that made cute, awkward angles if you didn't stay right on top of it. Like Lachlan's.

"I don't think you're supposed to be in here," I said, fishing Heidi's phone out of the travel contraption.

"Sorry! Do you need some privacy?" He glanced at the toilet stall and back at me, poised to leave.

"No. I just need to see who keeps calling." There were three missed calls from an unknown number, including one voice mail that said, *God damn, Heid, can you fricking pick up one of these times*: Krystal, who we hadn't heard from since she said she was going "off the grid," on a burner phone.

The soldier's boots hit the floor with a smack. "Captain Ch—" he started, hand out for a shake.

"I figured," I said, ignoring his hand and texting back—

**can't talk now—try drew if u need something**

—to my aunt. "Drew Hill," I said, because he looked like he was waiting for it.

"My pleasure to finally meet you." He beamed, rosy and expectant.

Fading petals of Renata Flynn's sanctimonious lilt passed the door, probably talking about the abstinence club she was always trying to start. Her voice prickled my neck more than Captain Chad West's, though, according to the portal, she had finally submitted the missing pieces of my application on the last possible day. I guess I owed her a pie.

"You look pretty perky for dead," I said.

"I'm made-up. Does that still count as dead?"

"Good question."

West stretched each muscley arm across his chest. His tee read USMC.

"I thought you were in the army. That's the marines."

He looked down at himself, unconcerned. "Yeah, Heidi got that wrong sometimes."

"I want to agree with you because she got a lot of things wrong, but since she made you up . . ."

He thought about that for a minute. "I'm just saying she could have researched better."

"True."

"And planned a little better."

"Also true."

A new text popped up from Aunt Nobody-Can-Prove-It's-Me:

that guy wants 2 schedule interview with Mom, fyi. i said she
lives with u guys.

There were more pending dots and then she added:

bc she does lives with u

Nice work, Krystal. Just in case someone besides Heidi (or me or Chad West, who was leaning over to see) was reading, that second text would divert any suspicion. Of course she does lives with us.

I looked at West, looking at the screen, till he looked up and smiled. "Did you want something?" I asked in the same polite way I would ask a real, living customer in the bagel shop who was taking too long to order. "Because I should probably get back to class."

"Oh, right. Sorry. I just wanted to check in about my boy."

"Ah."

"Lachlan."

"I know."

"Oh, right. Sorry. I wanted to make sure he's doing okay. With everything and all."

"Well, he doesn't really know 'everything and all.' He thinks Heidi's on an extended business trip. She went straight from Mexico to Canada."

The truth was that we weren't sure what Lachlan knew. Work travel should have seemed odd since she hadn't ever had a job, but he seemed strangely satisfied by the explanation. He didn't even ask what job it was. Then again, for a long time we couldn't tell if he still believed in Santa Claus or if he had too much invested in us believing that he believed. I didn't feel like getting into it, though, since the captain already knew everything I knew anyway.

"I gotta tell you, I'm a little worried."

"You're a good dad."

He smiled, proud. To be honest, he was showing more concern than Heidi.

"Fictional. And dead. But good."

"I just wish I could be there for him, you know?"

"Me too, man. Me too."

The bathroom door swung open and he slipped into an open stall without a sound. A freshman scuttled into the other toilet. She peed loudly and quickly, rinsed her hands, flashed me a shy smile in the mirror, and rushed out. West peeked around the stall door, then reemerged.

"So what do you want to know about Lock?"

"Everything you can tell me."

"Okay, he's eight, he's in second grade . . . I guess you know those parts. Um, he loves cereal, he just grew out of his snow pants, sometimes he lets Carna paint his toenails as long as she uses 'boy colors,' which apparently means orange and black." Chad looked unsatisfied.

"Is he playing hockey? Basketball?"

"I'm not sure if he's a sporty kid."

"Art, then? Animals? Magic: The Gathering? There must be something he's interested in."

"I mean, right now we're just trying to get by."

It hadn't been our best morning. We were already late and then Lock suddenly had to go back inside to pee, which took forever because he stepped in the puddle from his boots and had to change his socks, and then on the way when I asked if he'd locked the door, he said, "YES-YES-YES, DREW! Probably," which for sure meant that the front door was standing wide-open at home.

I had been driving him in case K-Darth tried to approach him when he was alone, but he liked the bus and the bus-stop kids. It almost felt like he was making the mornings hard on purpose so I'd put him back on the bus. That's what Carna would have done.

Of course. Crafty little shit. I shook my head.

The captain looked at me expectantly. "He's clever," I added. "And funny. And really sweet most of the time. When he's not, he feels guilty about it. He's pretty snuggly, like he'll sit right on top of you instead of next to you. I mean *right on top*." He laughed, leaning in, eating it all up. "He's smart, too. He's in the second-best reading group but he doesn't like the book they're reading so he wants to drop down to the third."

"Can he do that?"

"I won't let him. I told him he could get a new Beyblade when he finished the book."

The bell rang, meaning I had missed most of third period. Mr. Rice would assume it was period problems. Male teachers were willing to blame a lot on "period problems." I don't know what kind of problems they thought periods presented. "I should get to class. Thanks for checking in, though," I said.

"Yeah. Thanks." He nodded, but looked unsettled. The hallway was suddenly loud, like someone had turned the tap on the flow of humans. "Are you sure he's going to be okay?"

Another question from the captain I couldn't answer. "Maybe. Probably?" If I could think of any alternative where the answer was *yes, definitely*, my whiteboard would be clean. He looked sad, lost even. It wasn't good enough, and we both knew it. Sorry, imaginary dad. I know how you feel.

At the door, I turned back to him. "I should have said music," I offered. "He loves music. He loves to sing."

He looked up and smiled a little. "Music," he repeated, trying it on. "Hey, Hill?"

"Yeah, West?"

"No matter what happens, though, you'll stay together, right? All three of you. None of the rest of it matters. Promise?"

There were a thousand things beyond the control of a seventeen-year-old whose mom was dead and whose dad was a dud and who had no connections or money or power or lawyers or adults who weren't assholes. But I heard myself say it anyway to an empty bathroom, like a prayer. "I promise."

# CHAPTER THIRTY-TWO

- *grandma = agoraphobic, can't leave house for death star*
- *grandma = germophobe, can't let anyone in house*
- *grandma = ~~kidnapped~~ old-person-napped, can't come*
- *grandma = napping, can't come*
- *dress drew up as grandma since she's basically an old lady anyway*
- *grandma = joined cult, can't come*
- *burn house down + live in woods*

"You said we were brainstorming. You can't erase someone else's brainstorm," Carna mocked, pulling the eraser out of my hand. She rewrote "joined cult" on the whiteboard and drew a face with a triangular hat next to it.

"What is that supposed to be?"

"A cult hat."

As Krystal had warned, we'd gotten a letter requesting that Sharon Alberta Hill appear in person at one o'clock on the following Thursday at the Social Security Administration's field office in Madison. She should bring picture ID.

By then, it was clear we'd be better off saying our final goodbyes to Grandma Sharon even if it meant losing her deposits. I would have mailed in a spoonful of her ashes with a note that said, "You win," to get K. David Barth off our backs, except then he'd be even more determined to look for Heidi, and there was a solid chance he'd find her. So we were stuck pretending everybody was alive and living in a multigenerational sitcom until we could think of a better idea. Still, Darth was more than skeptical, even with occasional greetings from Grandma's Gmail and our judicious use of her credit cards. He'd even sent the letter certified, which meant we couldn't pretend it wasn't delivered. We'd need to produce our grandmother or a good reason for her absence.

Carna added:

- *grandma = arachnophobia, can't come*

to the board.

"'Cause there might be spiders in the office." She drew a spider with a cult hat.

"Can you *try* to help?" When I said encouragingly that no idea was too stupid, she'd committed to proving me wrong. Somehow, her being stupid made me the stupid one.

Mom had tried to convince me that not reporting Grandma's death started as an oversight, and that by the time she realized the money was still coming it had already been several months. But there had never been an obituary or funeral. Not even a Facebook post. It was like slowly loading your gun, asking someone to hold very still, and then claiming you shot in self-defense. She had covered it up from the beginning.

I probably shouldn't judge.

"This one is running out, too," said Carna, and threw the blue in the garbage on top of the black. "Your markers are trash. Plus your colors are boring."

She had added:

- *grandma = moved to africa, can't come*

The "come" was very light. She switched to red and outlined what was probably meant to be Africa, but looked like a cartoon steak.

Why had I dragged her down here? I could have made just as much progress (none) on my own, without anyone telling me my hair looked greasy.

I flopped back on my bed and stared at her latest entry to the list of useless ideas. And then I sat back up.

Darden's grandparents on his dad's side had done exactly this. Or not exactly—they weren't in Africa, they were in Sun City, Arizona. His mom thought the move showed insufficient devotion to Wisconsin, grandchildren, and associated hockey tournaments, confirmations, choir concerts, and birthday parties. Dard's dad defended them; he felt like there were enough people representing number 66 in the stands already (except me, who no one defended). It really was a reasonable thing to do, both because of the weather and because Darden's mom was a lot to take, but it turned into a competition between grandparents and a source of tension in their whole family.

"What if Grandma Sharon moved to Arizona?" I suggested. Carna drew a red giraffe next to the Africa steak. It had either two small triangle hats or pointy ears.

"Um, she's dead."

"Arizona is pretty nice this time of year."

Carna turned from the board to face me, looking thoughtful. "You know, it doesn't make sense for her to be out in this weather. She could slip and fall on the ice." She recapped the red marker and drummed it against her hand. "She *should* go to Arizona. She should leave soon."

"Yesterday," I corrected her. "She should leave yesterday. Right before that letter came. But just for the winter."

"Why? She might like it there all year."

"Well, for one, because it's really hot in the summer and she hates the heat."

"She's literally ashes."

"And also, because if we say she's there permanently, we probably have to get her a new bank. Plus they might transfer her case to Arizona, and maybe there's an Arizona Darth that's better than our Darth."

"Or an Arizona Darth that doesn't give a shit," Carna countered. We both felt like Darth had taken a personal interest in our family. Heidi had that effect on people even when she was dead. "Actually, that's pretty smart."

Brilliant, more like, but "pretty smart" was as big a compliment as she'd give me. The previous high point had been prom, when she said my dress didn't look as skanky as she thought it would.

"Thanks." I got up to erase the cult giraffes and spiders, feeling almost back in control for the first time in a while.

"Won't it seem a little shady if we just say she's 'somewhere in Arizona,' though?"

I licked my thumb and rubbed off a stubborn bit of Africa. The board looked clean. "We won't. We'll give them her new address."

Mom always said you were ride-or-die, Lisa-in-Phoenix. Let's hope that's true.

# CHAPTER THIRTY-THREE

My little brother is an excellent actor.

And by actor, I mean liar.

When I overheard him tell a kid at the second-grade choir concert that Heidi had "a 'mergency at work," I found myself wondering when she'd accepted a new position and what the emergency was.

He's also an excellent singer, even if he thinks he's singing falsetto like JT when really his voice is just that high. They don't choose soloists in second grade, but there were four or five out of sixty kids who really belted, and it was easy to pick out Lock's voice among them. He got to do the wood block on a song about woodpeckers *and* hold a flag for "This Land Is Your Land," so as far as we were concerned, he pretty much had the lead.

The smart thing would have been to nab Lock and slip out without drawing attention to ourselves, but he was determined not to leave without a square of Costco marble cake. Liam's mom was serving, so he was sure he'd get a piece with a flower.

I waited anxiously under the caged gym clock, smiling politely at people wondering what we were doing there instead of Heidi, though to be honest she probably wouldn't have come even if she wasn't frozen stiff. Carna sat on a folded-up section of bleachers, scrolling Heidi's Instagram and liking whatever needed to be liked. Lock finally emerged from the crowd, proudly carrying a Dixie plate with a large corner piece.

"Wow. That looks frostingy."

"It's the *most* frosting one."

"Congratulations. You really worked your connections. Did you get a fork?"

His face fell. "Hold this so no one takes it." He dashed back to the table, crawling under the legs of impatient dads clawing their way to the cake.

"Are you Lachlan's special guests?" Ms. Emily drifted up, her ID badge hanging from an LLES lanyard decorated with musical note pins.

"He's our brother," I said.

Lock bounded back with a plastic spoon and stopped next to the choir teacher. At that age, I felt like I worked for my teachers, and Carna assumed they worked for her, but Lock seemed to think he and Ms. Emily were friends. "Did you *see* this thing?" he said to her, taking the plate back from me. He spooned a whole purple rose into his mouth.

"Lachlan was excited you'd be here. I'm glad they let you out of class."

"We had a free period," said Carn, not looking up. She freed herself from a lot of periods.

"You must listen to a lot of music at home," she said. "I hear a lot about Justin Timberlake."

"Yeah, he was—is—our mom's favorite." Carn looked up at my flub. Lock kept spooning in cake. His tongue was black. "She had an emergency at work," I added.

"Totally understandable. What does your mother do?"

I blinked at her. "She's in sales," I finally said.

"That sounds interesting. I'm sorry she couldn't be here."

"Yeah. We all are."

"Well, you can tell her that your brother is such a good participator. Some kids are reluctant to sing, but not Lachlan. Sometimes I have to ask him to stop singing!" Carna tilted her head and squinted at her. "I mean, just if I'm explaining something to the class," Ms. Emily explained apologetically.

"We should probably get going, bud," I said to Lock, who had tipped his plate to his face to lick it. "You did a great job today."

"I wanted to ask: I'm starting a ukulele club after school. It's a good way to introduce a first instrument. Do you think that's something Lachlan might be interested in?"

I looked down at Lock, nibbling the edge of his plate, and remembered my conversation with Chad West about finding something that interested him. "We'd be singing a lot, too," she added.

"Lock, you think you'd want to do after-school music with Ms. Emily?"

"Right now?" He nodded enthusiastically, wiping a sleeve over his stained lips.

Ms. Emily laughed. "Tuesdays and Thursdays."

"*Both* days?" He beamed.

"I guess that's a yes," I said.

# CHAPTER THIRTY-FOUR

A re you sleeping?"

"Huh?"

"You were sleeping."

"No I wasn't. I was listening."

The last thing I remembered was Lachlan sitting in the papasan chair trying to learn the chords to "Can't Stop the Feeling" from a YouTube video while I tried to read. He'd come downstairs because Carna said ukulele sounded like a hungry Yorkie and she was going to carve the uke into a shiv and stab someone with it if she had to listen to one more minute. I liked it, though. Not necessarily the sound of the instrument, but the sound of Lachlan playing it. He was so determined.

Now it was dark, the kid was standing next to me, and I appeared to still be on page four of *The Kite Runner*, which was unfortunate, because it would be hard to write a three-page essay on only four pages of the book.

"Maybe I did fall asleep. I'm sorry, bud."

"It's okay. I think I never saw you asleep before."

"Yeah you have. You used to wake me up all the time when you were little. Mom would tell you to go ask me for breakfast."

"Oh yeah. Now you're always up before everybody."

"Yep."

"And you go to bed after everybody."

"Yep."

"You don't sleep very much."

"Nope."

"Except for this time."

"Right. But I didn't mean to. I guess I was tired." The last part came out as a giant yawn.

Lock looked down at the uke. "Maybe it was because you like when I play. Or maybe it's a magic one that makes people fall asleep!"

"Probably the first thing."

"Or maybe it's both things because I was the one *doing* the magic."

"Solid logic, bud." He beamed at me, a thousand watts of energy to my negative-one. It would have felt so good to close my eyes and go right back to sleep, just this one time, but he stood there, ukulele in one hand, waiting. "Um, did you want something else?"

"When's dinner?"

# CHAPTER THIRTY-FIVE

G reat. Now I'm Uber for hallucinations," I said, glancing at Captain Chad West, who had just appeared in the passenger seat. "Make sure you give me five stars in case the Tooth Fairy needs a ride."

"I don't actually need to go anywhere, but I'd definitely be happy to give you a good rating."

"You're very sincere, West." I sighed.

"Thank you, Hill," he answered sincerely. His seat belt was buckled, which was unusually cautious given that we were parked outside an elementary school, and that he was both imaginary and already dead anyway.

"So I checked with Lachlan about basketball and hockey and those were nonstarters. He said maybe baseball in the summer if Liam signed up, too. I didn't ask about piano lessons because we don't have a piano. Oh, and no to chess club."

"You asked him about chess club?"

"You wanted me to find out what he was interested in."

"It wasn't going to be chess club."

I shrugged, not offended. I didn't think so either. "But . . . gimme a drumroll here"—he drummed his hands on the dash silently—"he is an inaugural member of Ukulele Club!"

"Ukulele Club?"

"Yep. Meets after school Tuesdays and Thursdays."

Chad looked thoughtful. "Huh. Okay. Not exactly what I was expecting, but I could see it. It's basically a tiny guitar, right? Kinda *plink-plink-plink*?"

"Don't worry, man. He can graduate to a guitar in fourth grade. He mostly wants it to sing along to. I bet you can sing, can't you?"

He tried a few lines from a *Dear Evan Hansen* song Darden's sister belted poorly and often. Captain Chad West was, of course, Broadway-good (being fictional and/or dead lets you be perfect. (It only failed on Heidi because I knew her too well.)

"Lock and the ukulele are going to come through that door any minute." I pointed a mitten toward the school. "You going to stay and say hi?"

"Aw, you know I wish I could."

"Is that it? You just came for an update?" I hoped so. Usually, the otherworldlies showed up to make me feel bad about something.

A couple of parents crossed in front of us, heads down in the wind. Most people just lined up in running cars, but the seriously paranoid personally escorted their little Codys or Swee' Peas door to door. West watched them.

"I'm worried about safety."

"Hence the seat belt," I said, gesturing to his lap.

"'Hence'?"

"I need to write a will. I'm trying to sound more legal."

"Oh, that was pretty good. I like that. *Hence*. Have you tried *aforementioned*? That's a good one. Or *non compos mentis*?"

I glared at him. "Don't be a dick." He shrugged. The door to the building swung open and kids began to trickle out. "What about safety? You worried he's going to get lost on the way to the car?"

"Say, why are you in this junky car anyway? Don't you have a Range Rover?"

"Carna's got it."

"That figures. Anyway, I was thinking, your mom got lucky when you were little because you were such a, a, you know"—I snorted—"but Lachlan, he's a little more curious."

"Curious?"

"Like he's a kid who could get into stuff. Make, you know, curious choices."

"I'm familiar with my brother's curious choices." He had curiously chosen to stand on an empty fish tank to reach Liam's closet shelf, for example, and Liam's mom had to pick glass out of his shoes. "Just . . . it's your job to keep him safe, you know? You were kind of like a parent when you were a kid, but Lock, he's an actual kid."

The actual kid came out in a group of boys. I flashed my lights four times, which was our signal to find me in the line of cars. He waved with the ukulele case, then stopped to trade some special second-grade elbow bump with each of his friends.

West watched him, then turned to back to me. "If anything happened to him . . ." He looked like he was going to say something like "I don't know what I'd do," which was ridiculous since he couldn't do anything under any circumstances. But instead he trained those earnest eyes right on me and said, "It would be all your fault."

"Jesus, West."

The door swung open and Lock climbed into the seat Captain West had/hadn't been in. "It's cold as BALLS!" he shouted. Carna's influence. He pushed his backpack down into the well under his feet, pulled off his hat, and ran a mitten over his forehead to get his stat-icky curls off his face. It made it worse.

"Buckle your seat belt, please."

"I know, I know!" He snapped the belt in place, catching a mitten in the process, took off the mitten, fixed the belt, swiped ineffectively at the aura of his hair, gave up, and pulled his hat back on.

"Ready?"

"Spaghetti," he answered. A fan of hairs stuck to his cheek. "UGH! Hair! I hate hair."

He didn't look like he was in danger of anything but a hat.

"You want me to help with that when we get home?"

"Are you going to cut it off?"

"What? No. I'm going to introduce you to the miracle of condi-tioner." He looked skeptical. "Trust me, kid."


AT FOUR O'CLOCK IN THE MORNING, Lock was sound asleep, his head smelling cherry-almond, but I was wide awake, still thinking about safety. Stupid Chad West had brought it up like I might send the kid into grizzly country with a salmon-skin windbreaker, and now all I could think about were all the ways little kids might get killed.

Lock was too big to choke on hot dogs. He was too smart to shove a fork into a socket. There wasn't currently an open body of water in the state to drown in. Not enough traffic to worry about running out into, and he was way too suspicious of strangers to get into any vans promising candy.

Mostly, I was thinking about guns. Our guns.

When Carna was in fifth grade, she was almost friends with Berit Olziewski, who is not an insufferable suck-up like her big sister. (Carna would say the same thing about herself.) Professional Mother Brenda Olziewski called to arrange the details before she'd bring Berit for a playdate. It was one of Heidi's quintessential examples of why it was better to have a mother like her.

According to Heidi, Brenda called with a set of flash cards she got from uptight-yoga-bitch training, asking about screen-time philosophy, parental controls on the cable, if we had a "rescue" dog that might suddenly behave aggressively, if our bananas were fair trade or only organic, and how many ply the toilet paper was in case Berit needed to take a shit in the two hours she'd be at our house. Darden's mom was attentive, but Brenda O represented a whole other level of *involvement*.

Heidi went along with it, lying as needed (not about the dog, we didn't have one; and not about the toilet paper, if that was a real question, because we have good TP) because we all would have appreciated a friend for Carna for a couple of hours.

But then Brenda said, "I have to ask, Heidi, do you keep a *gun* in the house?" Heidi imitated this part like a whisper, as though the mere word put children at risk.

"Excuse me?"

"You know, with all you hear, we like to make sure that if our kids are going to be somewhere there are guns, that they are in a *gun safe*." Brenda sat there, waiting for Mom's response, while Mom sat on the other end of the line thinking about shooting her. "And that it's *locked*."

It was probably a standard checklist parents passed around on Facebook, but to Heidi, it felt personal. It felt like Brenda Olziewski had jumped from Heidi's not selling pails of fundraiser cookie dough to being too irresponsible to keep us from playing with firearms. You can imagine a meaningful pause here, where my incredulous mother organizes a dignified response, but you would be wrong. Heidi would never waste time composing herself.

"What the fuck are you suggesting, *Brenda*?"

"I'm not suggesting anything, Heidi. I'm just *asking* a *question*."

"What the fuck kind of question are you asking, *Brenda*?"

"Look, if it's too much trouble, why don't the girls play over here?"

"Oooh, that sounds like a carnival! Sign. Us. Up! But first I have to ask you, Brenda, have you put all your knives in a pirate chest and buried it in the backyard? Or do you just let the kids stab each other for fun? And have you taken all the laces out of the shoes? There are so many accidental strangulations involving loose shoes. You should get rid of the goddamn zippers, too."

"I didn't mean to offend you."

"No, no, no problem. Oh, by the way, do you keep your vibrator in a safe? And is it locked?"

The playdate did not happen. Carna and Berit did eventually hang out a few times, but not until middle school, when they didn't need their mothers to approve of each other, and not anymore, because Berit is a jock and Carna is Carna.

She could have just told her the guns were in a safe, because of course they were in a safe. And that's where I was at four o'clock in the morning.

The gun safe was a fireproof metal locker a little shorter than me and about two hundred pounds heavier. It sat with the water heater and dusty boxes of junk in the darkest and spideriest part of the basement. It must have been a few years since anyone had even opened the thing. If Carna and I shot at Malcolm's (usually watermelons and cans, which don't have seasonal restrictions and are surprisingly satisfying targets), we always used the ones up there.

The only things we kept at home were the .22s that Carn and I had gotten when I was eleven and she was nine, Grandpa Mitch's old 12-gauge shotgun, and a small handgun Mal had once given to Heidi as a gift, along with assorted ammunition and ear protection. The rifles would have stayed at Mal's except that he told Mom that "you and the girls should have some protection at the house down there." He was increasingly convinced that every hour you lived closer to Chicago, the greater the chance someone would kick in your door for drug money. I guess if my mother waving the Sig Sauer she'd only taken out of the box for selfies didn't do the trick, Carn and I could flank her with our deer rifles.

But even though Chad West was annoying, he might also be right. Lock had mastered the combination 013181 before he could properly count. That magic series unlocked Mom's phone, the iPad, paid Prime content, and the **iDiet Self-Locking Programmable Cookie Canister (★★★★★, have to think twice before I cheat)**. Sooner or later, it might allow him to open the gun safe, too. We needed a new code.

I opened the door to dial in a new sequence. Our tiny arsenal was there, untouched. Unless my brother could guess 181310 within six tries, he would be unable to open the safe and shoot somebody or (the more likely problem) lock himself inside. Before I shut the door, though, I noticed something poking out from the bottom cubby.

It was the strap of a purse, a big fake Gucci that Lisa had given Heidi a few years before, which had been pushed all the way to the back of the safe. My first thought was that maybe it hadn't been a fake after all, and she'd left it in the safe to protect it. But if that was true, she wasn't treating it very well, jamming it in the bottom of a musty-smelling gun safe.

As soon as I tugged to pull it out, my heart started racing. It felt heavy. Part of me wanted to shove it back behind the boxes of ammo and ignore it, rather than unzip another secret of my mother's I'd have to deal with, but I'd come that far. I'm not sure what I thought might be in there, but I definitely wasn't expecting a giant pile of cash.

Twenty-two thousand four hundred dollars, to be exact.

The money wasn't in neat stacks of hundos with paper bands around them, like in a movie. It was twenties and tens and fifties, held together in bundles with rubber bands and ponytail holders.

The rest of the night was spent counting, sorting, and standing over a spread of cash, wondering what it was doing there. For once I would have welcomed HalfHeidi to fill in some details about why she'd hid a bunch of money in the gun safe, but she didn't come when called and wouldn't have told me anyway.

It crossed my mind that maybe she had been working as a prostitute, until I remembered how bad she was at pleasing people. Or a drug dealer, but that didn't seem like her either. Maybe it was my college fund, tucked in with some twenty-year-old shotgun shells so FAFSA couldn't see it. Maybe she'd been running a Sunday-afternoon meat raffle.

I planned to talk to Carna about it first thing in the morning, but my "first thing" and her "first thing" were an hour apart. In that hour I found that she'd worn and not washed my first- and second-choice shirts for the day and was in fact sleeping in another, eaten the last of the yogurts, and failed to drop the last two bunches of packages at UPS, though somehow she'd run Heidi's car out of gas anyway.

By the time we were on the way to school, we were not speaking, which was why I didn't mention the twenty grand I'd found, at least then.

If I was going to have to figure out everything else on my own, I could figure out the money, too.

# CHAPTER THIRTY-SIX

"Make her pose with a cactus," Carna wrote across the whiteboard.

I muted myself. "A *cactus*?" Darden's grandma didn't notice. She was trying to give me a video tour of her place in Sun City, but she didn't know how to flip the camera on her phone, so I was mainly getting a tour of her chest.

"Something Arizonish. Cactus. Iguana. The Grand Canyon."

I unmuted. "Um, Mrs. Mac?"

"I know the headboard looks like it's wicker but it's something called *rattan*."

"Mrs. Mac?" She brought the phone close and flipped the screen several times before we were looking at each other. "Since it's so cold here, it would be fun if you could record the message outside in the sun."

"Good idea! Should I go to the pool? The pool here is very nice."

I glanced at Carna over the top of my phone. She shook her head and underlined "cactus."

"Sure." Carna drew an angry cactus on the board.

"Now where did my pool key go?" She set the phone down and I watched a ceiling fan spin for several minutes before she returned to view in a visor and sunglasses. "This is so sweet of you to do, Drew—I don't know why they're always saying you're not very warm."

She had to know that not flying back to Wisconsin for Darden's last-ever high school hockey sectionals would move more points from her column to the other grandparents'. The good-luck video message, though, recorded over FaceTime by me was going to get her out of trouble, which would have been rather thoughtful of me if I hadn't had my own motives.

Facing into the sun, half her face covered, she could have passed for any white Midwestern grandma saying hello from Arizona, which was my actual motive.

"Can you hold the phone up higher?" I was mostly talking to a PROUD GRANDMA OF A LARCH LEAP HONOR STUDENT T-shirt. (That would have been for Dard's sister.) "Okay, I'm going to start recording and STOP RIGHT THERE. You're good where you are, GRANDMA MAC!" She'd been trying to get the pool in the background by walking backward toward the edge of it instead of lifting up the phone. I didn't want to kill Darden's grandma while I was pretending she was mine, though if I did maybe I could teach Dard how to collect her Social Security, too.

All I wanted was a fuzzy screenshot to post to Heidi's social media ("Mom having fun in the sun while we freeze here" with some LOLz after it). Carna didn't get her cactus but we did get a nice row of palm trees in the background. The quality was pixelated enough we could have claimed it was Darth's own mother and he'd have had to look twice. Perfect.

Darden got the full recording, which included a lot of "proud of yous" and even a "leave it all on the ice, Dardy!" He cried when I showed it to him. He cried because it was his grandma and he cried because I arranged it, which he interpreted as romantic. If I was a crier I'd have cried, too, because I was dating a crier and because I didn't want to sit in the bleachers in a number 66 jersey while he left it all on the ice. I wanted to go home, finish my Spanish, five-star a shitty air fryer, and check into bulk dry-ice delivery in case the weather kept looking so good. But once someone knows you're hiding something from a guy with business cards, even if they only know only a tiny fraction of the trouble you're in, you can't break up with him. All you can do is say things like "I'm so glad I have your support right now," and try to mean it.

They won, 3–0, with two assists from Dard. He played better than he had all season, everyone said. I believe he played well because they played a squad of skinny, clumsy skaters from a town that didn't have its own ice. He believed he played well because I was good luck.

I am definitely not good luck.

# CHAPTER THIRTY-SEVEN

The second time I didn't tell Carna about the money in the safe, it was because Lachlan was with us.

We had decided we should have burner phones to communicate about anything Heidi, Darth, or otherwise fraud related. Plus I wanted Lock to have one for emergencies, like if Darth or child welfare or the ghost of his mother showed up at school.

The point of the burners was to be untraceable, so I drove to the Walmart in Pine Prairie and sent Carna inside to buy the cheapest prepaid phones that didn't look like the kind secret agents in movies were always breaking in half and throwing out their car windows.

"Use the rest for a preloaded Visa so I can pay for the plans online." I handed her six hundred dollars. It felt like I worked for a cartel.

She counted through the bills and looked up at me. "Where did you get this money?"

"How long is this gonna take?" I glanced back at Lachlan, who was paging through an old Dog Man book. "I'm getting really hungry."

"Ten minutes," I said to Lock. "ATM," I said to Carna.

"It's wrinkly," she said suspiciously.

"Can you just go?" I didn't want to talk about the money in front of Lock.

"Can you just go and bring me a snack?" Lock said.

"You said yesterday you hadn't been at the bank this week."

"I had some money. You don't need a snack. We're going home after this."

"Yeah, but by then it's going to be like eleven or something." It would be six. "Oh, wait, is that a McDonald's?"

"NO. It's a hospital with a big yellow M and drive-up shots for children. Do you want one of those? Carna, should I just go in and do it?" I held out my hand to take the money back, annoyed at both of them.

Carn got out of the car, but not without looking at me very suspiciously, which made me wonder why she would be so concerned about a little bit of cash.

# CHAPTER THIRTY-EIGHT

**ME**

have to go to pizza runch with dard—is lock in bed?

**CARNA**

runch?

**ME**

ranch.

**CARNA**

new phone who dis

**ME**

haha is lock in bed?

**CARNA**

he just started last jedi. win or lose?

**ME**

win:-| another game thurs:-/

The more nights this dumb hockey season lasted, the more nights I'd be out celebrating with the team and the more nights my brother would stay up till midnight while Carna convinced herself she was doing me a favor by making sure he didn't poison himself or burn the house down.

**CARNA**

did u change some combinations on things

My scalp prickled under my hat. I had changed the combination on exactly one thing. Did she try the safe? Was she looking for a gun? Had a ten-point buck blundered into the yard? Or did she knew what else was in there?

**ME**

why?

There was no reply for a full minute, during which I could see the shadow of waiting boots under the stall door. I couldn't risk Darden asking about the janky phone I was using, so I was tucked inside an ice arena bathroom. *Why are you asking about combinations now?* The boots shuffled. I rattled the toilet-paper roll so it wouldn't seem like I died on the toilet.

Carna's reply finally appeared.

**CARNA**

new phone making me paranoid about security. we should change heidis pws

It was either a legitimate suggestion or complete bullshit, and chances for each were about even. But if Carna had been trying to get into the safe, I wasn't going to be the one to ask.

**ME**

good catch. will do later

The girl in the impatient boots looked at me sympathetically when I left the stall. You have no idea, I thought.

# CHAPTER THIRTY-NINE

'm good at secrets."

"I know."

"I don't tell stuff I'm not supposed to tell."

"I know."

"And I know stuff I'm not supposed to know."

I looked up at him.

Lock pushed books into his shelf, one by one. I sat on the floor in front of his dresser, taking out clothes, refolding them, putting them back. "Come here a sec." An inch of boy stood out on either side of the shirt I held up to his back. The Milwaukee Bucks moved to the giveaway pile. "We'll get one that fits," I said, cutting off his objection.

The point of no return on his room had come. What started as a faint dirty-boy smell, a smell you might blame on wet feet or warrens of dust bunnies, had gotten sharp and sour, like the pheasant foot Carn had kept in a baggie the first time she shot one. Lock followed us around, saying, "My room doesn't stink! It doesn't stink! Oh, I think I can smell the smell. DON'T JUST THROW MY GUYS AROUND! Sometimes it's boots that stink. Maybe it was that dinner Drew made," while Carn and I thrashed around the swim of Lachlan's room looking for the source. Neither of us would have admitted it, but we had both become desperately sensitive to the smell of things rotting. If it had turned out to be a decomposing mouse, I might have completely lost my shit for good.

Not, thankfully, a dead thing: a split tube of punch-flavored Go-Gurt, tucked in the pocket of a pair of pants, stuffed inside a very old Hot Wheels garage, sitting half over the heat vent.

"That's it. You and me. We are cleaning this dump," I'd said, and he knew enough not to argue.

That's how I found myself spending the only Sunday I hadn't worked in months tunneling through chaos with JT in the background and my brother leaning dangerously close to demanding to know where our mother was.

"When somebody is a spy, the CYA says they can't even tell their family," he said.

"You mean the CIA?"

He looked at me carefully. "They think it's more safer in case the spy's kids are bad at secrets."

"Can we give away some of these?" I toed the pile of free plastic he got every time Heidi drove him through McDonald's.

He squinched his face but didn't say no. "A lot of kids are bad at secrets," he said.

"Lock?" I moved from the floor to the edge of his egg chair, careful not to sit on the stuffed monkeys he had arranged there as his first task. "Do you have a secret to tell me? Or do you think I have a secret?"

He studied me, unflinching, and I did the same. If this was it, this was it.

With the floor cleared and the shelves arranged, the room seemed twice the size. Neat. Rational. Orderly. I would send the **TurboSuc Self-Propelled Robotic Vacuum (★★★★★, always wanted a robot to clean** up after me) afterward to make napped lines of fresh carpet. You could imagine it as the room of a regular kid in a stable family with at least one and maybe two parents.

Lock said nothing, still. I picked up a monkey and twirled a loose eye while I waited. I'd sewn and resewn them when he was little, as determined that he not choke on a button as he seemed to be to choke on one. But now he was big enough not to bite off things he couldn't swallow. Or at least I hoped he was.

"I don't want to give away any of those monkeys, Drew," he said finally. He was answering my question by not answering my question.

I looked at the lineup behind me, simians tucked into some shape of family. "I don't blame you, bud. They're good monkeys."

He let out a loud breath. "I will when I'm ready," he said. He looked relieved.

I was relieved, too.

"That sounds like a good plan."

It wasn't a plan. It was a leap of whatever substitutes for faith if you don't have faith in anything. Hope, maybe. A leap of hope. Hope that by the time he was ready, Carna and I and the monkeys and the medical examiner and the family court would be, too.

# CHAPTER FORTY

We knew we'd become a personal crusade for K. David Barth when he stopped trying to give everybody Social Security Administration business cards and started lying about who he was.

He was at a table with his back to the door and the Roasted Badger's customer copy of the *Wisconsin State Journal* spread out in front of him when I stopped in to pick up my check. If the navy-blue Patagonia hanging on the chair back hadn't given him away, Audrey's eyes darting back and forth between him and me the second I walked in would have.

I ducked back out and waited. A few minutes later she texted, "All clear." I found her standing next to the empty table, folding the *WSJ* he'd left behind.

"He asked if you were working today and I said no. And then he tried to ask other stuff but I said I couldn't give out personal information. Who was that guy?"

I looked at her, suspicious. "Who did he say he was?"

"'Family friend.' But he had a real creepy vibe, so I was like, mmm, I don't know, dude. Oh. Sorry if he's, like, your uncle or whatever."

"He's not. He didn't even introduce himself?"

"Hullo, I'm Mr. Man's Man from the Zip Up My Jacket Company and I'd like three shots of espresso," she said in a dorky voice. "No."

"And he didn't give you his number?"

"Ha! Oh my god, Drew! He's like FIFTY!"

"No, no. I mean he tends to share his contact information. Sales guy," I added, thinking about how eager Stephanya was to trade numbers when anybody expressed the slightest interest in whatever she was selling.

She shrugged. "Nah, he just asked about you guys. Did I know your family, where was your mom working these days, was she working at all." She slipped in and out of her impression. "'How about Drew's grandma? You ever see her around?'" I tensed, remembering Audrey spooning Grandma back into her urn. She looked for my reaction; I tried not to have one. "But I was just like, 'Did you want a scone with that?' He finally gave up and just sat there. I swear he was reading obituaries. Super grumpy. No tip."

"Sorry about that. Thanks for not telling him anything." She shrugged it off, curious but too polite to press. He hadn't pulled his usual I'm-practically-the-FBI routine to interrogate Audrey, so maybe this investigation wasn't really sanctioned under the Office of the Inspector Gadget. I wasn't sure if that made him less or more dangerous. "My mom's ex-boyfriend," I offered. "We try to avoid him, but he keeps coming around."

Audrey raised her eyebrows. She wasn't one of those girls who imagine it would be flattering to have a boyfriend who can't get over you, like how millennials think vampires are hot instead of seven-hundred-year-old rapists. "Should I call the cops if he comes in here again?"

"NO! I mean, no. It's not like that. She might owe him money." That was actually true. "But I can handle it." That may or may not have been true. She looked skeptical, wanting to make sure. "Really. I'd tell you if it was a problem."

Audrey went back to pushing in chairs and picking up stray cup sleeves. "At least I can spit in his coffee for you if he comes in again." She's a really good person.

I picked up the eraser from the community chalkboard and wiped away the ELLA WAS HEREs and the DON'T CRY BECAUSE IT'S OVER SMILE BECAUSE IT HAPPENEDs and the penis outlines. Audrey watched, approving, as I added TRY OUR SPECIAL MAPLE-MARSHMALLOW LATTE in big bubbles, with a maple leaf for the *W*. If only Brandon could have served my mother the February special instead.

"What does he sell?" she asked.

"Wellness supplements," I said, adding a pyramid of chalk-art marshmallows to the board. "Glucosamine and stuff."

# CHAPTER FORTY-ONE

Don't tell people he's my ex! I would never date such a douche-bag."

"*That's* what you're worried about? Plus douchebag is your type."

"Oh my God, Drew! He's like FIFTY!"

"Move."

She slid off the lid of the dumpster and waved me by with her imaginary arms. I'd seen her through the window and offered to take the recycling for Audrey on my way out. The bag was full of glass Nantucket Nectars bottles, which shattered dramatically when they hit the bottom of the bin.

"Jesus. Chill out, kid."

"Why are you here?" You'd think that talking to your dead loved one would be helpful, or at least inspiring. That's what Harry Potter got. That's how it worked for Luke Skywalker and that cute kid from *Coco*. But Heidi was getting to be a drag. She must have been bored being dead.

"You think showing up here was *my* idea?"

Fine. Maybe I subconsciously loved torturing myself, but if you thought about it, you could blame that on her, too. I slammed the lid on the dumpster. "Have a nice death. Bye."

"Hang o-on! I have something to tell you."

"Sure you do."

"I do! You know how you were looking for those little butterfly studs that Dard gave you?"

"Yeah . . ."

"Well, remember how I said that they'd be cute in my third holes? Right before I left?"

"And I said it would be weird if you wore earrings my boyfriend gave me for Valentine's Day?"

"And I said you wouldn't even notice because you hardly ever wear them?"

I turned around and walked slowly toward her. She backed up to the dumpster, looking sheepish, if dead people can look sheepish.

First hole: long, fake–Native American feather earrings.

Second hole: plain silver huggies, like always.

Third hole: motherfucker, my fucking mother.

# CHAPTER FORTY-TWO

will give you ten dollars if you go out there."

"No."

"Twenty."

"No."

"A trillion."

"Deal."

"Carn, I did the computer. It's your turn."

"They're *your* earrings. Plus you don't even *like* them."

"Yes, I do. Darden gave them to me. I just don't change earrings much."

"You don't even like Darden."

"Yes, I do." I just don't change boyfriends much.

"Why are you so sure they're out there?"

"Hmm, what? I just remembered that she borrowed them."

WE OPENED THE DOOR to the fat ass of a possum greedily tearing a hole in Mom's tarp. It swung its deranged face toward us to reveal a row of tiny razor teeth.

"Shit!" yelled Carna.

"*Kkkkhhhhh!*" hissed the possum, jaw gaping, ready to defend itself from the giant invaders . . . and then promptly fell to the floor of the shed, catatonic. Its black, glassy eyes stared blankly at the bonnet hair dryer. If anything was still going on in that little brain, it was probably thinking about how that thing would never sell.

A half minute passed with no movement. Carna reached down, picked it up by its ratty tail, and pitched it outside. It landed in what was once our sandbox. When it woke up later, it would stumble home with a story the other possi wouldn't believe.

"Did it do any damage?" Carn asked, brushing her gloves off.

I pulled back the tarp where it had been gnawing. "Just the tarp." I was glad I'd put Heidi's mittens back on her.

"We need to figure out how it got in."

Carn inspected corners and floorboards with the light from her phone. As good a builder as Malcolm is, wood can get soft or seams split over time, and creatures looking for shelter in a northern winter are persistent. She swung the door shut to check for any light gap under the door. It seemed tight. When she opened it again, I realized I had been holding my breath in the dark.

While Carna rearranged boxes and looked for holes, I peeled back the tarp from Heidi's face and sighed. She looked mostly the same as when we'd found her, which was mostly the same as before we'd lost her. By now I had lost the braced unease that she might suddenly blink or cough or resurrect. I could look at her like you'd look on a memory. A three-dimensional memory that was eventually going to thaw.

The butterflies were where they were supposed to be, atop the cairn of piercings in each ear. The posts slid out cleanly. Carna said I was lucky, because if the body had had a chance to bloat, it would have been much harder to take them out. "Hashtag blessed," I mumbled. I zipped them into my pocket.

Outside the shed, Carna squinted up at the eaves. "That's got to be it." One of the soffit vents had been pulled back, leaving a several-inch opening.

The little motherfucker had climbed in through the roof.

## "GOT ANY GRASS SEED OUT THERE?"

"I don't think so. No one's been planting any grass."

"Birdseed? Suet?"

"I doubt it. We don't feed birds either."

"Usually if something wants to get in that bad it's because there's something to eat in there."

Carna and I traded a look. We had assumed that when the cold halted decomposition, it would also halt scavengers, but we should have known better. You only have to see an eight-year-old with an uncut freezie pop to know how determined someone can be.

"Or maybe it's just because it's so damn cold this year," Mal added.

Sure.

Lachlan was trying to teach me a dance move he invented that looked mostly like he'd misunderstood a video of moonwalking, while Carna consulted Malcolm over FaceTime: steel wool, contractor-grade caulking, whichever wood preservatives the EPA hadn't banned yet. They could have been two old farmers at the feed store, swapping tips for how to varmint-proof the barn.

Lock had been so excited about the idea of an animal faking its own death that he jumped out of the truck and ran out back the second we got home. "Parmesan," which is what he decided its name should be, was already gone. I wondered whether Carna had dispatched the thing with a shovel blade while I was picking him up from school, but she swore she hadn't. Besides, if she had found a quick way to dispose of a body with the ground still frozen, it would have been on my whiteboard.

# CHAPTER FORTY-THREE

The Last Will and Testament of Heidi Hill (ghostwritten by me) was very straightforward, with no surprise revelations, earmarked family heirlooms, or anything else that might pique the interest of a court. Downloaded for free from a legit-seeming website, it revoked any Codicils previously made by Mom, and sporadically Capitalized words like a SpongeBob meme or the German language. Lawyers must learn different grammar. Most important, it named Sharon Alberta Hill as the guardian "of the persons of those of My Children who are under the age of legal majority," and in case Sharon died, failed to serve, ceased to serve, was bitten by a rattlesnake in Arizona, found the metaphorical Lands' End, etc., it named Drew Krause Hill as the first alternate guardian, if she/I happened to be of the age of legal majority, which was still a couple of months away. We dated the will five years before, though, to look less suspicious, which is why Grandma was still in it, though even at twelve I would have been the better choice. If it had been really authentic, instead of starting I, HEIDI HILL, OF LARCH LEAP, WISCONSIN, DECLARE THIS TO BE MY WILL, it would have said I, HEIDI HILL, JUST NEED YOU TO DO THIS ONE THING FOR ME, DREW.

Carna's guardianship would automatically pass to our dad. There was nothing we could do about that besides kill him, too. He might agree to leave her in Larch with me and Lock anyway, though, or in a Walmart parking lot or really anywhere that wasn't his place. For her part, she had become so miserable she seemed increasingly uninterested in where she might end up, which might have been my biggest worry if there weren't so many bigger worries.

As for Lachlan, there was nothing to lead the court to the orthodontist, so they'd have to either buy our story of the stock-photo soldier being his dead dad or start collecting DNA swabs from Justin Timberlake's roadies looking for a match.

To make the document official, Heidi would need to sign in the presence of two adult witnesses. Her signature was easy, since my version of it was as prevalent as hers. But the witnesses needed to be real live people willing to swear that they had been in the room with Heidi while all three of them signed. That might be a sticking point for most people, but the adults closest to Heidi were as ethically flexible as she was. Hashtag blessed again.

As I printed out the will, Lisa-in-Phoenix and Aunt Krystal each got a text from Heidi:

> help! i dumped a coffee on a box of papers that had my will in it. *[A Heidimoji with her head exploded.]*

> i don't want to redo the whole thing. can you just resing the last page?

> sign

Aunt Krystal responded immediately:

> who gets kids if you die? not me right?

Love you too, Aunt Krystal. "I guess we don't have to worry about her suing for custody," said Carna. Once assured she was low on the list, Krystal said to just sign her name on whatever and that she was getting rid of this phone, too.

Lisa's reply to Heidi's text:

are u leaving me million$$$ *[A make-it-rain GIF, and several laughy faces.]*

Carna chose Simon Cowell saying "It's a no from me" as a response and threw in an eye-rolling Rihanna. Somewhere in the middle-aged exchange of Memojis and shade that followed, Lisa said no problem, just send it, and she'd overnight it back.

Either no one remembered that they'd never witnessed a will in the first place, or more likely, it fell under the less-you-know-the-better rule of their relationships. Mom never balked when Krystal's ex needed to leave a dented car in our garage for a few days "while things cooled down." And Lisa hadn't even questioned it when she got a text saying if any mail came for Sharon, just FedEx it back to us. Lisa took that to mean she could use Mom's FedEx account whenever she had any personal shipping to do. It seemed a fair trade.

I slid two copies of the signing page to Carna for Krystal's signature. "Date it around Christmas so they'd have all been in town."

"Got it," said Carn, looping the legs of the K like Krystal would have.

"I bet they would have gone out for drinks after while I babysat."

"Oh, poor you."

"Seriously, the amount she saved on babysitters because of me could have paid for that Range Rover."

"So is this the real will or are you going to add a part where you leave yourself all the money?"

"What the hell does that mean?"

"Nothing. I just thought maybe you were calculating your own back pay." She dropped the papers on the table and went to her room.

I bit my tongue and watched her go. She'd been pissier than usual lately, and I couldn't think of anything I'd done.

# CHAPTER FORTY-FOUR

need to talk to you about something."

The sweaty forehead told me that much. Either that or he needed to poop. "What's up, Dard?"

"I didn't want to bring it up because I know you're so busy and stressed and everything. But I don't want to not tell you." And anyone within a half-block radius. I dragged him down to my room to muffle his voice while Lock was sleeping. "I was hoping your mom would be back. Oh god, I'm sorry," he caught himself.

In Darden's world, my mom was in Nevada providing hospice care for a great-aunt I'd never mentioned—the same poor, suffering aunt we'd allowed to use Grandma Sharon's identity and Social Security benefits, for purely humanitarian reasons. Carna had come up with her on the fly the day K-Darth and Dard had accidentally met, and the story played beautifully to Darden's devotion to family, enough to overlook the unlikelihood of Heidi Hill reading psalms and sponge-bathing a cancerous senior of tenuous genetic connection. And now he'd put his foot in his mouth wishing that the old broad would hurry up and die already. "I didn't mean it like, uh . . ."

"She just keeps hanging on," I said. "Aunt Karen's a fighter." Wait. Was it Karen or Carol? Had we really done Sharon and Karen?

"That's good! I mean, is that good?" It was hard to figure out the right thing to say in a situation like this, but Darden was trying. He meant well.

"Mom says she's not in any pain." There was no reason to torture my fake aunt, especially since we needed her to survive as long as it took to figure out what to do about Heidi.

"Oh, that's good. So I need to . . . um, could you stop doing that for a minute?"

I looked down at the screeching roll of packing tape and stopped mid-flap. I'd had to reopen the package after Carna boxed it without giving me the model number for the **UShiine 10 in. Portable Selfie Ring Lite With Folding Stand (★★★★★, my brows have never looked this amazing; 25k likes don't lie)**. "Sorry, just need to"—the dispenser screamed again—"seal this up."

I set the package aside and sat next to him on the bed, determined to look interested. "Okay, what do you want to talk about?" He fidgeted like Lock when he didn't want to tell me where the rest of the fruit snacks ended up.

"Your hair looks wavy," he boomed finally.

"I slept with a braid."

"Oh. I like it."

I pushed my hair over my shoulders so it wouldn't distract him from the important thing he needed to say. (Unless that *was* the important thing he needed to say?)

Darden took a deep breath. "So a few days ago I got a call from a number I didn't know. Like a *call* call."

Had I butt dialed him from the burner and he overheard something?

"I didn't answer, because you know, you're not supposed to answer those, but then they called again. Twice."

Now my stomach twisted, picturing Dard's lock screen: Incoming call from Can-you-bring-your-girlfriend-in-for-questioning. "And?"

"And it was this guy from McKean University."

I gave him a blank look.

"Yeah, it wasn't really on my radar either. But it's got a good reputation. It's on the list of the top thirty small colleges people haven't ever heard of." At least half of that was true. "It used to be a girls'—I mean women's—college, but it expanded in 2012. So the men's hockey team is getting more established."

I started to see where he was going. "And so the guy who called you was—"

"The hockey coach." His face brightened. "A college hockey coach. He'd already talked to Kopanieck, and when he found out I'd been a captain for two years, he said he thought I might be exactly what the program needed." He looked up at me with either hope or pain, or maybe a bit of both, like a dog not sure whether you'll like the half-dead bunny he brought you. "He asked if I wanted to play for them."

"Oh my god! That's amazing! Darden! You're going to play hockey in college!" I hugged him hard. Darden loved hockey, always had. Someday he'd be one of those dads who played in the over-fifty leagues and coached Mites till he couldn't skate anymore. But going from high school captain to college player is super competitive. His applications to Stevens Point and Bethel and St. John's had been long shots hockey-wise, but he'd tried. But this was a real offer from a real coach, somewhere.

"How'd they even find you?"

"Ms. Flynn knew their admissions director"—of course—"and then the coach saw some of the videos my mom posted. She is so proud of herself right now." She should be. That was some Brenda Olziewski–level mothery.

"Yeah, but the playing was all you. I hope he saw her highlights reel from that first sectionals game." And not the one when they got killed. At least Dard hadn't been responsible for either of the own-goals. "Congratulations." I held his giant hand in mine. Goodbye, buddy. What a happily-ever-after ending for both of us.

And then I realized he was . . . crying? "What's wrong? What's the problem? Does it . . . cost too much?"

"No, my parents said they'd pay anything."

Of course they did.

"Are the academics bad?" And would that really be a problem for you?

"No, there's a business communications major or sports management, just like I wanted."

"Well, is the campus gross or something?" I said, grasping at straws.

"No, it's really nice, but it's in"—he took a giant, heaving breath—"*Pennsylvania.*" He said it like it was the outer edge of the known world, like transportation had stalled with covered wagons, and the mere act of getting overland through Indiana and Ohio might cost your life. "Babe, we'd never see each other."

"Oh" was the only thing I could think to say. Had the news just gotten even better? Darden in another state, playing hockey on a campus that overindexed girls-I-mean-women that would make me easy to replace? Had Heidi pulled some strings in the hereafter?

But Darden was distraught, like Lachlan when the school tortoise went home with another kid. Why couldn't either of these guys be happy about their freedom? "Oh," I said again. "I've never been to Pennsylvania. I bet it's awesome, though. I think, um, Ben Franklin's from there, right? And Will Smith?"

"There's two NHL teams," he sniffed. "The Philadelphia Flyers and the Pittsburgh Penguins."

"See, and we don't have any."

"If only it had been in like Minnesota or something."

"Yeah, if only." Wrong. Like Minnesota or something was way too close. Alberta, Canada, would be okay. They have lots of hockey, too. "But, Dard, you're going to love it."

He looked at me with a sympathetic smile and squeezed my hand. Oh god. He thinks I'm being brave, I thought. I looked down at my lap. His hand was so much bigger than mine I could have worn it as a glove. "This is the hardest decision I've ever had to make."

"What is?"

He looked at me curiously. "Whether to accept the offer?"

"You haven't accepted it? What are you waiting for?"

He furrowed his substantial eyebrows. "To talk to you first. This affects you, too."

It really doesn't, I thought. Or at least not negatively.

"Oh, Darden. I appreciate you thinking about my feelings. It's really sweet." And a lot of pressure to put on a person. "But you can't make a decision that affects your whole life based on who you're dating in high school."

Reluctantly, I gave Heidi some credit for what I considered my very realistic perspective on love. She wasn't anti-relationship exactly. She had boyfriends, she sometimes posted on dating apps under her real initials, she encouraged crushes and taking initiative (she'd hovered over my elementary-school valentine-making, trying to get me to draw a heart around Jacob T's name). But she was very clear that men and boys in general were not to be relied on. Decisions, even minor ones, shouldn't depend on someone you thought you were in love with at the time.

"That's exactly what my mom said." Cheers, Mrs. Mac. We found something we agree on. "She said, 'If Drew is the right girl for you, she'll still be there when you finish college.'" I am not and I will not.

"Yep," I said, promising myself I'd break up with him the second it became feasible. "We'll each focus on our own future and who knows?" I know.

"But what if I'm in school all the way in Pennsylvania and you're just stuck here?"

I pulled my hand back. "I'm not going to be 'stuck.' I'm going to UW–Madison."

"I mean, sure. Hopefully."

"I *am*." Maybe we should just break up now, Dick-Mac. "We're both going to be very busy." It came out slightly angry instead of sweet.

"You're always so practical," he said, like it was a bad thing.

"Promise me you'll write back to that coach tonight and accept the spot?"

He smiled up at me. "Okay, babe. I promise."

"Great." He kept just gazing at me, maybe inventing some future love story where we reunite in Pennsylvania, at a Flyers versus Penguins game. I glanced at the clock and back at him, staring at me.

I smiled. "You know, you should go home right now and write that message. It'll show how excited you are. Babe."

His eyes were suddenly teary again. "I just realized you're wearing the earrings."

I wished I'd left the goddamn butterflies in a corpse.

# CHAPTER FORTY-FIVE

s that your guyses' dad's truck?"

The F-250 sat in the driveway, dust sprayed across the sides. Carna and I looked at each other over Lock's head as we pulled in. I felt my ButterBurger in my throat.

"What is *he* doing here?" Carna asked.

I checked my phone and Heidi's, but there was no warning from Malcolm. "No idea," I said, swinging open the door.

Lachlan slid carefully from the truck, protecting the cup of ice cream he was working on. He'd earned the Culver's drive-thru when the bank teller was about to refuse my request to open a safe deposit box in Mom's name and Lock piped in, "Mom doesn't do things herself. Drew has to do them." She interpreted that as Mom being either permanently housebound or a high-powered executive, but either way, she gave us the forms and politely looked away when I signed them. Heidi's will was safely and unsuspiciously stored in a safe deposit box.

Lachlan didn't know why I kept high-fiving him on the way back to the car but he decided to be proud of himself for whatever he'd done. I'd even driven all the way to the Pine Prairie Culver's, where the custard of the day was Snickers instead of the blackberry bullshit Larch Leap had. When Heidi was around, I never got him stuff with any kind of nuts, just in case, and I was right when I predicted it would blow his little mind.

But sometime between Lock insisting they hadn't included any ketchup for the fries and Lock discovering he had been sitting on the ketchup pack the whole time, Malcolm had arrived.

"Go in and finish that custard at the table, bud." Lock punched the code on the garage keypad and ducked under the lifting door. "And see if you can find my sleeping bag to take to Liam's tonight."

Stomach tight, I followed Carna around the corner to the back-yard. We could hear Stephanya arguing that sauerkraut was *not* a good substitute for kombucha if you only ate it with bratwurst. If they had already opened the shed and discovered what/who was inside, they sounded pretty calm about it. Maybe our conversation would simply go "Bummer about your mom. If only she'd eaten more sauerkraut . . ." "Wait, was that my Christmas present?"

I stopped holding my breath when I saw that the lock was still hanging from the shed door. Mal and Steph were occupied with rogue forestry. He, gloveless despite the cold, was cutting an overhanging limb with a pole saw while she stood next to a pile of branches hold-ing a roll of chicken wire and chattering about probiotics.

"Oh, there you are," he said crossly when he finally noticed us, like we were late to this surprise visit.

"What are you doing here?"

"Steph had to be down in Madison for a meeting—"

"Achievers Breakfast and Next Level Visioning," she corrected.

"Steph had to be down in Madison to learn how to sell more magic beans," Malcolm said, "so I thought I'd ride down, too, and see about your possum. I see your mom finally put a lock on that thing."

"Yep," I said, eyeing the lock I'd put on the shed door. "No one's getting in there." Or out.

"Except your possum."

"I already fixed the hole," said Carna, annoyed. She seemed less stressed about him being one sheet of plywood away from our frozen mother than him questioning her workmanship. I hoped she wouldn't swing open the door to show him where she'd stuffed steel wool in the cracks.

"Yeah, but no use making it easy for him to try again. You never want a tree hanging over a structure like this." He directed Carna to pick up one end of an orange rope that he'd looped around a limb and went back to sawing. "Pull," he said as it started to give. "Harder!" Carna yanked the rope like a tug-of-war, snarling.

"You should probably move," he added casually to Stephanya at the same moment the branch broke loose and crashed at her feet. "There, now," he said, satisfied.

"Hey!" she yelled.

"I didn't want it to go through the roof."

"Oh, so you'd rather crush me than whatever's in the shed?"

Mom would have loved that.

As soon as the limb was out of the way, the sun shone full on the roof. I cringed. There's a reason people plant shade trees. It's to keep the bodies from thawing when the shed heats up.

Next he examined Carna's work on the overhead soffit. He gripped the sides of vent and tried to wiggle it. "You lay a bead of caulk under the edge before you screwed it back down?"

"Yeah," she said, rolling her eyes. "What's the chicken wire for?"

"In case there was gaps at the base. If somethin was digging."

"I TOLD you the foundation was FINE." My sister's cheeks, red from the cold, flared brighter.

"What'd you use for caulk? Something rated for cold, I hope?"

I realized that if it wasn't a possum, it would be Mal. If it wasn't

Mal, it would be a neighbor. If it wasn't a neighbor, it would be Darth. If it wasn't Darth, it would be a midwinter thaw. We needed Heidi out of there. Now. I just had no idea where to put her.

"I USED A HIGH-ADHESION SILICONE. OBVIOUSLY." Carna's jaw set. They would be a while.

Malcolm was mostly ice inside anyway, and stubbornness and rage could keep Carna warm a long time. But Stephanya was shivering so hard the chicken wire sounded like brushes on a snare drum. "Do you want to come in?"

She looked at me gratefully, then hesitated. "Is your mom home?"

"Not for a while," I said, with a quick glance back to the shed.

The blare of *Steven Universe* coming from the living room cut off abruptly when we opened the door. "I'M NOT WATCHING!" called a small voice.

"Yes you are, but it's fine," I answered. No seconds passed before Steven was back on, loud. Stephanya laughed.

She took a seat at the table still in her jacket, and I showed her our collection of coffee pods. "You don't have any herbal tea, do you?" she asked.

"We've got fake Keurigs, juice pouches, or a warm Monster Energy Drink. Unless my sister drank it."

"Oh good. I'm kind of tired of all the healthy stuff." She chose an Irish Cream Hot Chocolate cup and I pressed it in the maker. She wasn't judgmental about that kind of stuff, not really. How could she be, when she was living with Oscar the Grouchy Possum Hunter in a house that might be reabsorbed into the woods any day? And when her brother had a side hustle that was . . .

Oh shit. That was my answer. *Kevin.*

I responded politely to the regular questions about school (going fine, home stretch) and college apps (still waiting) and Dylan (it's actually Darden—no, don't feel bad, no one gets it right), and nodded along through her long and hard-to-follow explanation of the sales and reward levels she was trying to reach in the supplements business. There was a conference coming up in Tampa that she was dying to go to, but she didn't have the money. "They should do scholarships like they do for college," she complained.

"As long as you're here," I finally interrupted after she remembered to tell me that the stem cells of honeybees, now available in gelcap form, were the key to being more productive, "I was wondering if I could get your brother's number?"

She stopped short and squinted her eyes. "Kevin?"

"I have a job for him. It's for a friend," I added. "They're very private."

"Ahhh, of course." She nodded knowingly and pulled out her phone. "Dog or cat?"

"Dog," I answered, looking into my mug. "Big dog."

"Oh, poor thing. I'm sorry," she said sincerely. My phone buzzed with Kevin's contact info.

"Me too."

# CHAPTER FORTY-SIX

Kevin considered himself a shrewd negotiator.

"A lot of them places get you in there with 'starting at fifty bucks' or something, but what they don't say is that's only for a cat or maybe, like, what are them little Taco Bell dogs?"

"Chihuahuas?"

"Yeah! Chee-wahs. And the other thing they don't tell you is if you want your guy in there *alone*, it's a lot more. A *lot*. Otherwise he gets mixed up with other dogs and hamsters and everything else."

"That's terrible," I said. "Who would want that?" I squeezed the phone against my head with my shoulder while I uncapped a bottle of nail polish for Lock. He was bored with the stamper and was painting his own designs on golf balls instead. He wanted to make a ladybug to bring to Liam. *Be careful,* I mouthed.

"So by the time you get to something big like your friend got—what was it again, Irish wolfhound or Newfie or something like that?"

"Something like that."

"And then you want a private, all the sudden your fifty bucks is five hundred. *Or more.*" This point in the sales pitch was meant to scare me into agreeing to any number less than the looming five hundo.

For our "something like that," five hundred dollars would be a steal. But that wasn't a matter for the phone. "Wow," I said.

"And what I got is better anyway. I got a cleaner, better retort—that's what we call the oven, a *retort*—than they got in them places. No mixing whomsoever. So not only can I give you a better price, you're going to get a *better quality results* than you could get somewhere elsewhere." He'd practiced.

I was tempted to ask how he measured the results of one cremation over another, or why anyone would care about a little "mixing" when it came to a creature that probably spent half its life with its face up someone's butthole, but all I needed was for him to think he was providing a cheap way to dispose of Clifford the Big Dead Dog.

"You really know what you're talking about," I said, swooping behind Lock to wipe his fingers with a polish remover pad. He was trying to paint the entire ball, and his fingers looked like bloody sausages. "And I can tell you really want to help people," I added, remembering that Steph had said Kevin was a big softie. Maybe she meant his brain.

"I do. That's exactly it. So if you want to move forward, we just need to agree on a price. I could probably do it for . . . three hundred?"

"Done." I could almost hear his fist pump.

"And a time for the drop-off. Like my sister probably told you, because of my current employment situation, I'm working with the equipment in the off-hours. And I do like to keep things on the QT."

"That works out perfectly." I picked Stephanya's hot chocolate pod out of the garbage, peeled the top off, and balanced the golf ball in it. Lock went back to painting the exposed dome. I tried not to touch anything with my sticky fingertips. The fake AirPods from Christmas would have been really useful if the microphone hadn't died within a week. "Because I'd like to keep this on the QT, too. Could you do tonight? I can be there by midnight." Lock was going to sleep at Liam's, which gave us till eight the next morning.

"Oh jeez. Tonight? Are you, uh, in a rush? For a cat I tell people they can just clear out some freezer space, but with a bigger—"

"I'll pay you a thousand dollars. Since it's a rush job."

The days had been pushing up into the thirties, with a lot of sun. Overnights were still below freezing, but the weekend looked like it was going to be beautiful, unfortunately. If only Mal had finished the electrical wiring, we could have gotten a Sub-Zero out there (★★★★★, halts decaying, rotting, bloating, and decomposition until you are ready to say goodbye), and kept her forever.

"I'll see ya then. Cash or Venmo. No checks, if you don't mind."

Duh. This was obviously going to be a cash transaction. "See you tonight."

# CHAPTER FORTY-SEVEN

No one's on the road in northern Wisconsin at eleven thirty in the winter. The deer are bedded down, and there's a gap in drunk drivers till bars close at two thirty. It's too cold for anyone else.

The headlights bleached the rows of pine on either side of the road. It was the only light at all besides Carna's phone glowing up at her face. In the summer, the high beams are fuzzy with insects, but at this time of year, all the bugs were dead or drinking or unhatched. The light was pure and cold.

Once, before Lock, I'd sat next to Heidi on this dark drive. She'd come up to get us and stayed too long talking to Malcolm. They used to alternate fighting and flirting, before it leveled out to a steady sniping tolerance. That one had been a charmed night, with laughs and drinks and a borrowed flannel when it got chilly. Carna had fallen asleep on the couch, mouth open, eyebrows locked in whatever argument she'd been in the middle of when she crashed.

Mal had suggested we stay over, and Heidi looked on the verge of agreeing. The idea worried me. A lot. I was only six or seven, the age you are supposed to fantasize about your parents getting back together, but not me. I knew. I always knew. They weren't better together, even for a night. "Come on, Mom." I rattled her keys.

I can redraw the scene: Them both a little buzzed—one too many brandies but not three or four too many. Malcolm suggesting one thing—the couch, a sleeping bag—and Heidi interpreting another. My mother embarrassed when she realized her mistake. She didn't take rejection well, and rejection from him was the worst of all.

We cleared out quickly, someone prodding Carn just awake enough to drag herself to the back seat of Heidi's old Corolla. I said someone should carry her to the car but they left her to me, and I was a child, too.

Tiny Carn slept across the back, a seat belt around her ankles because I put it there. I sat in front with Heidi, who was fidgety and defiant. She talked to me, but not to me. Mumbled snippets of "Boys always make such a big deal about everything—remember that someday" and "I'd rather drive all night than wake up in that depressing shithole."

And then, at some point, in a different voice, she said, "God, it's dark. We really are in the middle of nowhere. You see how dark it is, Drew? There's not even a moon." I tilted up to look over the dash, but it didn't seem dark. Her headlights showed exactly where everything was—where we were going. But before I could disagree, she clicked them off—*snap*—and the trees, the bugs, the road disappeared.

We were in a starless space. I could tell we were still moving, because the car bumped and the wheels made noise, but our direction could have been anything. She laughed.

My stomach fell to my feet.

"Turn them back on, Mom."

I could just make out her face, a grin.

We'd have seen any other car by its lights. Deer would probably be sleeping. And the shoulder, should you start drifting, will chase you back with rumble strips, or "drunk bumps" as people up there call them. She wasn't self-destructive. She just liked not seeing where she was going. I didn't.

I don't.

"Turn them on," I said again, louder.

"It's crazy, right? How you can't see anything?"

"TURN THEM ON, HEIDI." Tears in my eyes and in my throat.

It was a few seconds in the dark, but it split me from her in a way I didn't understand at the time.

She made a disappointed grumble as she clicked the lights back on. I watched while she did it, so I would know how myself. I watched everything after that.

And now, on the same two-lane highway, lights shining bright and a laden deer sled sliding around the bed of the pickup, I wondered whether I'd missed something.

"Check out how dark it is." I flicked off the lights and glanced over at Carna.

"Are you high?" she said. Not scared, but not amused.

"It's crazy dark, right?" My hand hovered over the wand, anxious to turn the lights back on, pretending not to be.

"Yeah. *Crazy*. The turn is in six hundred feet."

"Crap." I flicked the lights back on and hit the brakes. "You were supposed to tell me when it was coming up."

"I just did."

# CHAPTER FORTY-EIGHT

Northern Lights doesn't cremate on-site. That part of its operation is in a warehouse on a big parcel of land shared with an indoor boat-storage facility. Kevin explained it all on the phone, even though I'd been there once before to jump his car with Mal. He also said that the funeral home was planning a new crematorium with a reception area and place to watch, which was becoming very popular, but would make his side jobs harder to do. We were lucky, though, because the current one was "out in the country," which also meant he could kill us with a chain saw, bake us in the oven, and no one would ever know.

Kevin didn't have any surprises, though. We did.

He was waiting in his car like he'd promised when we pulled up. He got out to peer over the back of the truck. "Oh, that does look big," he said, scrunching his eyebrows.

He dropped the tailgate and pulled the sled toward the end. "Can one a you girls help carry?"

Kevin and I each took a side of the sled, unconventional pallbearers for an unconventional funeral. Carna opened the door to a small, plain room with a few framed certificates on one wall and a white ceramic cross on another. We heaved the sled on a long metal table with a loud clang.

"Glad you found the place in the dark," he said. Carna raised an eyebrow at me.

He reached to loosen a bungee cord and I grabbed the hook to hold it in place. "So, Kevin. The situation is a little more complicated than I was able to explain on the phone."

He stepped back with the look I would have had if he had met us with a chain saw in the parking lot. "Hey, whatever happened to the dog is none a my business. It's over now. And you gotta believe, I seen *a lot*." He reached again for the tarp.

I put my hand on top of it, feeling a chill. "We'd really like things to be as . . . private as possible." I looked to Carna, who nodded. "It's probably better for you that way, too."

"You mean like . . . you wanna keep the tarp on?"

"That would be best."

"We're not supposed to put anything in there besides them cremation caskets." He motioned to another room, where they kept overpriced cardboard boxes to put your loved one in before you torched them. "And, well, the thing that's supposed to get cremated."

"The tarp and the deer sled are both polyethylene composites. At the temperatures you use, full combustion won't be problem," Carna said. She'd done the research. "Probably wouldn't want to breathe what comes out of the vents, but the chamber will be just fine, if that's what you're worried about. It will all go up." She made a poof motion.

*"You wanna put in the sled, too?"* His eyes got wide. "It won't melt or nothin'?"

Carna gave a confident shake of her head.

Kevin suddenly looked terrified of us. I can only imagine what he imagined might be under the tarp. "I don't want to get involved in any—"

"We don't want you to," I interrupted.

"Look, I'm just trying to make it a little more easier, more cheaper, for people when they—I don't want to do nothin' that's illegal or—not like serious illegal."

"You don't need to worry about that," I said, which was a lie. I took a big, patient breath. "But since we're asking you to do something you're not totally comfortable with, we've included a little more than what we talked about. For your time." I gestured to Carna, who slid her backpack off her shoulder and took out a manila envelope.

Kevin looked conflicted but curious. He opened the envelope and peered inside. He couldn't have counted twenty-five hundred dollars in cash that quickly, but he could tell it was a lot. There was no way he was going to say no.

Carna watched him paw through the envelope and turned back to me with eyebrows raised. I hadn't told her how much was in there, but it was clearly more than I could have withdrawn from the ATM that afternoon. I looked away.

If everything went well, Kevin would never know who or what he'd cremated and he'd never ask. He'd probably convince himself that we'd run over an exceptionally large dog, maybe while drinking or doing something stupid, and didn't want it discovered. I hoped that's what he'd think, even though it hurt my pride that someone would think of me as that irresponsible.

But between the improper disposal of a corpse and the actual amount of money he was making from fraudulently using Northern Lights' equipment, I had turned his misdemeanor side hustle into a felony. It made sense to be generous with the money. Now we both had reasons to make sure no one ever found out about it.

"Sure, we'll keep it covered if you want," he said, nearly hyperventilating. There you go, buddy. Failing to find a pocket big enough for his envelope, he slid it into the waistband of his pants. Probably right not to trust us to hold it.

IT WOULD BE A FEW HOURS, Kevin said, first for the cremating, then the cooling, and finally the grinding of any larger fragments. Neither of us would have wanted to watch even if Northern Lights had already opened its new reception room.

As Carn and I went back out into the cold, I said, "Look, about the money—I thought we should give him enough—"

"Yeah, whatever." She climbed into the bed of the pickup. "I don't really want to talk about it."

She pulled a down blanket around herself and took a Monster drink from her backpack. I grabbed a tall thermos from the front seat and slid in next to her. "Here. This is still hot."

"Nah. I'm going to need caffeine." She took a big swig of Monster.

"There's four shots of espresso in this hot chocolate." She grinned and lifted up the blanket to make room for me.

We leaned against the cab together, legs touching, taking turns with the cocoa, waiting. The world was so perfectly silent, it was impossible not to notice the muffled buzz start up from the building. We both tensed. I wondered when was the last time she'd sat so close to anyone but Lachlan.

"Oh! I almost forgot!" I dug the new **SonicPulse Bluetooth Speaker with Lights (★★★★★, good upgrade from the MeJamz Personal Speaker, big bass and LED lights turn any night into a party)** from my bag.

We played with the color settings as the little lights flashed the beat to the playlist I'd queued at work a few days before. After a bit,

Carn held out her hand for my phone and said, "I can't listen to bagel-shop music anymore."

It was quiet again while she searched, no chirps or howls to interrupt the cold white noise of the machine inside. Then from the speaker came JT's thin, plaintive voice: "Hey, hey . . ."

I leaned my head into hers and sighed.

"Did you know," Carna said, "that she kept changing her birthday back a year on Facebook?"

"That's one way to make sure you never get old. The other way is, well—"I glanced at the building and down again. "Did you change it for her in January?"

Carna let out a little laugh. "Yeah. I actually did."

"That was kind of you." I dug a granola bar out of my bag and offered it to Carna, who wrinkled her nose but took it anyway. "Kinda cool she never got caught by Social Security. That was lucky. For her," I added.

Carna raised a finger. "And she never had to see the engagement ring Steph posted on Instagram."

"It's some kind of agate. She would have thought it was ridiculous."

"True. Do you think they'll actually get married?"

"Does it matter?" I shrugged.

"I can't even imagine Mom old," she said through a mouthful of granola bar.

"Can you picture her with one of those wobbly necks? Or forehead wrinkles? She would have hated it."

"She would not have let that happen," Carn said with confidence.

"At least Justin would have gotten old with her. Too bad she didn't get to see him again." For the first time, I let my mind wander to that night before the New Year, to the time between looking for the suitcase and dying, between being excited to go and being gone. "It must have happened really fast, right? I mean, she didn't even come back to the house."

"Yeah," said Carn. "She probably didn't even realize what was happening." After a long time she added, "I wonder how she would have posted about it? Dying to try out this 5-star zebra suitcase—"

I choked on my cocoa. We weren't that good at finding bright sides, but on the bright side, we weren't that bad about dwelling on the dark side either. Heidi would have jumped right in. I almost expected her to.

The song finished, but she'd queued it to repeat. We'd learned *NSYNC songs the way other kids learned "Itsy Bitsy Spider."

"Bye bye bye bye bye," I mumble-sang. Too soft, like Ed Sheeran (sad British nerd, according to Heidi) instead of the sexiest man alive (also according to Heidi). It felt like we would be crushed by the weight of winter.

Carna looked at me briefly and set the thermos aside. "Come on." She pushed off the blanket and stood up. "Come on!" She pulled me to my feet, and turned up the volume.

Because Heidi had taught us the moves, too. Maybe all our moves.

We danced our eulogy in the bed of the pickup. Stomped and pumped fists and called our goodbyes to the stars. Replayed, replayed, forgot and remembered choreography, forgot and remembered everything. When Kevin woke us later, the speaker had run out of battery and there were wispy white trails like loose strings across the sky.

I wished, still wish, Lock could have been with us, but he was too young. We were too young, too.

Bye bye bye.

# CHAPTER FORTY-NINE

Carna's head vibrated against the window, fog expanding and contracting in front of her mouth. Heidi sat between us, in a plastic bag in a cardboard box in a plastic bag, which is the unceremonious way they hand you your family member if you don't bring a decorative urn.

I envied her sleep. Carna's, I mean. She'd offered to drive, but I didn't trust her in the dishwater light. Deer again, plus other things roused for early mornings. When we got home, she retreated to her room wordlessly and shut the door.

I thought about mixing the ashes with Grandma's in the too-big urn, but Heidi wouldn't want to be trapped for eternity with her mother any more than I would. I tied the handles of the bag together and slid it under my bed.

Liam's mother greeted me with a plate of bacon when I came for Lock in the Range Rover; the truck felt too hearselike that morning. She told me she shut them down at midnight, but Lock said they'd only *pretended* to go to sleep. The last number they'd seen on the **iFUN Touch Tablet 4 Kidz** he'd brought (★★★★★, Affordable starter device if you factor out compatibility and speed. Only tablet that comes in

**orange!)** was 12:57. His personal goal had been 3:00 a.m., but that had been ambitious.

He had been eating Pull 'n' Peels, farting in my sleeping bag, and playing knockoff *Minecraft* while Carna and I waited outside the building where Mom was being incinerated. I wouldn't ever forget that night, but he would. I was glad about that.

He was sound asleep in the back seat when we pulled into the garage. I propped open the door and carried him.

# CHAPTER FIFTY

D rew! Door!"

I sent Lock to his room and pocketed a box cutter. I was trying to Tetris the fourteen parts of a **MyRetreat Dehydrator and Vacuum Sealer Food Storage System (★★★★★, Made and sealed squirrel jerky packs for the bug-out. Compatible with generator or solar. A must for gourmet survivalists.)** back in their box. Reviewing and selling stuff to preppers had especially high margins, but spending time on sites run by people stockpiling for an apocalypse makes you a little edgy.

Char Yancy of Boise (aka @NakedButNeverAfraid), who wanted to pay for the dehydrator in crypto, would always keep a box cutter handy.

"Sorry," I said. "Nobody's home right now. Didn't anyone tell you that my grandma's in Arizona?" Of course they had. She'd told him herself via her Gmail account, and we'd told him unofficially through well-devised social media posts.

"I was actually hoping to catch Heidi. She's not home much, is she?"

I shrugged.

"Working?"

I didn't answer. He looked comfortable on our step. He should; he spent a lot of time there.

"You know, I went to her work. Dr."—he said the name of Lock's father—"office? Thought maybe I could find her there. That's where she works, right?"

I narrowed my eyes. "You went to the office?"

"And I'll tell you what's strange: The receptionist said Heidi Hill didn't work there!" He overplayed it like a hammy TV detective. "This gal said she didn't remember a Heidi *ever* working there and she's been there seven years!"

Fucking Janelle. Even if she didn't know the specifics of the arrangement, she had to know there *was* an arrangement. She worked for a very shady guy. Besides under-the-table child support, he had all kinds of side hustles. For example, it was an open secret that he offered parents a prescription for painkillers every time he changed their kid's bands. The more messed up Junior's bite, the better chance Dad ended up in rehab. For Janelle, the right response to "I'm an investigator looking for fill-in-the-blank" should always be "Let me get the doctor for you."

"I was a little surprised when I heard that," K-Darth said, wrinkling his nose in a mocking way. I wished the windchill was still zero, because he hadn't looked as smug when it had been colder out. "Because according to her income statements, ha-ha, she does!"

"Did you talk to her boss?"

"Well, no. But it would be strange if the person at the front desk didn't know the other employees." He kept pronouncing *strange* like it was a scientific term. It was getting on my nerves.

"Not really," I said, glancing back at Carna, who'd wandered over. She mirrored my unconcerned look. "Mom only works from home. She does the accounts and the insurance stuff. I don't want to get anybody in trouble but she's found bills and insurance claims that were . . . *strange*. It's better if she can review everything in private in case anyone, you know, tries to take advantage."

"Mom's got so much integrity," Carna confirmed. I laughed through my nose and pretended it was a sneeze.

"Who did you say you talked to? Was it the one with the hockey hair?" The last time I'd been in, there were several lady mullets at the office.

"I guess it you could say that," said K-Darth, considering.

"Janelle," I said to Carna knowingly.

"She's one of the strange ones Mom has been looking into," Carn whispered loudly. I stifled another laugh, which apparently made me look shocked. "I'm sorry, Drew, but he's in the FBI. I can't *lie*."

When he finally stalked back to the Honda shaking his head, I burst out laughing.

"Did you hear him? 'I'm not FBI. I never said I was FBI,'" Carn blustered in her K-Darth voice. "I bet it says it on his Bumble, though."

"I bet he wears an earpiece and dark glasses in his profile picture."

"Who's Janelle? Do you think we got her in trouble?" Carna asked. Carna never had braces.

I didn't care what happened to Janelle, remembering the way she'd send the kids waiting with their parents back first while I sat there alone. ("Um, excuse me? Can you not rumple the magazines?") I also wouldn't mind if the orthodontist got taken down for writing bogus prescriptions, tightening wires like a sadistic freak, or trophy-killing a lion. But mostly I hoped that Darth would abandon the ortho office, because I didn't want anyone figuring out *why* he paid someone twenty hours a week not to brush any teeth.

For some reason, the man was fixated on us, when any normal person would have calmly waited for Sharon to not show up to her scheduled meeting in the spring and then start issuing warrants. We needed him off our backs before he opened the wrong door (or jar or plastic bag in box in bag) and called in the people with guns and dogs instead of business cards and clipboards.

"We've got to kill off Grandma," I said reluctantly. "It's time."

"Yeah," Carna said, and sighed.

I rubbed my eyes with the heels of my hands. "We should tell Aunt Krystal first in case she wants to open a credit card in Grandma's name or something before it's too late."

"You're really too kind," said Carna.

# CHAPTER FIFTY-ONE

Urban preppers are a paranoid bunch. They're what you'd get if DIY YouTube and conspiracy theory Twitter had a baby, and then that baby grew up and met an environmental doomsday cult leader at a gun show and they had another baby and instead of vaccinating it, they never filed a birth certificate and taught it Morse code. Sort of a distant cousin to my dad.

But they loved shopping online.

Carna had been getting to know Char Yancy (not her real name), who bought the food dehydrator, through a chat room, at first swapping high-protein recipes and simple designs for car battery circuitry, and slowly edging into complaints about getting the government off her back. Yancy, who I imagined as the off-the-grid version of Brenda Olziewski, knew everyone in prepper world. You wouldn't assume that there'd be a master networker among a group of avowed hermits, but you'd be wrong.

Yancy told Carna she knew someone who could provide a legal death certificate in the state of Arizona. It wasn't clear if it was a real doctor or someone with fake doctor credentials, but they promised a person could be declared dead of natural causes, sight unseen, no questions asked. The preppers figured a lot of people had legitimate reasons (not paying taxes, stockpiling ammo) to disappear from Uncle Sam's record book. All they wanted was a pinky swear you weren't trying to escape murder, rape, or kidnapping charges, and three hundred bucks.

We were in the market for such a service. If Grandma Sharon could suddenly die while she was away in Arizona, K-Darth would have to leave us alone. It would mean the end of the Social Security payments, but that was mostly just covering the payments on Heidi's car, which we could sell if we needed to (sorry, Carna). Plus everyone has to die eventually.

I'd even written a nice, short obituary to put in the *Wisconsin State Journal* as soon as everything was ready. (No picture. That cost extra and attracted more attention.) It was not so different from writing a product review. ★★★★★, she enjoyed winters in Arizona, crab legs at the casino, and illegitimate grandchildren.

We were counting on none of Sharon's old friends noticing, or if they thought they remembered her already being dead, worrying it was a sign of Alzheimer's and keeping it to themselves. We decided to suggest memorial gifts be sent to children's cancer research, which sounded like the kind of cause a grandmother would have liked. Not ours, probably, but we couldn't ask for donations to the Social Security Fraud Legal Defense Fund.

# CHAPTER FIFTY-TWO

What did you expect? She can be such a bitch when she wants to be." Dead Mom had a knack for showing up when I most needed help, in order not to give it.

"Can you stop calling people bitches? Especially your own daughter?"

I'd come downstairs to get money to mail to Aunt Krystal, who needed five hundred bucks for "expenses." (Krystal had been low-key blackmailing Heidi their whole lives.) Carna was on her way up. My room was in the basement—as was the laundry that had somehow become 100 percent my job—so I had plenty of reasons to be down there, but Carna didn't.

"What are you doing?"

"Sorry, didn't realize this was your private space." I raised my eyebrows. She hesitated, just for a moment. "I thought there might be something with Grandma's signature on it in the storage room. Yours doesn't look very authentic," she added.

"It's fine," I said, temperature rising. For a couple of days after the cremation, it almost seemed like we were getting along, but that had gone up in smoke, too. We were barely talking, unless growling or flipping each other off counted as talking, and I had stopped asking for her help or opinion. I didn't want her near the storage room, the gun safe, or anything of mine, and I really didn't want to hear another example of something I was doing wrong.

"Yeah, if she had a stroke and had to write with her left hand."

"Fuck off," I said, but she was already past me up the stairs.

Now there was five hundred dollars on the floor next to me and I was angrily trying to rethread the tie through a pair of Lock's sweats, a task I could at least claim to be competent at since I had to do it every time he wore them.

"I know you agree with me." Heidi rolled her pretend eyes. "Fine. She's an asshole, then." They weren't like dead eyes, not empty or buttony like in *Coraline*, but they didn't really look like they were looking at anything. "Am I allowed to say that? She's a real 'asshole' when she wants to be." Air quotes on the *asshole*.

"If you're not going to be helpful, you can go." I pointed to the door, like she'd need a door. She fluffed the pillow behind her head.

The real problem wasn't whether Carna was an asshole or a bitch or a buttpoop (Lock's latest redundant slur; "That doesn't even make any sense. What other kind of poop would there be?" Considers. "Buttdiarrhea?"). It was the "when she wants to be." Carna was a buttpoop even when she didn't want to be.

"One time Grandma said to her 'you catch more flies with honey than vinegar' or whatever that saying is and you know what your sister said?"

"Why would I want to *catch* flies," I said.

"Why wouldn't I just kill them," we said together.

Flies or humans. She had finally pissed off the last remaining people at school who semi-liked her, besides me and her teachers (and not all of them either). Nothing even really happened. There was a group project. She didn't like the group or the group's ideas, and she didn't bother to pretend like she did. Two of the members were theater kids. *Sensitive* theater kids.

When Stellen, who had been her right hand for the first semester of ninth grade and who was still who she ate lunch with if she bothered to go, tried to mediate, Carn doubled down about how idiotic and fake and ridiculous his friends were, even though they had only ever been nice to her. One girl had even invited her to her cabin over the summer. But just because someone was nice didn't mean their contributions to an eight-slide presentation about the Scopes Monkey Trial weren't bone-crushingly stupid, apparently.

What I didn't get from Carn I pieced together from Darden, whose sister knew the theater kids. Carna became more withdrawn than usual. She missed days of school. She spent most of her time in Heidi's room, where there was a bigger bed and a TV, or putting pointless miles on the Rover, which she'd now taken over entirely. If I asked her to ship stuff, she did it. If I asked her to reset the Wi-Fi, she did it. If I asked her anything else, she pretended I was a fly and waved me away. At least she didn't kill me.

She was barely nicer to Lock. She didn't snap at him, but there were no midnight Cheerios, no shipping box forts, no selfies with rainbow barf filters. The worst part was not that he looked sad when she ignored him, but that he didn't. He looked like he expected it.

When I finally reached out to Stellen in an attempt to run interference, he sent me a screenshot of their last exchange:

**STELLEN**

I'm trying to help, but I'm exhausted, C. I can't be the *only* person in the world you don't hate.

**CARN**

consider urself off the hook

It felt like a gut punch.

But having your dead mother agree that your sister is the bitchy one is not a morale boost. It's just lonelier.

I concentrated on my lists. Checked off what was checkable. Fixed what was fixable. Important things, like pants.

I sat on the floor against the bed methodically working the tie through the waistband. Mom flipped forward onto her stomach so she could watch over my shoulder.

"You're practically killing yourself so she doesn't have to go live with Mal and Bob Ross Girl up there, and she can't even be nice. She doesn't appreciate anything." The voice was so real, right in my ear. I breathed in deep, looking for the scent of her moisturizer, which was made with retinol or stem cells or glucosamine but smelled like oranges. It wasn't there. Only mine was. "If you would've reported me that first night or the next day—hell, even the next week—it would have been so. Much. Easier. You could have stayed down here with that girl from the coffee shop. You did all this for your sister. And it's your senior year."

"Audrey," I said, working the string through, letting her words worm in. She watched over my shoulder while I stretched the sweats to check my progress and lost half of it. Heidi would have just thrown them away, but they were Lock's favorites. "She's the one from the coffee shop."

"Yeah, Audrey. She seems cool even if she let Brandon serve me that latte."

"It wasn't her fault. She didn't know about your hazelnut thing."

"I always forget if it's hazelnuts or walnuts."

"You forget what you're allergic to?! Were allergic to?"

"No, I mean which one Nutella is."

I glanced up at her. "Hazelnut." She laughed, one dark "ha."

The end of the string was just under the hole. I bit it and tugged it through. Victory! With the ends liberated, I tied fat knots to keep them from disappearing down the tunnel the next time Lock got fidgety and tried to pull the string all the way out. I smiled at the pants.

"Congratulations! You just saved the life of a pair of sweatpants. You the real MVP, Drew." I should have ignored her, but I couldn't do that when she was alive either.

The Ghost of Mom Present was there to remind me that while I could keep all the balls in the air, all the sweatpants tied up tight, even keep multiple frauds of varying complexity on track, I couldn't keep my family from falling apart in any of the ways that ultimately mattered. What if I kept them from splitting us up, but we couldn't stand to be together? I pressed my face into my palms, wishing there was anyone real to talk to in the world.

"Why do you think she was really in the storage room? Do you think she knows about your money?" she whispered.

"I never said it was my money." I whipped my head around, but she was gone.

# CHAPTER FIFTY-THREE

People at school couldn't think of anything to talk about besides acceptances, rejections, waitlists, and what was taking BlahBlah University so long. The people enrolling in two-year programs or training for EMT/fire/aesthetician certifications or who already signed with a navy recruiter tolerated the ones who buzzed around thinking everyone else was on pins and needles waiting for *their* big announcement, like their own personal finale of *The Voice*. Britelle was everywhere, rattling off her acceptances like I'd list bagel varieties. So hard to choose between poppy seed and Northwestern!!!

Dard got more excited about McKean as more people told him how exciting it was. He drove down with his dad and came back with a T-shirt for me, a bumper sticker for his mom, and a lot of enthusiasm for the Commonwealth of Pennsylvania. We'd already talked about Will Smith, Ben Franklin, and two NHL teams; it turned out there was also steel, Amish people, cheesesteak sandwiches, and the Declaration of Independence. Darden was going to be just fine.

Audrey was arguing with her parents about why they could afford Bethel University, a private Christian school in Minnesota, but not Macalester College, a few miles from Bethel with a reputation for turning out what they considered political radicals. The most likely outcome was that Audrey would end up at Lawrence, which she liked except that it was too close to home. She'd looked guilty as soon as she said it, knowing I was planning to live in Larch and commute, and covered with "Only because my family is impossible. Not like yours." Most everybody else slowly lined up behind Eau Claire or Michigan or Northland or Northern Illinois as acceptances rolled in each day.

I was still waiting.

Last fall, I'd decided on Kronshage Hall, right on the lake, as my first choice for housing. I'd picked out a meal plan, looked up plans for lofting my bed (hoping Malcolm or Carna would build it), and followed a bagel shop on State Street I was sure would hire me.

A lot about the plan had changed. No dorm, of course. I'd commute more than an hour to campus to keep my siblings in Larch. I'd work close to full-time to cover our expenses. So a reduced course load, no clubs or study groups, a few extra semesters to finish. But it would be worth it. I'd be in college, starting over in a place where no one would think that my mother not filling in a read-a-thon pledge sheet meant I couldn't read. I'd graduate from a great college and find a great job and live, eventually, anywhere I wanted. The plan, most of it, was still the plan.

I wrested my Wisconsin shirt back from Lock so I could post a picture wearing it as soon as the message came through.

And then it did.

# CHAPTER FIFTY-FOUR

got an email and I just wanted to double-check that it's right."

"Yeah, I'm sorry. It's right, though. We check them all real carefully before we send 'em."

"Oh. That's . . . disappointing. Can you give me any feedback? Was something missing from my application?"

"I mean, I'm just a work-study, but probably not? Because then they would have asked you for it?"

"Could you check, please?"

"Hmm. It looks like we got all your stuff . . . Hang on, did you do the ACT? . . . Oh yeah, it's here. No, yeah. We got everything. So in that case it's just that we had a lot of strong applicants this year and we can't take everybody . . .

. . .

. . .

"Are you still there?"

"Yeah, I'm here. I'm exactly where I've always been."

"I was saying that some people reapply the next year and get in. A girl on my floor did that. She didn't get in, so she did a gap year and the next year she was accepted. She went to Kenya in between."

"Can you tell me anything else about the decision? Or is there an appeals process?"

"I can see what's in the notes. We're not supposed to say anything unless someone asks."

"I'm asking."

"Hmm. Yeah. It was really just that there were a lot of strong applicants this year."

"Right, and you can't take ev—"

"And the committee didn't think your application had spark."

"'Spark'?"

"That means they didn't think it was very interesting."

"'Interesting'?"

"I mean if you're not like in the top something percent, you really have to stand out some other way. Like your essay. Or recommendations—did you have good recommendations? Or activities or whatever. Like everybody kept talking about this one kid who rescues llamas 'cause that's so random, right?"

"You're saying I didn't get in because I'm not very interesting?"

"I'm saying your application didn't, like, jump out to them."

"Like an interesting person's would."

"Look, it's not personal. They just can't take everybody. I mean, sometimes I don't even know how I got in."

"It's kind of hard not to take it personally."

"Well, hopefully you'll get into one of your other schools!"

"Fingers crossed."

"If you want, you can apply again next year."

"If I do anything really interesting between now and then, I'll let you know."

# CHAPTER FIFTY-FIVE

didn't tell anyone. Everyone assumed I was in, that I was in control because I always was. I smiled through the day, accepting congratulations I didn't deserve. What did it matter? My whole life was a fake anyway.

The only person I wanted to talk to, despite everything, was Carna. Even though she was perpetually angry at me, I thought she'd be angry *for* me, too, and that would feel something like solidarity.

Before I had the chance, a text buzzed on Heidi's phone.

ur girl did great! i think she'll like it. remind her aquaphor for a couple days while it heals

I reread the message a dozen times waiting for Carna to get home. How should I reply?

Kyla, tell me you're not saying what I think you're saying

Or

I hope you said goodbye because her sister is going to kill her

Or

When my 8 yo comes in, he'd like a giant Groot across his chest

I settled on,

                                                           tx! ur the best!!!

Lock and I were on the couch when she walked in, him engrossed in the *Vampire Diaries*, which he was definitely too young for, me clicking between application information for a community college and the full-time manager trainee program of a local grocery chain.

She tried to breeze past, but I stepped in front of her with Mom's phone open to the message from Kyla at Blue Violet Tattoo and Piercing. She registered it, met my eyes, and shrugged. If I had known what body part would be sore, I would have slapped it. She stepped around me and started toward her room without a word. I kicked my foot out to keep the door from slamming in my face.

"What did you do?"

"It sounds like you know what I did, Nancy Drew."

"You're under eighteen. You can't just walk in and ask for a tattoo."

She exaggerated a sigh. "Mom gave me permission as long as it was 'something small.'" She was mocking me, me or Heidi or Kyla the tattoo artist or all of us.

I scrolled back up the chain of messages There was nothing between last fall, when Heidi sent a picture of a Norse Helm of Awe that Kyla said would look awesome on a shoulder blade, and the message that afternoon, congratulating Heidi on baby's first tat.

Carn rolled her eyes at me, took the phone, and deleted the last two messages. "Ta-da. Like you've never deleted a text you didn't want me to see." Of course my sister kept things from me; I was keeping things from her, too. But this was pointless and stupid. There were nine thousand ways we could have gotten caught every day, and she was adding to them.

"So what'd you get?"

"Why do you care?"

"I just want to see."

"No."

"Seriously?"

"Calm down, Drew. You're not Mom."

"No kidding. Just show me."

She turned her back and slid out of one side of her jacket. I had done everything I could to hold us together—each of us and all of us—and she was turning her back to me, smug with some stupid secret, the kind of secret you can't even keep secret, the kind of secret another set of sisters at another time might have conspired about, fretted over, held hands and dived into together. And she wouldn't even show me. It was the most alone I'd ever felt. As the left sleeve was coming down, she pulled at the cuff gently, holding it away from her arm.

I grabbed her hand and shoved her sweatshirt up to her elbow, twisting it palm up. She gasped.

Just above her wrist, covered in plastic wrap, was a tiny perfect circle, plain black, with a thin line through it. I recognized it from math, but I had known it before. My mother used it as shorthand when she filled out forms for Lachlan, in the blank for medications, the blank for allergies, the blank for "parent two."

It was an empty set: the set that contains nothing. Or no one.

I had believed that no matter what, at least the three of us belonged together. *We* were a set.

That tattoo wasn't pointless. There was a point. And I got it.

"There's Aquaphor in the bathroom," I said, and slammed the door.

# CHAPTER FIFTY-SIX

Carna is equal parts Heidi and Malcolm. She has Heidi's hair—
thick and tangly, like dirty-blond willow branches, with accidental sun streaks. Hair that would do whatever she wanted
it to do if she wanted it to do anything besides clog the drain. The
two of them are the exact same height and almost the same weight—I
made her try out the deer sled first, to see how Heidi would fit. But
you can also see Malcolm's German angles in her face and her shoulders, like a soldier hiding under a civilian body. She has Malcolm's
long fingers, too, and like his, they are always moving.

All three of them are smart. Malcolm is a straight-up boring
know-it-all (though to be fair, he does know most of it). Heidi never
cared what anyone thought, so she didn't bother showing it off. Carna
is simultaneously uninterested in proving herself *and* annoyed if you
fail to recognize that she is smarter than you.

Heidi could be harsh, but she could get along with almost anybody when she felt like it. Her hair stylist talked about church too
much, but she was good at hair and Heidi respected that. One of the
neighbors put up a purple Vikings awning and a matching mailbox,
but she forgave him because he plowed our driveway when the snow
was really heavy. She and Stephanya shared a pitcher of margaritas

at Malcolm's fortieth, and we all know her feelings about Stephanya. Heidi didn't like everybody, but she didn't really hate anybody.

Malcolm, on the other hand, lived by a rigid code. It was simple, once you figured it out: Respect people and machines. Take care of your own property. Steer clear of mine. As long as you followed the commandments, you were good, no matter what you ate for dinner or where you went to yoga. But there weren't exceptions and there was little forgiveness. It's why he had such a hard time with children.

Carna had Heidi's bite, but with Malcolm's rigidity. The world was black and white, in or out, yes or no. There weren't second chances; there weren't even really first chances. It was like this: She couldn't just pick the olives off a pizza; once it was an olive pizza, it was an olive pizza. It was why she couldn't understand my thing with Darden. She couldn't overlook that Dard was a bit oversensitive or that he talked too loud, even if he was also pretty thoughtful and fun to tube down a river with. He would always be an olive pizza. Most of Larch Leap was.

The feeling was mutual. It's hard to like someone who doesn't like you. Stellen, her one best chance at friendship, stuck it out the longest. He tried on a bitchy boy persona that wasn't really him, and when people found out he was actually really friendly, he tried being her apologizer, pretending she didn't mean what she meant. The problem was that she did, and it's tiring to make excuses for someone who doesn't want to be excused. Carn didn't see his patience fraying until it was too late.

By the time Mom died and everything went south and she started to realize it was exhausting to fight with everybody, it was impossible to find her way back. It was no longer a matter of overlooking a few olives. Carna had burnt down the pizzeria.

# CHAPTER FIFTY-SEVEN

Darden wants to have a surprise party for your birthday."

"Oh?"

"I thought you might want to know."

"Yeah . . . I don't like surprises."

"I figured you wouldn't. I was like, 'Are you sure that's something Drew would like? She's kind of a control freak.' Sorry."

"Can you hand me the chive cream cheese?"

"He said you seemed so stressed lately. He thinks you need something to cheer you up."

"I'm . . . going to do something with my family that weekend. My mom is planning something."

"Really? That's great! Darden was worried she might not even remember. He says she's been traveling constantly."

"Yeah, well, she wouldn't miss my birthday. Please tell him not to plan anything."

"Drew, I know you're a very private person, but if I can help with whatever's going on—"

"Nothing's going on. We're just all busy. You've got customers on your side."

"Be there in one sec! Seriously, if there's anything you need—"

"I'll let you know."

# CHAPTER FIFTY-EIGHT

f that lady in that movie had kids, would they have got new names, too?"

"What movie?" I clicked between accounts, adding in my head. My spreadsheet was off by several hundred dollars.

"The ninja movie."

"The *Ninjago* movie?" Nya? Wasn't she too young to have kids? How old were Ninjagos? And what happened to the money from the two tablets we'd sold? Carna said she'd route PayPal to Heidi's checking. And there was a two-hundred-dollar withdrawal from Grandma's bank, but no two-hundred-dollar deposit to Lock's savings. I checked my numbers again, half listening to Lachlan.

"Not *Ninjago*! The one with woman ninjas that sing."

"I don't think I saw that one, bud." There was a transfer but only twenty dollars. I must have screwed up a decimal point.

Lock sighed loudly, which meant I wasn't paying enough attention. "I'm sorry, kiddo, I need to figure this out. Hey, did you get a math sheet today? Because I'm doing math and then we can both do math at the same time." He rolled his eyes; I rolled mine back. "GO." He slumped off for his backpack.

We worked next to each other for a while, him working on place values, me checking the payment history in our seller accounts.

Frustrated, I gave up for the night and moved on to writing reviews. I would have saved the **Scyence Lyfe Rock Tumbler Kit and Display Box (★★★★★, the insulated tumbler is whisper quiet)** for Lachlan if the real reviews hadn't said the thing was so deafeningly loud.

Singing ninjas. "Do you mean ninjas or nuns?" *Sister Act* had been one of the suggestions on Disney+ when I showed him how to find *High School Musical 3*.

"Nunjas?" he guessed.

"Pretty sure they're just nuns. But I haven't seen it."

"Nuns," he repeated, like he was learning a new language. "They were pretty good singers but they weren't that good of dancers."

"Nuns aren't really known for dancing. Why are you asking about that movie?" He looked down at his page, pretending to concentrate. I Wikipediaed the synopsis:

> After Deloris witnesses her gangster boyfriend Vince LaRocca execute an informant, police lieutenant Eddie Souther places her in witness protection. She is brought to Saint Katherine's Convent . . .

Witness protection. So he hadn't been convinced that Heidi was still working in Canada. It had seemed plausible—Liam's dad traveled so much that Lock had only met him once or twice. (Carna was sure the guy had another family in Dallas who thought he traveled to Wisconsin for work.) Up till then, Lock hadn't questioned that Heidi—whose actual résumé included brief stints at waitressing, event management, selling furniture, and a lot of under the table stuff—had launched a new career that immediately included managing all of North America. But somewhere in that eight-year-old head the wheels had started turning, and they had rolled right over to witness protection.

I wondered if he thought she was posing as a nun or a ninja.

It was funny to think of Heidi as some kind of whistleblowing hero. Dude, she is for whom the whistle blows.

I would tell him everything—well, not *everything*—eventually. But not until I could make a promise about custody. And save more money. And get the rogue federal vigilante to stop following us around thinking we wouldn't recognize him if he was wearing sunglasses.

"I think if the lady in the movie had kids, she would want to make sure they were safe," I said carefully. "That would be the most important thing."

"They would go with her?"

"Well, not necessarily. Not if there was someone else who could take really good care of them. Like their sisters. For example."

He looked at me knowingly. "The nunjas are sisters."

"I mean just regular sisters."

He studied me for a long time without blinking. I coughed. He was thinking I was either very wise or very full of shit. I tried to look the first, which basically proved the second. Finally he pushed a page over to me and said, "Is this supposed to be four in the tens spot or forty in the ones spot?"

**"FYI, LOCK THINKS MOM IS IN WITNESS PROTECTION."**

Carna, who had wandered in from her bedroom to fill up a water bottle, stopped short. "Witness protection?" I nodded. I'd been starved for anything besides business or bitterness from her, and was glad for something to talk about besides UPS or 5-star junk or how loudly I chewed. "Who's after her? The Menomonie Mafia?"

I repeated the whole conversation, complete with ninja references. Carn got the *Sister Act* reference right away; she had watched a lot of musicals when she was friends with Stellen.

"At least he doesn't think she's in prison anymore," she said, yawning.

I choked on my Pepsi. "WHAT?"

"He never said that exactly. He said, 'Do we know anybody who lives in jail?' And I said, 'Not at the moment.' That was it."

"Why didn't you tell me that?!"

"I thought you knew everything." She stretched her arms over her head. She'd been wearing the same grimy flannel for days, since I banished her from my clothes, and only long sleeves since the tattoo.

I ignored the edge in her voice. "Why would she be in prison?"

Carna raised an eyebrow.

"Right, okay, but why would *Lock* think she would be in prison?"

"Maybe the kid is smarter than you think," she said, and went back to bed.

# CHAPTER FIFTY-NINE

Carna was in such a bad mood she didn't even comment on the sad group of protesters lazily holding hand-drawn signs that said CHOOSE LIFE and ABORTION STOPS A BEATING HEART. They sat just over the edge of the women's clinic parking lot in fold-up camp chairs, taking up three spaces in the back of Chick-fil-A. They seemed bored by their own activism, maybe because there wasn't much traffic in and out of the clinic. Most of the clients—older women, transgender women, very obviously very pregnant women—probably didn't fit the profile the protesters were looking out for. There was no chanting, only chatting about whatever it is half-assed pro-lifers assigned a quiet beat in central Wisconsin chat about after football season is over.

But our arrival was exactly the kind of thing those four ladies and one man had trained for. Two teenaged girls without a parent? Slamming the car door so hard the air shook? An angry snarl of "I don't want to be here either"? Their interest was piqued, to say the least. They stood up and stared.

Almost too late, one of them remembered to call out, "Excuse me! Could I have just a minute of your time?" crossing one foot boldly over the line into the clinic's private parking lot.

Carna raised a middle finger high behind her and continued to the door. I should have, too, but the voice was familiar. I turned to see a middle-aged woman in a shaggy bob and sweatshirt that said, SMILE! YOUR MOTHER CHOSE LIFE. Her mouth dropped open in horrified recognition.

Of course this was how Renata Flynn spent her weekends. I followed Carna inside without a word or a middle finger.

When they called Carn's name, she stood up and waited for me to follow her. I had assumed she'd go alone since that's how she preferred everything, but I underestimated how nervous she was. The nurse deposited us in a small, neat exam room with some instructions and a thin white sheet. I looked at the posters—anatomical illustrations, admonitions about prenatal nutrition, resource numbers and websites for sexual assault survivors—while Carna stepped out of her jeans and positioned herself on the table with the sheet over her lap.

We'd left Lock home alone with a bag of pre-started clementines, no TV limits, and his burner, which had only my number and Carna's programmed, though he was hoping Ms. Emily would share hers, too. It wasn't ideal, but neither was bringing him to the clinic while we got Carna's itchy vagina looked at. I had been younger than Lock when Heidi left me and Carn alone for the first time. I'd figured out how to start a load of wash after she squeezed a Capri Sun over her ladybug Pillow Pet. Maybe Lock would be inspired to throw in some towels.

Just as the door was clicking open, Carna said, "Why do people draw penises on everything but not vaginas?" She had been staring at a poster showing a uterus, fallopian tubes, and ovaries arrayed like a bodybuilder in a "most muscular" pose.

"It's technically the vulva you'd want to draw, I think. But it's hard to do well if you're rushing." Dr. Bareket shut the door quickly and dropped her computer onto the desk. "Penises have such a simple, iconic shape." She drew a classic penis and balls squiggle in the air with her pen. "You just *get it* right away."

Under the Providers tab on the website she had a long list of impressive credentials, research and fellowships all over the world, but the woman in the lab coat and Vans seemed completely at ease talking about graffiti genitals. "The way people draw testicles, though, that's completely ridiculous. Like Mickey Mouse ears. Hi. I'm Dr. Bareket."

"Carna," said Carna.

"Let me change that on your chart," she said, tapping her keyboard.

"Oh no. Carna's not her legal name," I interrupted, wanting to get everything right.

"I'm not a lawyer," she said, shrugging. "I like to call people what they want to be called." She finished making her changes, then looked between me and Carna.

We were used to people asking where our mother was, even before the answer was "in a plastic bag under my bed." When she was in middle school, Carna used to make up elaborate, unnecessary lies to make me uncomfortable. I'd say, "Dentist?" She'd add, "She broke a tooth biting into a lamb kebab at the Greek restaurant that used to be a Burger King." I'd say, "Work?" She'd say, "Her boss won't let her take any more time off because she's the only one who knows how to work the machine since the last guy lost his fingers."

A plain "unavailable" would have sufficed.

But Dr. Bareket didn't ask about Heidi at all. She made a quick assessment and said to Carna, "Big sister can wait in the lobby."

Carna shook her off, though. She'd have rather been alone in a room with a wolf.

The exam was fast and thorough, starting with a few questions about symptoms, which Carna mumbled through much less descriptively than she had with me. (To Bareket's "Have you had itching or burning?" she said "Some" instead of "It feels like a maxi pad made out of poison ivy.") When the doctor positioned herself between Carna's knees to take some swabs, my usually fearless sister looked like she might throw up. Any doctor was bad, but one with her head between your legs talking about discharge? It was like her Achilles vagina.

Dr. Bareket rolled her stool backward, tossed her exam gloves in a bin, and helped Carna sit up. There would be some lab verification on the swabs, but she was sure they'd confirm that it was just a bad yeast infection.

"We've got two ways to treat it, and either one is good. I can give you a tube of cream that you squirt inside with a plastic applicator." She mimed pressing the plunger on a syringe, like the way we used to give Lock Baby Tylenol, except not. "Works, but it's a little messy. Or a pill to swallow. Works, but some people don't like pills." She looked to Carna for a decision.

"The pill, I guess."

"Flu-con-a-zole." She typed as she talked. "We've got a pharmacy here. They should have it for you."

"Thanks," mumbled Carna.

"It's still probably going to itch like crazy tonight. The pharmacist will give you some topical stuff in case it's too bad. I'd ditch my underwear for the night, too—sometimes that makes it worse."

"Should we switch detergent?" I asked, paging through the list of recommendations I'd brought up on my phone. "Does she need a fragrance-free one?" Carn looked like she hated me again.

Dr. Bareket sighed. "You can, and you can start eating more yogurt and drinking cranberry juice and experimenting with all kinds of supplements. They probably sell something made out of, I don't know, elm bark and witches' tears." Steph probably had a recommendation from the BestU BestUterus line. "But since this is the first one, I wouldn't worry about making a lot of changes. The antifungal should do it." She smiled and stood up with her computer. "Oh, and never follow the advice of anybody who wants you to steam your clams."

Carna snorted, the first normal sound out of her since she put her feet in the stirrups.

"Really! It was a thing on the internet for a while. People do weird things—especially when it comes to vaginas. Or maybe that's just the ones I see." She bulged her eyes wide, and this time, we both laughed.

CARNA SWALLOWED HER PILL with a swig of Sprite. The activists from the Chick-fil-A were gone. "Make sure you post a review of that," I said, nodding to the silvery tube of anti-itch cream the pharmacist gave her. "Five stars. This little tube relieved my burning crotch and whitened my teeth!" No response. Now that Carna was sure she wasn't dying from a rare form of vag ooze, all vulnerability was gone.

"Can we get going?" she said.

When we got home, Lock was watching a baking competition in what was now his UW shirt, legs folded inside with only a row of bare toes sticking out. He reported that no doorbells had rung, nothing had broken, and he was very interested in lunch.

"I can make quesadillas," I said, looking Carna's way, hoping to recapture a little bit of the warmth from the doctor's office.

"I'm not hungry," she said, picking a clementine from Lock's bag. She disappeared to her room.

Lachlan watched her go. "She's mad *again*?"

I sunk into the couch next to him and pulled the edge of the shirt over the tips of his toes. "Not at you, buddy."

# CHAPTER SIXTY

L eave it."

Carna was halfway through a public post to a prepper group calling out Char Yancy for entrapping freedom lovers and true Americans when I leaned over and flattened the cover on the computer.

She glared up at me.

"Delete the user name, delete all the posts. Delete your design for running an air conditioner off a car battery. And take down any products we've got listed under Conspira-C-Bitch."

"I've got a good bid on a pack of Mylar-lined emergency ponchos."

"Mylar? Like shiny balloons?"

"For hypothermia. They retain ninety percent of your body heat, so if there's a—"

"Actually, I don't care. Even if it's the only way to survive the secret threat of global cooling or the socialist anti-balloon agenda or whatever they're all paranoid about. If you sell them, someone can track where we shipped from."

She looked at me, annoyed. "Now who's paranoid?"

"You know I'm right. Shut it down."

"Then let go of my computer."

The humming tension in the house had gotten louder, like cicadas before a storm. The imposter doctor who was supposed to sign off that Grandma Sharon died of natural causes in Phoenix had turned out not to be an imposter doctor, but a real law-enforcement officer posing as someone selling forged death certificates. An imposter imposter doctor.

Luckily, I'd insisted on a trial run first, in case anything went wrong. It did go wrong. But instead of going wrong for us, it went wrong for one of Aunt Krystal's exes. He stole money from Krystal and said Carna "ate like a chubby little Guernsey," so we didn't hesitate to use his name to beta test the State of Arizona death certificate. Within days, he posted to Facebook that someone had issued a "death warrant" for him, which was not accurate but was tempting, and now he had to go to court to prove he didn't try to fake his own death. It had cost us three hundred dollars, but kept us out of trouble.

I don't know what the government does with the money undercover cops collect, but maybe they could take it off what we owed Social Security.

Carna seemed to take the whole thing personally. She'd found people as disenchanted with the world as she felt, even if they were paranoid, gun-waving, shopaholic weirdos, and they turned out to be assholes like everyone else. And now I needed to find some other way to get Darth to close our case before he came after us with more than suspicions and business cards.

It turns out, it was already too late.

# CHAPTER SIXTY-ONE

What are you doing here?" Carna stopped short, surprised to find me home when there was another hour left of school.

"So you're the only one who can miss sixth hour?" I shuffled the papers in front of me, sliding one on top and then the other. I'd actually missed everything after 10:00 a.m.

"Seriously, Drew, why are—" The toilet flushed down the hall. "Is Darden here?"

"Lock. He's in Mom's room watching—I don't know what he's watching."

"Is he sick?"

"I just wanted him home."

Carna had made a habit of storming by and slamming her door, but now she hovered. She used Heidi's email to excuse herself early a lot, but me? Never. And Lock? Never ever. I could feel the questions she wasn't asking, the way she shifted between thoughts. I stared down at her feet, tensing as she shifted her weight back and forth. Those socks had been mine once; nothing was now. A minute passed, or maybe two, or maybe none. She should go back to her own unhappy world. Still she stood there, trying not to go or trying not to stay.

I looked up finally, saw my dad's jaw, my mom's hair, and my own eyes looking back at me, not angry this time. Scared. "Drew?"

"We're going to lose the house," I said finally. "And then we're going to lose Lock."

She sat down hard.

**K. DAVID BARTH** had found the secret to getting someone to answer Heidi's phone. His text at the end of second period said:

Drew, we both know you're the one reading this. Get somewhere you can talk. I'll call.

He'd timed it for the school bells. The period ended and I bolted. My hands were shaking as I pushed past half the musical cast, in costume, setting up for the first big promposal of the year. "Everybody has to watch this!" someone yelled as I flew out of the building to the parking lot.

The phone rang right at ten. I leaned into the brick wall, prickling with sweat even in thirty-five degrees. He recited his full name and title, as though we hadn't been on a nickname basis for months. It felt serious. It felt real. I slid down to a squat and pressed the phone hard to my ear.

What he knew wasn't everything, but it was enough. He knew that Sharon had been dead for four years. Not the exact date, but close, because he'd finally stumbled on June, to whom Heidi had sublet Sharon's apartment in the senior complex. June was not supposed to have jumped the waiting list to get in, which should have ensured her silence, but if you were seventy years old and someone from Social Security knocked on your door, you'd probably spill your guts, too.

Once he got that close, he'd been able to find the doctor who had recommended the hospice nurse who'd never come because Sharon died too fast, and soon he'd find the gullible funeral director who had given Heidi the death certificate to file herself.

The big thing he couldn't find, of course, was Heidi.

He'd been watching the house and knew that she hadn't been there in months—knew, in fact, that every time he'd "just missed her," I'd been lying. That didn't surprise me. His questioning had always seemed like an elaborate game of chicken. I had hoped we could agree to be chickens for a while longer, but Darth was done.

The part that he had gotten very wrong, though, was believing that Heidi was still out there somewhere telling us what to do. She was the puppet master and I was the puppet, trying not to trip over the strings. And that was why he was calling. He wanted me to pass on a message. She should know that besides paying restitution (about $50,000), she could be sent to prison (which wasn't the threat he thought it was) and charged an additional fine of up to $250,000 (which was).

Given how elaborate the cover-up was (he'd seen the posts of Fake Sharon in Arizona), how she'd involved minors in the deception (umm . . .), and how there were other financial irregularities to be looked into, and how he basically saw himself as an Avenger, he'd be encouraging the department to go for the maximum penalty. I could do that math in my head: Two hundred fifty thousand dollars meant seizing her bank accounts, the Range Rover, and everything she owned, including the house. Unless, of course, she wanted to turn herself in and negotiate a deal.

My heart started beating so hard my brain was beating, too. Or maybe my brain started it and told my heart to man up.

"Look, Darth—sorry, Mr. Barth. She, uh, can't do that," I stuttered.

After all that time hiding what had happened, we had reached an unforeseen point in our story where we would be better off with the truth. *Alive* meant she was a fugitive, and all kinds of people asking all kinds of questions. Assets being frozen. Some kind of temporary court-appointed custody, probably with strangers since Krystal would be implicated, too. Investigations. Police. *Dead*, on the other hand, just put us back where we started, which had seemed like the worst place until we got ourselves here. I made the only decision I could. "I probably should have told you this earlier, but . . . she died."

An awful sound cracked through the phone, a combination of triumph and rage and disbelief and an ill-bred hyena.

Darth laughed.

"Oh wow. Wow. She died, huh? So you're telling me that your dead grandmother is alive but your live mother is dead?"

"They're both dead."

"Ha!"

"I'm being serious. It happened before she even knew about you. She had an allergic reaction. Carna and I were worried about our brother, so we didn't—"

"Sure, sure. And where is she now, then?"

"It's . . . hard to explain."

He laughed and laughed. Involuntary at first, but he kept it going, like he wanted to prove a point.

"Frankly, I expected more. She's going to have to come up with something better than 'don't bother looking for me, I just happen to be dead now.' You seem like a decent kid. I know your mother has put you in a tough spot, so I'm going to do you a favor. I'm going to give you through the end of the week to talk some sense into her while I get the rest of the approvals and processes in order."

"But—"

"It's going to be way better for all of you if she just turns herself in."

"I'm telling the truth!"

"You might need to reexamine your understanding of that word. Just make sure Heidi knows: No funny business. I'll be watching."

WHEN I FINISHED EXPLAINING, Carna's eyes were huge and her cheeks flushed. She looked younger than fifteen. "What are we going to do? What's the plan?"

"There is no plan."

"But you'll figure out a plan. Let's get the whiteboard." Carna sprang up for my room.

"There is nothing to put on the whiteboard, Carn. We're fucked. It's over. It's all over."

"No, it's not. We can still stay together. Lock is our responsibility. Even if they think Heidi's hiding out somewhere, someone has to be in charge."

"Yeah, someone who's eighteen and has a house and money and isn't under surveillance."

"There's a little money," she said.

"We need *a lot* of money."

"Kevin can prove she's dead! And then they can't charge her, right?" Carna's cheeks were getting hotter. Things were unraveling and I wasn't tying any knots.

"Kevin didn't actually see her, remember? We didn't let him? And why would he say he did? He'd be in huge trouble."

"We can tell them it wasn't his fault. Steph can talk to him."

"No. Even if they believed him and somehow didn't charge him, it would still make us look like psychopaths. A court's not going to let Lock live with underage psychopaths."

"We're not psychopaths," Carna said defensively. "And you're almost eighteen."

"We might be psychopaths, but that's irrelevant."

"We'll get an apartment. I'll get a job." Carna was furiously tapping into her phone, "Look, there's a two-bedroom apartment—oh goddamn, that's a lot. A one bedroom, though—we can share and Lock can sleep on the pullout. Dad used to do that."

"The pullout. Great. The orthodontist put in a pool last year. And a sauna."

"Lock doesn't need a pool."

"No. But he needs something better than a pullout couch and two teenage sisters who barely even speak to each other." We could argue about wastebasket hoops versus private half-court basketball, an off-brand Switch versus a home gaming theater, but it wasn't only the money. It was the scrambling. The quicksand. The barely hanging on. She knew it, too.

We'd been so determined to protect Lachlan from everyone else, we'd failed to protect him from ourselves. The sun shifted while we sat there, turning a bad day into night.

# CHAPTER SIXTY-TWO

ock's father had always been a looming threat, someone who could pull the pin on our complicated little world if he wanted to. The irony was that being an asshole was the only thing that prevented him from doing it. When Lock was in preschool, the guy briefly found religion when he and his wife separated. He reached out to Mom, wanting to "make things right." But then the wife took him back, Jesus said never mind, and Lachlan went on naming action figures Captain Chad West.

They weren't better people than us; they were probably worse. But they had a couple of boys in middle school, and Lachlan might like brothers. They had a couple of dogs, and Lachlan would love a dog. They could send him to the Catholic school and sign him up for hockey. If they were ever investigated for anything, they had lawyers and friends and friends with lawyers. Even if they never quite loved him like we did, they'd at least make sure he got into college. Maybe music school. Oberlin, like Darden's sister was planning. Or Juilliard. Or *The Mickey Mouse Club*.

Orthodouche and Toothwife would get used to the idea, and pretty soon, Lock would, too. It would be like when Malcolm discovered a protected turtle species nesting on his property and had to abandon his plans for a new dock. At first he was angry, but he grew to appreciate the turtles, eventually, kind of.

I hoped they liked Justin Timberlake.

**THE DOOR RATTLED DOWN THE HALL.** Lock padded out and Carna scooped him into her lap and kissed the top of his head. He pretended he didn't like it, but he stayed put. It had been a long time since he'd been in that lap.

"What's up? Getting hungry for dinner?" I asked.

"A little hungry, but not for regular dinner." Carna walked her fingers up his shoulder and around his ear. He squeezed his head against his shoulder, trying to trap her hand, but her fingers scrambled away over the top. He lolled his head to the other side.

"No? Then what kind of dinner are you a little hungry for?"

"I'm hungry for popcorn dinner."

I raised my eyebrows at him.

"But also . . . I would eat a fruit?" he tried.

"Is that a question?"

"Yes?"

I smiled and rubbed the tired spots under my eyes. "I could go for popcorn dinner. With grapes."

His eyes got wide, like he couldn't believe it had worked. It was upside-down day and Drew was agreeing to fun. He pressed his luck: "Guys? I just thought of a idea. Let's pretend tonight is a party. Starting now."

"Don't you have any worksheets tonight?" I asked.

"It's *Monday*," he said, like who would ever give out a worksheet on a Monday?

"Me neither," piped in Carna. I looked at her skeptically. "It's *Monday*."

"Well—"

"It could be a sleepover party!" Lock added, "In Mom's bed!"

They watched for my reaction. Carna arched an eyebrow. "You don't have any worksheets tonight, do you, Drew?" she asked, squeezing Lachlan a little tighter. He held his breath.

Homework in three classes, a Spanish oral exam to practice, jobs to apply for, free law clinics to search, custody agreements to research, files to find, messages to draft, dirty boy clothes everywhere.

But no worksheets. And nothing to lose I wasn't already losing.

"Not on a *Monday*," I said. Lock jabbed a fist in the air and knocked Carna in the face.

When someday I ask him what he knew or thought he knew then, he won't remember. But I will remember that he knew enough to think that day was precious and fragile and fleeting. I remember it that way, too.

# CHAPTER SIXTY-THREE

We partied like it was the end of the world, because it was. For Lachlan that meant unlimited Capri Suns, popcorn and grapes and toaster waffles for dinner, a JT karaoke dance party, and falling asleep in the middle of the second *Guardians of the Galaxy*.

It was mostly the same for me and Carn, except our drinks weren't Capri Suns. And instead of crashing at nine thirty, we passed out at around two.

"Can you brush your teeth, bud? Lock? Just use the bathroom, and then you can go right back to sleep." Dead weight. "Hello? You're going to have to pee in the night." Not even an eye twitch. I carried him to Heidi's, brought in all the monkeys, and threw the blanket over everybody. There's your sleepover, buddy.

When I got back, Carna was at the table in the kitchen, playing with the strap on the purse from the safe.

"You need to find a better place for this unless you want Darth confiscating it with everything else." Carna slid it across the table and set another stack of bills next to it. She rolled her eyes at my surprise. "It took about three guesses to figure out the combination. Mom and Justin's birthday backward? Real sneaky, Drew."

I stared at it, shaking my head for a minute, then took out the bottle of margaritas Taylor had left in the freezer on New Year's. I filled two Packers souvenir cups and handed one to Carna.

"How did you know it was in there?"

"Um, duh? I was the one who put it in there?"

"*You?* Where would you get this much money? You've never even had a job. Is it stolen?!"

"Oh. My. God. Calm down. Mom had it with her in the shed. What's left in the purse anyway. The rest I started saving after you changed the combination." She tapped the pile.

"Why was Mom keeping that much cash in a knockoff Gucci?"

"To bring to Mexico, I guess."

"For what? How much could a Justin Timberlake T-shirt cost?"

"I know, right? I kinda wondered if she was going to bring back a bunch of prescription drugs or something. You could make a lot more selling oxy than kitchen appliances. But that's pretty sketch even for her." It was exactly what I'd thought. "But once we had her computer, I checked her search history. She did bookmark an article about counterfeit Rolexes, so I thought maybe it was something like that . . . until I found a bunch of websites for Mexican clinics."

"Clinics?"

"You know," Carn said, "face-lift, butt-lift, that jiggly-arm thing, boobs bigger, boobs smaller. You can get all kinds of stuff done cheaper there. Look up 'mommy makeover Mexico.' It's a thing."

"Are you kidding me right now?"

"Drew, think about how much she dreaded getting older. And how much she liked getting a deal."

"You're not fucking kidding? Plastic surgery? Zero dollars for college but twenty thousand dollars for jiggly arms and Botox?" Not that I needed a college fund anymore anyway.

"I don't know why you're surprised. Would it have been better if she was dealing black-market Adderall? At least this way she wasn't going to kill anybody." Yes, Heidi was practically a hero, just like Chad West. I grabbed the bottle from the freezer again and brought it to the table.

"Why didn't you tell me about it?" Carna had not only found a hoard of cash, she'd tried to hide it from me.

Carna got up and got a couple of paper-wrapped drive-thru straws from a drawer. "To be fair, you didn't tell me about it either. I wasn't positive you'd found it, and then when you gave that big wad to Kevin, I knew." She dropped the straw in her cup and took a long sip. "Maybe he'll go to Mexico to get his ears fixed . . . They're so weird . . ."

"I was going to tell you. You haven't been exactly easy to talk to."

She looked at me steadily, reluctant. "Probably not."

I fanned through the extra bills Carna had given me, another thousand dollars or so. She must have been skimming out of our accounts to make up for the first stash, which explained why my spreadsheets were off. "So what were you going to do with it?" But as soon as I asked, I realized that the answer was already hanging there between us, just waiting for one of us to pluck it out of the air. It hit me like a snowplow. "You were going to run away."

I wished I could be Carna, even if she was miserable most of the time. Or my parents, even if one of them was dead. I wished I could divide us up so easily. Draw a neat line between each, like lanes on a track, each in their own race. Me. Her. Her. Him.

Lock.

Carna rubbed her face with her hands and sighed. "If I had to." She folded the straw wrapper into an accordion. "I couldn't go to Starling. I just couldn't."

"We were figuring it out!"

"I didn't think . . ." She stopped, considered, started again. "You know how you have always done exactly what you were supposed to do? Like always, even when no one else would? I couldn't believe it when you didn't call 911 the second we found her."

"I tried to. You talked me out of it!"

"I didn't think you'd really listen to me. The next day I was like, 'Drew must have been in shock. Today she'll change her mind.' Same the next day. And the next. I figured sooner or later you'd come to your senses, but it kept going, and it was even kind of working. But even when we were in the middle of it, I knew that once you graduated you'd choose Madison like you planned your whole life"—I winced, realizing she still didn't know—"instead of being stuck here with me and Lock. I wanted options. Options that weren't Dad's place." She added, "I never would have left without telling you first."

I turned this over in my mind. Carna had a backup plan. The backup plan was primarily a pile of cash and an excellent sense of direction, but my sister could get a long way with just that.

Where the fuck was my backup plan?

She skimmed the pages I'd left on the table earlier. The letter to K. David Barth said that I'd lied to my siblings, who until recently thought Heidi was on a long trip, and had nothing to do with anything. It explained that she really had died, and that I'd paid someone on the urban prepper network to bury her. I hoped he'd decide to believe me. It would make it easier for him, too. I included birth dates, death dates, accounts, aliases, and Social Security numbers. The hardest part to type had been the contact information for the orthodontist.

I hoped Lachlan would forgive me someday.

Carna frowned at the pages. "You know, I always thought the reason you were such a rule follower was because you were boring."

"Wow, Carn. Thanks." I couldn't exactly be insulted, because I'd thought the same thing—and the UW admissions department had, too, apparently. Whenever Heidi or Carna or Krystal would brag about getting away with something, instead of feeling right, sometimes I just felt jealous. I poured more strawberry slushie.

"No, just listen. Mom—"

"Was definitely not boring." I lifted my drink in a toast. My head was starting to feel a little wavy.

"For sure not boring. Opposite of boring. But I think she wanted to seem spontaneous. And fun. Like with every stupid thing. The thing is, though, she wasn't fun. She was reckless."

Carna folded the papers together, then proceeded to tear them into tiny bits of confetti. I appreciated the gesture, even though I'd have to print them out again. "I couldn't understand how you got to be like you are living here. But I think maybe now I do. You're not boring. You've just always been trying to control the chaos." She let the bits of paper fall from her hand like slow, soft snow, then scooped them into a pile. "I'm sorry. About all of it."

A tiny, hot drip escaped from my eye, and while I was wiping that one, another teetered on the edge. Carna had never said sorry for anything in her life. I pressed the cold glass against my eye to freeze the rest in place.

I said, "I'm sorry, too, because now we're fucked."

"Looks that way." Carna sighed and took a big slurp. "Not because of us, though. We're fucked because of Mom. And K. David Barth," she added.

"Yeah, fuck him," I agreed. "Also, fucked by Aunt Krystal."

"TRUE." She refilled each of our glasses. "And super fucked by the orthodontist."

"RIGHT. But not by Captain Chad West."

"Of course not. He'd never. Fucked by the prepper fuckers."

"Definitely. Char fucking Yancy fucker." Slushie freezer margaritas can get you wasted without ever noticing you're on the way to wasted, especially if you've spent most of high school driving drunk hockey players or parents around. But I couldn't remember the point of being responsible anymore, since it hadn't actually gotten me anywhere. "Fucked by the University of Wisconsin Department of Admissions," I declared.

Carna gasped. "What?"

I shook my head or it shook me. "Lot of strong applicants. Can't take everybody," I singsonged.

"You didn't get in? How is that—"

"It's fine," I interrupted. "Well, it's not fine, but I don't want to talk about it."

"Drew, oh my god. I'm so sorry. That's total bullshit."

She looked like she might hug me, which would have wrecked me. "Lots of things are, but there's nothing I can do about it right now and my heart is already broken enough for today. Let's go back to saying things we're fucked by. School guidance counselors."

She frowned, but didn't press. "Okay, fucked by . . . um, I'm running out of things."

"Yeast infections?"

"Oh, no, actually, that's better!" She brightened. "That medicine cleared it up fast."

"Aw, I'm so happy for your cootchie." I was definitely drunk. "I'm gonna make a toast. To flucozocanol!" We drained our cups.

"Wait. That wasn't it. Difooligan?"

"No, that was the fancy one. You got the generic. Flucanolaoil?"

She took out her phone and said "what medicine itchy" out loud as she typed. "Wait . . . what the hell . . . Shit, Drew. Did you know you can have butt worms?"

I choked on a laugh. My coughing fit blew the confetti confession off the table.

Carna started laughing, too, her real laugh, with her real smile. "Please let me be the one to tell Lock there's such a thing as butt worms!"

She crawled under the table to pick up scraps and whacked her head against it. I crawled in next to her and petted her hair. She looked up from my lap and said, "I wonder if you can bait a hook with butt worms. I'm gonna try that for the opener if we're not in jail."

Somewhere way, way upstream, weeks or maybe years upstream, a dam broke. I didn't have to be right. Or boring. She didn't have to be mean. We laughed at nothing and complained about everything and plotted our terrible futures and finished the liter of margaritas, while Lachlan dreamed in a pile of monkeys down the hall. It was the end of the world, which was too bad, because it felt like a beginning.

Before she dragged herself up to go to bed, Carna put her hands on my shoulders and said, "Don't send that letter to Darth. And don't say anything to Lock."

"I won't."

"Seriously."

"I won't!"

"We're gonna figure something out."

"Absolutely," I lied. "It's going to work out." I couldn't bear to tell her she was wrong.

On her way out she looked down at the cash, still sitting on the table. "If you want to keep all that, I haven't gotten you a birthday present yet." She flashed a huge smile.

Birthday present. Right, I'd be eighteen on Friday. Eighteen, which we'd thought would solve all our problems. Happy fucking birthday.

# CHAPTER SIXTY-FOUR

I stayed up to put things away and bring the bottles out to recycle (I may have been half wasted but the other half was still me). It was cool, but not cold, and the ground smelled wet, like melting. Even in April, the banked snow was stubborn, sitting there dirty and shrinking. When it finally disappeared into the ground, everything would look clean and fresh for a while, but not yet. My head was heavy and tired, but it spun less out in the dark.

I wondered if this was how an unarmed general would feel the night before a battle; the troops asleep in their bunks, her hoping for a miracle—or even a missile strike if it would mean the next day never had to happen—but counting on nothing. They will be okay, I told myself. We will be okay. I thought it, but didn't feel it, which used to be enough for me. I let my fingertips get cold and held them under my eyes.

Somewhere in the back of my mind, I had assumed that one day, we would just start telling people that Heidi had gone away and never come back. No one would pinpoint the moment, and no one would especially care. That was the plan C or D or Y that I hadn't actually made. But if Darth made her an actual fugitive, someone would notice us. They'd start digging. They'd ask questions. They'd take away everything. Maybe even the egg chair and the monkeys.

And even if we could prove she was gone, then what? What kind of happy ending was this place? I had been so sure of my own future, so sure I could see where I was going, that once all the eggs I'd counted into that basket broke, I had no clue what else to do. Carna needed a new start more than anything, maybe more than she needed to avoid our dad. And Lock deserved so much more than floundering, disappointed siblings lying to him about where his mother is. I couldn't keep the three of us, in this same house, in this same place, in this same cycle. It would bury us.

Tomorrow I would send the letter to Darth. I would make the call I should have made.

When I came back inside, Heidi was at the table, waiting, admiring the bills stacked neatly in front of her.

"You look like you've been having a real good time," she said unhelpfully.

"You look like a zombie." It wasn't true, but I knew she was sensitive about being dead.

"Drinking on a school night with your baby brother in the house? What other kind of trouble have you been getting into?" She fell into snorty giggles.

"I haven't heard from you in a while. I thought you were gone."

"Did you worry something might have happened to me?" She laughed at herself again. I slid the piles of money away from her.

"What do you want?" I asked, tucking the cash into a Fry Magic Air Fryer we couldn't sell after news broke about it starting electrical fires **(Review removed due to product recall)**.

"Nothin'. Just sayin' hi." She looked over my shoulder into the fridge as I put the grapes away. "Yuck. I thought those were Snack Packs but they're yogurt." She slid up onto the counter, knocking her heels into the cupboard door below. It didn't make any sound. "You know you should drink a lot of water before you go to sleep. That'll help with . . ." She pointed at her temple and clicked her tongue. I'm not sure if she meant my blooming headache or my grip on reality.

I took my cup to the sink and filled it. It tasted like watery strawberries. A quick wave of nausea almost brought it all back up, but I swallowed hard. She smiled small. It looked sad.

She never used to look sad.

I pulled myself up on the counter. I was so tired, but if I lay down, I was pretty sure I'd throw up. After a long time, she said, "I wasn't trying to create chaos."

"You weren't trying not to."

She sighed. "That's probably true. I did the best I could." And then, before I could, she corrected herself. "Aw, that's probably not true."

I laughed in spite of myself. A truth. A truce. The heat clicked on. A twenty had slipped the pile and fluttered in the vent under the sliding door. I hopped down to grab it and smoothed it over my knee, sitting with my back against the cold glass. And then Heidi was right next to me, the warm air blowing through her.

"Did you know how much trouble we were in before you left?" I asked.

"Mmm, not exactly. A couple things had been off. Krystal had gotten really sloppy. I knew it was possible, I guess."

"Is that why you were so determined to go? Even though Lisa couldn't? And you didn't have a passport?"

She didn't say anything.

"And I asked you not to?"

"It was JUSTIN TIMBERLAKE, Drew! Of course I was determined to go!" She rolled her eyes, trying to be playful.

Suddenly, I was more tired than nauseous. If I didn't go to bed

soon, I'd fall asleep on the floor. I pulled myself up and finished another cup of water. "I'd love to stay up chatting about the *NSYNC
years, but I gotta get some sleep. Big day tomorrow. Pulling the rug
out from my siblings, who for some stupid reason trusted me."

I expected her to follow me, but she stayed put. Finally, she called,
"You never asked me not to go."

I stopped at the door and thought about it. No, I guess not. I
never said no to her. *Just do this one thing for me.* And I always did.

But that wasn't the point, was it? She looked up from her spot
over the vent, searching my face. "I shouldn't have had to," I said.

There was a risk in thinking too hard, especially when you've over-
done the slushies. But there was something gnawing, a thought like a
busy possum that I couldn't leave alone. "Would you have come back
for us? Knowing what you know now?"

The question caught her by surprise, which, given the circumstances, I didn't know was possible. Her look of shock turned to
something like understanding, and then urgency.

"God, Drew. Yeah. Yes." Tears sprang to her eyes, or else they were
mine. "Same now. If there was any way . . . You don't know that? Tell
me you know that?"

I believed her. I believe her. How could I not? Even then, she was
still there.


LOCK WAS SPLAYED FLAT ON HIS BACK, mouth stained fruit-punch
pink, covers kicked off and monkeys everywhere. He wore light-blue
boxers with Lightning McQueens printed on them, and an old T-shirt
of Carna's from hockey camp.

Carn was curled toward him, her face inches from his. It looked
like she'd fallen asleep whispering stories or secrets, whatever truths
or lies he needed to hear or she needed to tell. Her arm draped across

the pillow over his head. There was enough light to see the outline of the tattoo on her wrist.

My room, my bed, my toothbrush were too far away. I lay down on the other side of Lachlan, mirroring Carna like two parts of a Rorschach.

I brushed my hand over my brother's hair and touched the mark on my sister's wrist.

Maybe we were always meant to be an empty set.

"I'm sorry," I whispered. "I love you."

# CHAPTER SIXTY-FIVE

Rough. Morning.

The hot, crawling, hard thing inside my skull, which demanded I hold still or it would stab hot needles into the backs of my eyes, was only the second thing I noticed.

The first thing was that my shirt was cold and wet and clinging to me in a way that did not feel good. That's when I sat up too fast and my head almost exploded.

I think the pee smell was right after that, the third thing. My **Fashion-Tech Smart Watch (★★★★★, but I hope this thing is waterproof)** read 7:52, which was possibly the latest I'd slept in my entire life and eight minutes till we needed to leave if anybody was going to make it to school.

I don't know why we went that day. Who goes to school when there is an asteroid headed for your town? I'd say it was something about wanting to prove something or needing to get at least a B on my Spanish evaluación or giving Lock one more normal day, but really I think it was habit—and being covered in urine. If Lock hadn't wet the bed, I might have dropped my head back on the pillow and stayed there till Darth kicked the door down.

Juice pouches work in mysterious ways.

"Guys! Up! We overslept. Get up," I said. Every single word tapped the head rock against my eye sockets.

Carna rolled her head to one side without opening her eyes. Her nose scrunched in disgust. "What the hell? Oh, fuck my life." Lock sprawled coma-like, unconcerned. Carna gave his shoulder a hard shove. "Dude. Get up. You peed on me."

The next eight minutes were a scramble of stripping sheets; arguing with Lock, who claimed it wasn't him, even though those soaked Lightning McQueens told a different story; calculating and downing the maximum number of Tylenol I could take without immediate liver failure; and stuffing books, papers, and a couple of unmicrowaved microwave pancakes in Lock's bag. There wasn't time to shower him, but Carna did as much of a wipe down as she could with a wet towel. She couldn't have felt great, but she moved at a nearly normal pace without having to grip the wall every three steps to keep from puking, which was better than me.

On the way out the door, Lock said, "My legs feel sting-y." He fidgeted with his pants, trying to pull them away from his thighs.

"Does it itch?" He nodded. "Does it burn? Does it feel hot?" He thought about it and nodded. I looked at Carn. "Can you get that stuff from Dr. Bareket?" Lock dropped trou, and I slathered the tube of vag cream we'd gotten from the clinic on his prickly thighs. "Bath the second you get home from school, okay?"

The halls were mostly empty by the time we got to school. Carna meandered in the general direction of her class, in no rush, checking over her shoulder at me. I moved as quickly as I could, each step like a hammer coming down on my head. *More Tylenol,* I thought. *Liver failure can't be worse than this.* Something shifted into the wrong organ and everything I'd eaten in the last week was in my mouth. The ancient drinking fountain outside the main office was the closest place to throw up that wasn't my own shoes. Good thing the drain holes were big.

It felt like an exorcism, like purging some evil out of my system. My head was no better but I could stand up straight. I almost puked again when I saw Renata Flynn watching me from the window of the office. I took an icy slurp from the fountain, washing as much down the drain as I could, and hurried the rest of the way to Spanish.

Besides getting confused about some diacríticos, it went okay, but every minute the chance of me puking somewhere even less ideal than a drinking fountain went up. I tried to focus on holding my head perfectly still, but the walls kept tilting. One of the deans slipped in and handed a note to Maestra Olson. She read the note, looked up at me, and said "Claro" to the dean, waving him off.

I wasn't surprised Maestra stopped me on the way out with instructions to see Señora Flynn in the office before my next class. "¿Estás bien? ¿Te sientes enferma?" Even she could tell I was on the verge of barfing. Flynn was probably going to chew me out for coming to school sick. AS IF, Renata.

# CHAPTER SIXTY-SIX

"Come on back, Drew." Renata Flynn was waiting for me in the main office, watching the door eagerly, which is a way no teacher, counselor, or other school administrator has ever greeted me. "Can I grab you a water or something? Cheryl keeps apple juice in the nurse's office if you want that."

I understood immediately. I had not woken up hungover. I had died in my sleep of alcohol poisoning. In this weird hell, Renata Flynn worked for me.

"I'm good," I said. "Wait. Water would be good."

We settled into her office, me in the same seat I'd been in before, but this time she wheeled her chair to the side of the desk to be closer. She was wearing a burgundy cardigan buttoned to the top instead of her YOUR MOTHER CHOSE LIFE sweatshirt. If I didn't black out from the headache, I would black out from how surreal this was. She closed her door.

"So, Drew. I wanted to check in about your plans for next year, and see if maybe I could help with anything."

I looked around her office, expecting to see a sign that I was actually still at home dreaming in a lake of urine. The only thing different from before was that the little box microwave was gone. I could get her a new one for free. "Well, I got rejected from Madison, so I'll probably try to get a job and take some classes at county." Like you probably expected me to.

"Oh, I wasn't aware that you hadn't gotten in. It's very competitive." Thanks, Renata. "I have so many students to work with, I wonder if sometimes people think I'm so busy they can't ask for help. But that's what I'm here for. For any kind of help, really." She kept looking at me like she was hungry. I didn't know why she'd summoned me, but if it wasn't to yell at me for throwing up in the drinking fountain, maybe she wouldn't mind if I threw up in her candy bowl, too. It was deep and mostly empty, with just a few flavored Tootsie Rolls and the odd Kiss. I took a sip of my water and swallowed hard.

"Do you know you can come to me for help, Drew? About anything? And you can trust that anything you say in this office is confidential?"

The most personal request I would have trusted Renata Flynn with at that point would have been to eat my shit, so I said nothing. Maybe a Tootsie Roll would remind my body that things were supposed to go down, not up. Oh, but one of them was banana, and just thinking about a banana Tootsie Roll made me feel worse.

She blinked at me, then shifted. "You know, I'm just going to come out and say it then. I know you saw me at the clinic this weekend. And, well, you can call it coincidence if you want, but I don't believe in coincidence. I believe we are put in places and situations where we can help people. And I know I'm not supposed to say this because of the 'First Amendment' or whatever, but I want you to know: I prayed for you."

My thinking wasn't too fuzzy to think that wasn't weird. She prayed for us? Did Jesus cure Carna's yeast infection?

"And then when I saw you back at school and feeling"—she laughed a little—"let's just say 'under the weather,' I knew my prayers had been answered. I knew you hadn't done anything drastic yet."

Holy fucking shit. I was definitely not too hungover to understand *that*. She thought I was pregnant. She thought I went to the women's clinic, made the "right" choice, and was having the happy nausea of first-trimester morning sickness. She laid a hand on my hand and I promptly threw up in the candy bowl.

She went for apple juice. Came back with paper towels. Took the bowl. Came back with apple juice. In the meantime, I tried to explain I was just hungover and Carna was just a fungal nightmare, but before I could get any of the words out, she pulled out some pages she'd printed and handed them to me. My first thought was, they never let the teachers print in color.

My next thought was, someone should warn you that day-after hallucinations are a side effect of drinking that much.

My next thought was, is this what I think it is?

Instead of pictures of smiling embryos and their fully formed nine-week-old fingerprints, the top page of the stack said "St. Dismas College: Investing in Family Futures Initiative" under a collage of old stone buildings, a modern library, young people in lab coats looking at beakers, and a smiling baby in a Dismas onesie.

The first page was a fact sheet. St. Dismas College was a small private college in upstate New York with thirty-eight undergraduate majors including a new entrepreneurship in the digital economy track; a long history of teaching laureates, brainiacs, and interesting people at a campus that looked like a stock photo for "ideal college campus" (the library had a view of Lake Ontario); and admissions statistics that rivaled Lawrence, Carleton, and Grinnell, none of which I would have bothered applying to.

The next pages were about a new program that some billionaire alum had endowed to provide tuition and housing for students with dependent children. There was a long, lofty description of outcomes for children of young parents and educational attainment of unwed mothers as a predictor of blah-blah-blah, written in the language of well-intentioned wealthy yoga bitches. I scanned the pages as quickly as my hurting head would allow.

What was missing from the description was anything that said the dependent children had to be babies you had recently decided not to abort. There was nothing that said they couldn't be eight-year-olds you were pretending were orphans or even fifteen-and-a-half-year-olds whose dads probably wouldn't care if they moved with their sister.

The wheels in my head clicked to life, working double speed to make up for the miasma of hangover. Snips of Flynn's voice filled in gaps: Dean of admissions was a sorority sister—the AOΠs keep in touch. Already made a call to see if they'd look at a late app given the *circumstances*. No guarantees, but a good rec from a trusted advisor would go a long way. Of course it all depended on me being *eligible* for the program, on me making and not making certain *decisions* about my future, which meant it depended on me having a dependent.

Checkmate, Flynn. I've already got two.

She was even grosser than I'd imagined. Finally willing to do her job, as though I were a Britelle Olziewski or a Darden McMurray, as long she could tell her friends with the signs that she'd saved lives. Not mine. Not Lock's or Carna's. Just the imaginary one that didn't actually exist. Someone should tell her what a hypocritical, diabolical ass of a human she was. It would not be me.

"Do you know if there's a hockey team?" I asked instead.

"Hockey? Oh, no, I don't believe there is."

"I'll have the application done tomorrow."

# CHAPTER SIXTY-SEVEN

The pain in my head turned into a loud ring, but I couldn't tell if it was the hangover or the electrical storm of planning. There were a million things to do—I needed a whiteboard! a spreadsheet! an iced coffee!—but first, I needed Carna. The bell hadn't rung (unless that noise in my skull was the bell?) so she should be in second period if she hadn't gone home already.

But as I stepped out of Flynn's, there she was, leaned over the counter in the main office filling out a form, her hair hanging like a tired curtain over her face.

"Carna?" She turned, startled, and moved an arm over the paper. "What are you doing here?"

"Okeydokey," said Mary Pat Brown, tugging the sheet from under Carna's elbow. "I'll get goin' on gettin' yer transcript sent up north. Technically we need your mom to sign, but just have Heid gimme a buzz later when she's feelin' better." The bell rang.

"What are you doing?" I repeated more firmly.

"Thanks," she mumbled to Mary Pat, and grabbed my arm to steer me roughly out the door. The hallway was already teeming. She pulled me into the bathroom where Chad West had introduced himself. There were no military boots under the stall doors.

"I'm transferring to Starling. I've thought about it and it's really not that bad."

"What the—? Uh, no, actually you're not."

"Yeah, I am. Don't try to talk me out of it. When I was falling asleep last night, I realized that I can't just rely on you to solve everybody's problems. You need to focus on reapplying to schools and figuring out what you're going to do and where you're going to be and you can't do that if you're trying to support us."

"Carna."

"You can apply anywhere. You'll get a ton of financial aid, because Darth is going to take everything and people will feel sorry for you because they think Mom's a fugitive. It will make your application 'interesting.' It doesn't even have to be in the state if you don't want."

"Carna, stop!"

"And Lock's dad might be a dick but it's not like he's going to hurt the kid. And I can handle Dad."

"Listen to me! Neither of you is going to live with either of them."

"Drew, I appreciate what you're trying to do, but it's the best we've got."

"'Best we've got'? You would be miserable in Starling. You don't know anybody."

"I'm already miserable. And all the people I know here don't like me anyway."

"There's not even a room for you there!"

All the usual angry was out of her face. "Come on, Drew. What's in Larch for me? I know a lot is my fault but I just want to start over. I could like, join debate or go back to hockey or something. I'll be nicer."

Carna being nice seemed unlikely, but I could imagine her trying robotics or drone team, if they had them—something she'd be so good at it wouldn't matter if she wasn't very friendly.

"Just let me go." She stood with the resignation of a soldier heading into a war she was all but certain she wouldn't return from. She wasn't doing it for me, but she wasn't not doing it for me.

"Never," I said, and my smile broke wide.

# CHAPTER SIXTY-EIGHT

A ll right. She's on the lam." I'd sent a note to Darth saying I was gathering the information he'd requested and could he please not like our Instagram posts because it was creepy. He responded by saying that my mother should know they had jurisdictional authority across state borders and he didn't have unlimited patience.

"'On the lam'?" Carn mocked.

"I want to see a lamb." Lachlan popped into my room from nowhere. "Baa-aa."

"What are you supposed to be doing right now?"

The lamb looked sheepish. "Learning 'Happy Birthday' on the ukulele so I can make you happy on your birthday."

"Do you need me to find the chords on YouTube for you?"

"No. I need you to find me a snack, though."

"Do you want some lamb chops?" Carna suggested.

"Gross!"

I sent him upstairs to find a banana. "Finish the banana before you touch the ukulele this time, please? I'll be up pretty soon. I've gotta talk to you about something."

When we were sure he was gone, Carna said, "K. David Barth must be shitting his Dockers he's so excited."

"I hope he won't think she faked her death," I said.

"Well, he'd be half right."

After we sent the application to St. Dismas (a team effort: Carn proofread my essay and wrote a very moving recommendation from a nursing home I'd never worked for; 5-star volunteer, obviously), Carna and I had come up with a plan to prove Heidi was gone. There were three possible outcomes: It works perfectly and we're home free, it doesn't work and I am tried as an adult, or it half works and Carna and I die a miserable death in northern Wisconsin. In short, it was either the most practical or the most reckless idea of our lives: our family, in a nutshell.

"Is this a terrible plan? It is, right?" I said.

"No! It's super solid." I raised my eyebrows. "I mean, hopefully not *too* solid. Just the right amount of solid. What's the forecast say now?"

I checked my phone. "Still below freezing overnight, but sunny and clear during the days. Seriously. Doesn't this feel like something Mom would do?"

"Yep," Carna said. "That's why it's going to work."

# CHAPTER SIXTY-NINE

We have to talk about something, bud." I switched off the mini-speaker and sat next to him. I couldn't avoid talking to him any longer, and he couldn't avoid listening. Soon the whole state would know Heidi was dead. Lachlan deserved to hear it from me first. Usually, wherever my brother was, there was noise, but this time there was only quiet and waiting; the silence felt heavy and strange. "It's about Mom. But first, I want you to know that no matter what, Carna and I are going to—"

"She died?"

I choked on my carefully rehearsed statement. He was so perfectly matter-of-fact. *Double-checking here: Mom's dead, right?* Just confirming what we all knew, like if you looked out into a lightning storm, rain in buckets and electrical strikes all around, and said, "Canoe trip canceled?"

I suddenly wanted to deny it: "What? No way, silly! Those aren't lightning strikes, they're just a laser show to make it more fun! Everything is better than ever. And Mom is alive and well and is directing a choir of nun ninjas in a reboot of *The Mickey Mouse Club*."

"Yeah, bud," I said instead. "She died."

His shoulders dropped, turning the stripes of his pajamas into curves. I ran my hand over his back, wishing I could straighten them out. "I thought so."

"Why didn't you say anything?"

He shrugged. "I dunno. Because in case maybe she wasn't?" I understood that perfectly.

I reached behind him for a monkey. He sat it in his lap and absently twirled its tail around one finger. "How did you know?" I asked.

"'Cause she wouldn't leave us for so long. Not even for work or Justin Timberlake or a space trip." Space trip was new. "She'd at least FaceTime us."

I don't know when I lost the conviction that we were the top of Heidi's priorities, but seeing it in Lachlan made me wonder if I'd ever thought it.

I remember a storm one spring where the rain came down so hard the bus had to stop twice because the driver couldn't see. Kids screamed the worst words they knew at the top of their lungs to see if they could hear themselves over the pounding. At our stop, the lights of Britelle's mom's car winked hello. "Hey, kids," they seemed to communicate, "I'm right here where you knew I'd be, right when you needed me." She sprinted to the bus with an umbrella the size of a circus tent, hot chocolate and rainy-day scrapbooking probably already set up in the craft room at home.

Half a block later, Carna and I were soaked to our underwear. Our shoes overflowed. Everything in my backpack was ruined. The Olziewskis pulled alongside us.

"Girls! Get in! I'll take you home." Carna stopped but I pulled her along. "It's me, Britelle's mom! It's all right!" Carna made a step toward the street. A blurry smudge of Britelle waved from her window to confirm this was not a kidnapping.

"NO THANK YOU! WE'RE OKAY!" I yelled over the thunder. "WE LIKE RAIN." I steered Carna away by the elbow. We didn't take help from the yoga moms.

By the time we got to the door, my fingers were frozen, my nose was running, and I couldn't find my key in the pulpy jumble of my pack. The gutter over the step was clogged with leaves, and the rain poured onto us. When we finally pushed inside, Heidi was at the table, dry, bored, eating a bag of pretzels. "Crazy out there, huh?" she said. Thunder boomed and she laughed. "You guys are soaked!"

I was Lock's age then and already past expectations. But Lock had still somehow believed that a warm, dry car might have come for him with our mother behind the wheel. What a beautiful, lucky lie it had been.

Then again, someone would have come. It would have been me.

"You're right," I said to him. "She'd miss you too much."

He nodded, confident. "And you. And even Carna!"

I took another monkey from the pile and straightened its ear. A piece of me wanted to tell him he was wrong, to burst that naive bubble he was floating around in, but most of me wished I could crawl in there with him. "I'm sorry I didn't tell you before."

Lock set the first monkey on my lap next to the second. He twined one long floppy arm over the other's shoulders. "You didn't want me to be sad."

"That's part of it."

"But I'd be way sadder if she didn't come home just 'cause she didn't *wanna*."

And that was the mercy behind Captain Chad West. Heidi was a perpetual liar who'd say anything to make her life easier, which often made it harder for the rest of us. But the myth of the captain had been her trying to protect Lachlan in her own fucked-up way. She'd figured it would be way sadder if your dad just didn't wanna be around. The truth hurt worse.

Someday, he'd have to know. Someday, he'd get curious about genetics or extended family or military benefits for surviving children. And someday, he'd be very, very angry. But not yet. For now, maybe it was better to be an orphan than the son of an asshole.

"Buddy, there's another thing I have to tell you. You can't tell anybody about Mom. We have to pretend for a little while longer."

"How come?"

I sighed, adjusted the monkey arms. "Because there are a lot of rules about where kids can live and who kids can live with. And right now, we're kind of breaking those rules."

His eyes got wide. "What rules?"

"The rules say if you can't live with a mom or a dad, it has to be someone else who's an adult. And Carna and I don't count."

He folded his eyebrows in. "But you always take care of me."

"People think somebody older would do a better job."

"Like who?"

Like your father who uses orthodontics as a front for selling drugs and considers Mom a part-time employee. "Like anybody who's older. Aunts or uncles or—"

"Aunts?" he asked.

"Sometimes aunts."

"AUNTS?! Aunt Krystal isn't even good at babysitting!"

"I agree with you. That's why we're going to keep it secret for just a little bit more until you can stay with me."

He considered this. "And Carna?"

"And Carna," I said, more wishful than sure.

"Okay, but I think it's a dumb rule."

"Doesn't make it not a rule. Remember when we were at the

waterslides and they said you couldn't go on the big red tunnel because you weren't tall enough? And Carna said she'd take you anyway?"

Carna had tried to get Lock past the cranky sentry in the SLIDE CITY USA polo, but the woman had seen them coming and planted herself in front of the entrance. She pointed at the dotted line over a cartoon swimmer: Rules were rules. I offered to take him down the blue twisty again, even though I was dry and done for the day. But Heidi couldn't stand no, especially for something as stupid as a height restriction.

She bought a swim diaper from the concession stand, folded it on top of Lock's head, and pulled my swim cap over it. He looked like the Brain from *Pinky and the Brain*, but it gave him the extra inch to hit the line. He and Carna got in one glorious slide down Big Red before the cap popped off, the diaper floated to the filter, and the manager asked us to leave.

Heidi retold the story a hundred times, the way another family might reminisce about finishing a marathon on a sprained ankle or cooking a turkey in a trash can when the oven broke. Except our stories were always about getting away with something instead of achieving something.

I hoped we were doing both.

Lock remembered. He remembered the cold spray, the dark tunnel, and the high five Heidi had offered when we were packing up our towels. A small smile. Pride, I think. "Some rules are good for protecting people, but some"—I couldn't believe I, of all people, was saying this—"have to be broken to protect people. Or, well, let them go down a waterslide."

We talked through what to say to friends, what to say at school, what to say to Aunt Krystal someday. He caught on easily, which was good for our current situation but concerning for his overall moral development. "Oh boy, we have a lot of secrets," he said.

An understatement. "All families have secrets, Lock. But most of them don't tell the kids." Another proud smile.

When I finally tucked him in after a lot more questions and a few more answers, he rolled over, bending around me like a little moon.

"Actually? I was kind of scared about that slide. I wanted to go on it, but also a little bit I didn't want to." This family had a way of pushing you into things you hadn't asked for.

"Me too," I said, not meaning the slide. "But you did it anyway. I guess that means you're pretty brave."

"I guess you're pretty brave, too."

I kissed a monkey and the monkey kissed Lachlan.

Lock's tunnel was scary, but it had a light and a family at the end of it. I hoped mine would, too.

# CHAPTER SEVENTY

When I got to my locker, there was a tuft of white fur sticking out. A half-dozen balloons floated out when the door opened. They were tethered to a giant stuffed bear who was wedged in so tight his paws were pinned.

How had Darden managed to remember my locker combination?

"Aww," I heard a girl coo. I grabbed the doughnut and card he'd left up top and slammed the door on the bear's snout. Then I opened it again, pushed the stray balloons inside, and shut it. Popping them would have drawn even more attention.

*I wish I could see you tonight! Have fun!* A bunch of skinny hearts and his spiky *Dard.* Not a signature, really, because at eighteen, the boy could still only print. He had never signed his own permission slips.

The way I'd skirted a surprise party was by telling Darden that my mom had planned a girls night in Chicago for my birthday. Audrey had agreed to stay with Lock, who was excited to teach someone new the sliding maneuver he thought was a moonwalk.

The doughnut was a fluffy glazed from Hy-Vee. He would have gotten himself two powdered at the same time. Or maybe not, because in the petal-strewn, hockey-scented mind of Darden McMurray, it would have been more romantic to get me a doughnut on my birthday if he didn't get one, too. I wished there was a way to regift him to someone who would appreciate him. Regift him, but keep the doughnut.

He was waiting at the door of my class. "Happy birthday, ba—" He caught himself and trailed off on the "babe."

"No. *Feliz cumpleaños*, Señor McMurray," corrected the maestra on her way in.

"Thank you," I said, letting him hug me. "That was so sweet." The white dust on his sweatshirt meant he'd gone ahead and gotten himself breakfast, too. Good.

"Did you get the balloons?" he said, looking concerned about missing balloons.

"Yeah, of course. I thought they'd be disruptive in class, though."

"Oh yeah. Probably. You could bring them to lunch!"

"Maybe!" I said.

Darden left for history, and because he had a voice like a Monster Truck Pull announcer, everyone in Spanish heard it all. If everything went according to plan, soon there'd be emergency court orders and a hot dish from Brenda Olziewski, and they'd all feel extra sorry for me when they remembered it had been my aniversário.

A string of texts pinged from Malcolm, one after another:

Happy birthday
I guess you're an adult now whatever that means
Steph says it means I'm old
Try not to get into trouble

Malcolm at his sweetest.
I typed back

I never do! How's Tampa?

The SuccessQuest by BestU conference at the Tampa Ramada was designed to unlock your potential! teach you the power of positive thinking! take your brand to the next level! and expand your BestU Wellness business to include nutrition and life coaching and real estate investment!! No wonder Stephanya had wanted to go.

The price to unlock your potential was $1,999, but Steph had gotten a last-minute email from the director of entrepreneur identification and empowerment saying her registration had been anonymously prepaid because she'd been nominated as a "distributor to watch." Steph was willing to overlook how suspicious the last-minute offer was in order to accept a free trip. She was heading into some life-changing sessions; Mal was on his way to charter a fishing boat.

We didn't care if the conference took her supplements business to the next level or turned her into a regular old drug dealer. All that mattered was that our little scholarship had gotten them off the lake for the weekend.

# CHAPTER SEVENTY-ONE

W hat exactly did Mal say again?"

"'I shoulda pulled that damn house off the ice. It's liable to go through.'"

"Is that a good sign or a bad sign?"

"I don't know."

Most years, all the ice-fishing houses would have been off the lake already, but the extra-cold, extra-long season meant that they were still measuring eight to ten inches of good ice on April first. Technically, you weren't supposed to leave them out overnight after mid-March anyway, but the year-round residents and winter anglers on the Lesser Starling Chain minded their own business, not the Wisconsin DNR.

The homemade shelter would have been a prepper's dream if it wasn't in the middle of a frozen lake, where it was completely visible to scavengers or zombies from every possible angle. At the start of the season, Mal towed it out mid-lake with his truck, but it was too risky now for the F-250. Eight inches was still enough for the side-by-side, but he'd been waiting on a part for it. They'd decided on the last-minute trip to Tampa, and so the house still sat on the dodgy ice while the weather had been warming.

Carna had followed me up in the Range Rover, which she'd parked at the Petersons' before walking back to Mal's place over the deer trail. The Petersons were hardly ever there, and we'd always helped ourselves to their land, their dock, and now, their driveway, so there wouldn't be extra tire tracks in ours.

While she checked the cabin, I swapped the key to my truck onto Heidi's key chain, and put the Gucci purse with her wallet and an unused passport in the passenger seat for the divers to find, if they ever sent any.

I hated the idea of Carna ending up here. Mal's place looked like the lair of an abominable old man-bear who'd skin anybody who dared to stop by after school. The druid Steph had painted on the mailbox didn't make it more welcoming, just weirder.

We walked down to the shoreline, stepping on the rockiest parts of the path to avoid extra footprints. Pieces of the dock were piled on the shore, ready to be rebuilt after ice-out in a month or so. The lake denizens had welcomed the long freeze: ski tracks, snowmobile tracks, and animal prints zigzagged over what was left of the snow, though only two ice houses still dotted the surface: Mal's and the Petersons' new wheeled trailer from Starling RV and Recreation. It was exactly the kind of expensive toy a banker from Chicago would buy so he could invite up a bunch of other bankers to be "outdoorsy."

Compared to that, Mal's looked like a weathered outhouse. If the DNR had come, they would have assumed it had been abandoned to sink.

Carna pressed her toe to the ice where it met the sand; a thin line of water seeped from the edge. She looked at me and shrugged. We set out cautiously, bouncing here and there to make sure it held.

Like in the cabin, Stephanya's touches in the ice house were limited, but nudging. She'd brought out a couple of candles, which added a whiff of almond to the smell of cedar and cold. Pinned to a stud was a small watercolor of the frozen lake, grays and dirty whites, just like the real one, with *Starling winter* in tiny, neat pencil alongside her signature. Her proportions were way off as usual, but she'd somehow managed to capture the cold.

I snapped photos with Heidi's phone around the shanty, but none of them screamed "ice house" like I wanted. A picture of the cot looked like a spare bed in someone's basement. The vignetted closeup of the washed-out WHEN HELL FREEZES OVER I'LL ICE FISH THERE TOO mug didn't seem like her. I showed them to Carna, who wrinkled her nose.

"I have an idea." She plopped on the bed, unlaced her boots, and replaced them with Heidi's **Shuggs Genuine Sheepskin-look Fashion Boots (★★★★★, the cutest vegan boots I've ever worn, and the Furr (tm) lining is made from recycled coffee pods)**, which we'd brought to leave behind. She propped her heels on the space heater under the window and took a leg selfie. Steph's painting was visible in the background.

Caption: **Chillin' at my new crib?!?** *[Laughing crying face.]*

Geotag: **Lesser Starling Chain of Lakes.**

Carn gave it the retro-lighting/Mom filter.

I laughed out loud. "Perfect."

"Think he'll figure it out? I can change it to 'Shh. I am hiding at Malcolm Krause's. Don't tell @kdavidbarth @SocialSecurityGuy. This is Heidi, by the way.' We could give him the coordinates, too."

"Let's give Darth a little more credit," I said. I had texted him earlier saying I couldn't ask my dad if he knew where my mom might be because he was out of town for a few days and not at his semi-secluded cabin in Starling, which our whole family liked to visit. His Spidey-sense should pick that up. "Come on. It's getting dark."

"Can't we just wait here till Lisa-in-Phoenix likes it? Oh, wait . . . there's the heart already."

On our way out, Carna found a good spot of still unmarked snow near the shanty to leave Heidi's boot prints in.

Now all that was left was to drive my truck through the ice.

# CHAPTER SEVENTY-TWO

We'd whiteboarded which car to sacrifice with "drew's car sucks ass, rover = awesome, rover *safer* family car, rover worth more, drew's car sucks balls" on the side of sinking mine, and "why would heidi drive drew car (bc she's on the lam, duh), car insurance pays $$$ (get brand! new! rover!)" on the side of sinking Heidi's. (Carna was the one with the marker, and Carna, who still had no license, *loved* the Range Rover.) She won the argument, not because she was right, but because by the time we got to Starling, I was so worried about the state of the ice that I thought the heavier vehicle might break through before it got anywhere near the middle.

My stomach felt like a fist as I eased the truck onto the lake. I rolled the windows down and hung my left foot out the door, ready to bolt at the first sign of trouble. It wouldn't be the latest date the ice was still good—locals still talked about the year they snowmobiled across on the last day of April—but I couldn't shake the images of glaciers collapsing in places more arctic than this. Carn directed me in the fading light, signaling like the ground crew at an airport. The weakest spots would be on the side where the spring connected the lake to the one above it, but it was shallow over there. She had been operating the depth finder for Mal since she was little and knew the deepest places, where recovery would be next to impossible. The truck cruised along like it was going through the Culver's drive-thru instead of hanging over seventy feet of water.

I parked where Carna stopped me and left the engine running, relieved to be out before it started to sink. We watched to see what would happen when the waves under the surface subsided. There were cracks and sighs, but otherwise, nothing. The truck sat there.

"I guess we've got to help it a little." I grabbed Mal's eight-inch hand auger from the bed of the truck and found a spot just in front of the truck. It punched through with a few dozen turns of the blade. I looked at Carna warily; it should not have gone that easily. I moved over a few inches and tried again. Same thing. We looked down at the pretty little circles, a pair of black holes the size of salad plates. It was already too dark to see well, so Carn took off a mitten to reach into one of them.

She looked up, alarmed, and held her fingers about four inches apart. We took several steps backward in unison. With only four inches of ice under it, that truck should have been on its way to the bottom of the lake instead of sitting there purring happily.

The stupid thing was too light. "We should've used Heidi's car," I said. I started another hole, and another, perforating the ice. It reminded me of punching holes to put assignments in a three-ring binder.

Carn ran back to the ice house for a crowbar Malcolm used to loosen the runners if it froze in place. She brought the sharp claw down hard near the edge of a hole, where it bounced back with a few shavings and a loud metallic clink. She struck again and made a divot.

"Shhh! That sound carries all the way across the lake!"

"So? Who's here?" she said, gesturing around, but she switched to prying at the edges instead of slamming into the ice. We worked side by side, busting up a lake with hand tools like ice farmers. Sometimes Carn would get leverage in the right spot, and a chunk would dislodge. Sometimes the bar would slide and splash ice water over our ankles. I started to sweat inside my jacket. My right hand threatened blisters. The moon brightened and the last bits of the day faded. "We should have used Heidi's car," I said again. If it was up to Carna, she'd spend all night carving a hole big enough to push the truck into instead of giving up on the Rover.

"What do you think?" I asked, surveying the collection of openings we'd made. It looked like the squirrel from *Ice Age* had been there.

Carna windmilled her shoulders and stretched her neck from side to side. "There's no way *that* holds. Let's give it a shove."

We leaned hard into the back tailgate until the wheels began to turn. Once the heaviest part of the truck was over the holes we'd made, the lake would happily swallow up the truck. The ground under it would crack to bits, and we'd be out of the way.

The truck rolled forward and caught a tire in a hole. I grabbed Carna's arm and we scrambled ten feet backward, ready.

It just sat there. Running. Waiting. Spewing carbon to melt the wrong ice. My lifetime of following the rules for ice safety (substitute: doing homework, showing up on time, washing my hands before returning to work, being honest, not eating undercooked eggs) felt like a giant prank.

We came around to the front, stepping carefully between the holes, and peered under with a phone light. The front driver-side tire was balanced across an opening like a bowling ball in a rack. Carna pressed down on the hood over it, bouncing a little. Nothing. She slid herself up so she was sitting on the hood. It popped in and back out when she moved, like a can.

"Maybe we should have used the ten-inch auger," Carna said. She tipped her head one way and the other, thinking. "I wonder if Mal has a welding torch."

"We're not going to melt the ice with a welding torch."

"Do you have a better idea?" The better idea would have been a heavier vehicle.

The ice interrupted us with a boom, a sound like thunder, but with none of the rolling or rumbling before or after. It doesn't mean anything, usually. Just one of those ghosty things frozen lakes always do. They make all kinds of weird noises: snaps, crackles, pops. Moans.

But it's creepy when you're alone in the dark on thin ice and no one knows you're out there and you were basically daring the lake to break.

"Hey, maybe you should get down," I said, reaching out an arm.

She pulled herself up to standing. "Maybe Ms. Flynn prayed for the safety of your unborn child and that's why the ice won't break." She bounced up and down on her heels. The truck bounced with her.

The wind picked up a little, sending graupel skittering. It sounded like a thousand tiny creatures on the move. "Come on, Carn. Let's go back to the cabin and warm up. We'll think of a different plan."

"It's going to work, Drew. It has to." She jumped up and down on the hood, the ice amplifying the sound of pounding on steel.

"SHHHHH!"

Her boots slipped and she landed on a knee. "OW." Carn slid off the truck, frustrated. "This stupid truck is so shitty the lake doesn't even want it." She kicked the door.

"Come on. Let's leave it running and maybe it will melt through." I started back toward the cabin, but she got into the driver's seat and slammed the door. "What are you doing?"

"Switching cars," she snipped through the open window, yanking the stick into drive. "You were right."

"Carn, no, that's a bad— Hey, is this loose?" The ground under my feet felt suddenly shifty, like standing on a floating swim dock.

She'd gone a few feet when a rear tire caught in a hole and began to spin in place.

"Damn it. Can you push?" Carna said.

It was too dark to see much, but I could feel it, the ice flexing, moving, detaching. "Carn? I think you should get out—"

It wasn't even loud when the ice broke, just some pops and crumples. Not a dramatic fault. It just split into a dozen pieces all at once, like it had been a puzzle, like it was never really whole at all. The front of the truck dropped headfirst, and for just a second it looked like it was rolling down a steep hill. Except that hill was heading through seventy feet of freezing water and my sister was in the driver's seat.

"Carna! CARNA!"

It went way faster than it was supposed to. I flew at the disappearing truck, but the ground tipped. I fell back, sat down hard on the ice, which bobbed violently. I stood up again and felt the world slope. I dropped to my knees, the ground rocking.

Not the ground. A floe. Untethered and tenuous and barely afloat.

Like every day had felt.

I stared ahead at the place we'd been carving up just a few minutes before. The moon off the ice was enough to see black water, the sinking pickup bed, and no Carna.

"CARNA!" I knew not to go in. I was going in. I clawed at the laces of my boots. "No-no-no-no-no . . ."

Her head broke the surface, gasping. She was treading, looking wildly around. I started to stand, tipping again, then dropped in the sick realization that I could not simply grab her. We would need to balance each other.

"Carn! I'm here." The pale moon of her face twisted to me. "I don't know what part is still solid. It's all cracking apart." I looked around but didn't dare take a step. "Just, come to me. Come my way." I lay on my stomach and pulled myself toward the edge.

Fragments of ice bobbed around her freely like misshapen animals. She paddled toward me, her mittens lost to the lake. She put both hands on the surface to push up, those strong, busy fingers slight and cold and shaking now. "Elbows," I said, Mal's warnings about the ice coming back to me. "Distribute your weight."

She flattened her arms out long, but I couldn't reach them. I wriggled toward the water like a bait worm. *Swwwish. Swwweep.* It felt slow and weak and against every instinct. What other emergency would you meet lying down? The closer I got, the more it felt like the ice was tipping. I stretched, trying to keep as much of my weight as far from the hole as possible.

"Stay flat. Try to slide yourself up." She pulled hard but it was too slippery. She lost her progress, and her shoulders sank back to the water.

Ice water saps the strength out of you fast. First your skin hurts and then your muscles hurt and then your bones hurt, and then your brain decides it would rather not move them at all. You have to get out quickly to survive, but the only way to get out is slowly.

"You got this, Carna." But she didn't. She tried to lift up on her hands again, and the edge snapped under her, forcing me to back up to maintain our balance. "No, you're doing it wrong." It helps to know the rules.

"Gimme a f-f-break." If she wasn't busy trying not to die, Carna would have thrown an ice chunk at me.

She managed to get her whole chest flat on the ice that time, but her arms were sliding.

I needed her out. I needed her. "Kick! You've got to get your legs level."

"I can't," she said, sounding strangely fuzzy.

"Yeah, you can."

She tried to push up again, and ice snapped against her chest. I pulled my weight backward to counter.

"CAROLINE HILL, YOU KICK YOUR FUCKING LEGS RIGHT NOW."

"I said I can't!" But she did it. She kicked and kicked till her legs were at the top of the water, propelling her forward with arms splayed like a demented seal. One hand was almost to mine, clawing at the ice, but slipping. "Drew. Help."

I rose to my knees and launched myself, digging my fingers so hard into her wrist I might have broken her bones if it weren't for the padding of her down jacket.

The ice tipped toward the open water but I rolled backward, pulling her with me. It felt like rolling up a hill and sliding down it at the same time, but I kept pulling and twisting until I was flat on my back with Carn's arm over my chest, more of her out than in, and the ice settled slowly to a rock.

The taillights on the truck shorted and blinked on, just before it disappeared with a gurgle. The ice stilled. We had done it. "Carn, it worked," I panted. "It's gone. It sunk. And we didn't. Our stupid plan worked."

"Hurray," she mumbled. She was shaking hard. "Bye, you stupid fucking truck."

"We gotta get you inside right now." I didn't want to let go of that arm, though. Under the wet down, alongside the null set tattoo, there would already be bruises starting from my fingertips, but I didn't ever want to let go.

She tried to stand. "Careful!" I snapped, and yanked her onto both kneecaps. "We're on a loose part. We need to stay low till we get to where it's solid." I handed her my mittens.

Carna army-crawled forward, dragging her soaked body ahead by the elbows. It was easy to find the place where the ice had separated, because there was now a couple-inch gap between it and the solid part of the lake, a tiny evil river we were on the wrong side of. Carn dragged herself across with me as a counterweight. Once she was on the safe side, I managed it with a leap to her hand. When we got to our backpacks, she stripped off her wet jacket and pulled out a small bundle.

"What are you doing? Come on."

The moon caught the Mylar as she pulled the emergency poncho over her head. I laughed. "I bet you're glad now I didn't let you sell those."

"I sold six of them," she said, still shivering. "I kept the rest." She put on her boots from the bag, which I tied so she wouldn't have to take off the mittens. Only one Shugg had made it out with her. She launched it into the open water. Someday some kid will think she caught something big and be very disappointed, and some investigator will say it's proof that Heidi is down there somewhere.

"When we get back," I said, "you get under the covers in Dad's room and I'll put your stuff in the dryer."

We'd be gone long before morning, when Darth would hopefully show up to capture the fugitive and, being the brilliant investigator he was, determine she had fallen through the lake in my truck and died. We had left him a trail of bread loaves.

"Crank the heat. Malcolm probably left it at fifty."

Huddled under the prepper cloak and shuffling across the nightlight glow of the barren ice, Carna looked like a low-rent Jedi. I was about to tell her so when she stopped suddenly.

"What the hell?"

# CHAPTER SEVENTY-THREE

White-blue headlights flickered through the leafless trees between the main road and the cabin. "That can't be . . ."

It was. The lights—two pairs—turned into Malcolm's drive.

"Why wouldn't he just wait for morning?" Carna growled. She took off, angling toward the lot on the other side of Mal's, where the trees came almost down to the shoreline. Those people hadn't bothered to take their dock out in the fall (personal and property failing, according to Malcolm). Our boots thundered across the boards.

The two vehicles reached Mal's driveway as we reached the tree line. Carna could find her way through the woods blindfolded, or, as it turned out, in the dark and half frozen. I followed the occasional glint of foil to the base of a twin-trunked tree.

Some deer stands are just a board nailed to a tree so you have something to balance on while you wait for a deer to walk under and get shot. Some are freestanding camo guard towers so you have something expensive to sit in while you wait for a deer to walk under and get shot. Ours was neither. Picture the world's smallest, saddest tree house: a splintery platform wide enough for two bored little girls and one grumpy man built between the trunks, with a partial railing around three sides to keep your kid or your lunch from falling off while you wait for a deer to walk under and get shot.

Or while you make lists of goals based on your eleven-year-old wisdom.

Or while you stew up there mad at your family.

Or while you fall asleep.

Or *bonus use* while you spy on an overeager Social Security agent and two local sheriff deputies out in the middle of nowhere because of an Instagram tip about a nonviolent (and actually dead) conwoman.

I climbed the steel spikes that zippered the tree and crawled in next to her.

The sheriff's SUV, still running, sat behind Darth's Honda. The deputies leaned against it, looking uninterested. The motion-sensor light over the door of the cabin flashed on as Darth approached it, spotlighting him like a soloist. He pounded so loud I thought he'd crack a knuckle. "HEIDI HILL! HEIDI HILL! I'D LIKE TO TALK TO YOU. MALCOLM KRAUSE?"

"Doesn't he know that banging on someone's door in the middle of the night up here will get a shotgun pointed in your face?" I whispered.

"This is the first time in my life I wish Dad was home," she whispered back, leaning over the side to peer through the trees.

Back on the ground, Darth walked around the cabin, shining his phone in the windows. The locals didn't seem interested in participating in his sting operation.

"Looks pretty dark, man. Are you sure your guy is here?" called one of them.

"She's not a guy, and she was here earlier."

"How do you know?"

"I *know*."

Carna shook violently next to me. I took off my hat and balaclava and pulled them over her head. "What am I supposed to do if you freeze to death up here?"

"Keep the possums off me."

She contorted inside her poncho, nearly knocking me off the platform. She produced her wet sweatshirt and hung it over the edge, and stood up to peel off her pants. She held one hand against the tree trunk while she worked her pants over her boots, then sat down with her legs crossed under the poncho. I pulled the edge over an exposed knee. She still had on her long underwear, the good lightweight wool ones. She dug out another emergency poncho, wrapped it around her legs, and tucked back under the poncho.

One of the deputies was vaping while Darth stormed the perimeter of the house.

"There's no vehicle here," she offered. Darth paused. Carn and I automatically looked toward the lake. It was as quiet as ever, as though it hadn't just swallowed up a small truck and almost swallowed a medium girl. From the shore in the dark, there was nothing to see besides empty dark, and the wink of a couple of outdoor lights all the way across. We didn't want anybody to discover that hole till morning, when we were safely and innocently back in Larch. "So if she was here, she's probably gone now."

"Where would she go around *here*?" Darth spat. Sounding like a snobby city guy was not going to win him help from the deputies.

"Town? 12-Point is just across the lake," tossed off the cop. "If she was even here in the first place."

"We should break down the door," Darth announced, sounding authoritative.

The vaper laughed out loud. The other deputy said, "You don't even got a warrant."

"I can probably get one."

Carna snorted.

The first deputy stretched her arms wide in a full-body yawn. "Look, man, the guy who lives here? Not someone who would be real happy with us right now. We only came out with you so you wouldn't get yourself in trouble. We need to get back to work." The business of Starling County was not often urgent—most calls in the winter were about people hitting deer; lost, drunk snowmobilers; or kids breaking into cabins—but they had run out of patience for Darth from Chicago and his Instagram hunch. The two deputies got back into their car.

Darth stood watching with his hands on his hips, while they cut a wide circle around the clearing and rolled out.

"I kind of feel sorry for him," I whispered.

"I don't," Carna said, pushing her wet clothes into her bag.

"He's just trying to do his job."

Carna shrugged. "He doesn't have to be so douchey about it."

That was fair. No matter what your job, you don't have to be douchey about it.

I watched from the tree as he dragged an Adirondack chair into the circle of light by the door. He sat down and opened a pack of hand warmers.

"Shit. He's not going with them? How long do you think he's going to wait out here?" Carna chattered.

Multipack survival ponchos, even those with 5-star **you could survive an actual ice age in this thing** ratings, aren't intended to keep you warm all night long if it's twenty-eight degrees and you're in nothing but wet long underwear. It was too dark to tell, but I thought Carna's lips looked pretty blue. We needed to get going, but Darth looked like he was just settling in. I started to take off my jacket to wrap around her and tried to remember what the first symptoms of hypothermia were.

There were a couple of sharp cracks and then rustling in the trees. Probably just a mink or a raccoon, but small things sound big in the dark, especially if you are from a place where most of the animals are on leashes. "Hello?" Darth said, sounding less authoritative than before. The rustling stopped, then started again. He stood up and peered toward the woods.

There was just enough moonlight to see the spark in Carna's eyes. She felt around the stand for a loose stick and found a short one an inch or so thick. She flung it hard in the direction of the cabin. It whispered through some dry branches and knocked into a tree. Darth jerked his head at the noise. "Mr. Krause?" he said, backing toward his car.

We tossed a few pine cones, which there were plenty of in the stand, but most of them were too light to make much noise. Carn reached for a thin, dry branch, which snapped and fell directly below us. Darth stopped at the edge of the porch light. We wanted the creepy noises to draw him away, not toward us.

Darth took a tentative step toward the woods in our direction, holding up his phone for light. I threw my jacket over Carna's reflective parka. We needed to move his attention away from our tree. We felt around the floor, but there was nothing heavy enough to throw any distance. I clawed through the backpack as quietly as I could, dismissing my wallet, granola bars, and car keys. "Hello? Heidi?" he called out.

My hand closed around my mother's phone. It had been indispensable to maintaining our lives/lies over the last months. It had been, practically speaking, Heidi. But now that part of our lives was closing and we were in a tree, and there was a guy deciding between being suspicious of the woods or terrified of them. I offered it to Carna, who stood up and threw as hard as she could.

A cell phone is very different as a projectile than a pine cone is. It sailed through the trees and smacked hard into the side of the cabin, dropping right around the corner from where Darth was. "WHO'S THERE?" The reason I knew he didn't carry a gun was because anybody with a weapon would have taken it out right then. Instead of running to his car, he froze in place, too scared to move.

But then something *was* moving. The sound was right below and then moved by us. The snaps and brushing were slow and steady and deliberate, not like wind or branches dropping. Like movement. Like something large walking (or crawling or slithering) through the forest toward the cabin. Even Carna tensed up.

It was all Darth could handle. He darted back into his car and flicked on his brights. I'm sure he locked the doors. The car whipped around the clearing and out Mal's long drive. He probably spent the rest of the night googling "what kind bears northern WI" or "wolf sighting Starling" or "walking dead real?"

"Let's go," I said. I dropped the packs over the side and started down the tree.

"What the hell *was* that?" Carna asked, climbing down after me. "It sounded big." I had an idea, but I'd never say it out loud.

On our way past Malcolm's place, we searched the ground for Heidi's phone, dragging our feet through loose grass where it should have been, but it must have bounced harder than we thought. "You know what? We don't actually need it anymore. Can you wipe it remotely?"

"I think so," said Carna. "Yeah."

"Perfect. If anybody ever finds it, it will look like she lost it on her way to the lake."

We crossed the deer trail to the Petersons'. Once we were in the car, Carna aimed all the heat vents inside the poncho, blowing it up like a parade balloon. "You should thank me. I saved your life tonight, you know," she said to the Rover, putting her cheek on the dashboard.

Once we hit the paved county road and turned toward home, my heart slowed down for the first time since we stepped onto the ice. Maybe since January. Carna stopped shaking, peeled off the hat, and finger-combed her wet hair. She smelled like the lake, but I didn't mind.

There was too much to say to say anything. Carna dialed through Mom's Spotify lists. She skipped around *NSYNC's first album, all grammatical disasters and *Glee* harmonies, played the McDonald's theme song and a couple of his other early singles, and eventually landed on "Man of the Woods," which isn't really about the woods, but we didn't care.

WE PULLED INTO THE DRIVEWAY at about 3:00 a.m. I could see Audrey through the window, asleep with the TV on. Carna had somehow dozed, blinking awake when I turned off the car. I leaned my forehead against the wheel.

"What's wrong?" she asked.

"I don't know. It just feels weird."

"Weird like we forgot something? Weird like you feel guilty?"

"No . . . just weird. Like we can stop pretending."

"Not quite. There's a bunch of stuff to take care of. And we have to be very surprised when we get a call from up north tomorrow."

"I know. But it feels different. Like if we're not pretending she's still here, she's really just *gone*."

Carna let out a deep breath. "I knew she wasn't actually in the truck, but part of me kept wanting to dive down after her anyway in case I could bring her back. Stupid, right?"

"Not at all."

A minute passed. Carna turned in her seat to face me. "Thank you, Drew."

"For pulling you out of a lake?"

"No. For keeping us together. For keeping me."

I said, "I didn't know what else to do with you." And then I leaned over and pulled her tight.

**AS SHE OPENED HER CAR DOOR,** Carn said, "You think maybe it could have been a coyote out there? Usually they'd lay low if people were around, but maybe it's got babies to look out for."

I glanced in the rearview mirror, where just for a second, I thought I saw Heidi, wearing a camouflage hat and jacket. She caught my eye and winked.

"Yeah," I said. "That was probably it."

When I turned around, she was gone.

# CHAPTER SEVENTY-FOUR

Darth wasn't the one to find the break in the ice or the tire tracks leading to it the next day. He was at the Badger State Motor Lodge when the county sheriff's office got a call about a big spot of open water on the lake, and weren't those shanties supposed to be off by now, and could someone come check it out and probably fine the owners? The caller refused to give her name. She didn't want any trouble with those crabby fellas on the other side of the lake. And then the caller threw her burner into the garbage at a Culver's.

The sheriff's office might have ignored it, but not long after that call, the Petersons' expensive trailer house really did go through. That wasn't our fault; that was because it was too heavy, too late in the season. Mr. Peterson, who was as usual nowhere near Lesser Starling, heard about it from someone else on the lake, and called in Great Lakes Diving & Recovery. They sent in a submersible drone camera to confirm location and condition, which also captured images of a mini-pickup, as well as a canoe that looked like it had been there for ages. The dive master called the lake "gorgeously deep" but said any retrieval would have to wait for ice-out, and prepayment by the owners of the respective wrecks. That fancy ice house was unlikely to see the light of the sun again.

According to Malcolm, who, as the registered title holder of the truck, was contacted in Florida, Peterson was thoroughly pissed off, because the same company that took in his dock, sucked out his septic tank, and managed the annual chipmunk invasion was supposed to have taken the ice house in. (He would be even madder the next month when he brought some business associates up for the fishing opener and saw that someone—the crew building the new Finnish sauna, perhaps?—had driven over the wood-burnt welcome sign that said PETERSONS' PARADISE. I swear it wasn't on purpose.)

With only the shortest, vaguest series of cryptic and legally inadmissible texts, Malcolm performed beautifully. I'd always thought my mom was the virtuoso of lying, but damn if my dad isn't an artist himself. It helped that he was mistrustful of any governmental employees besides librarians and the crews who haul dead deer off the roads. Yes, that had been his truck. No, he didn't drive it anymore. Yes, his ex did sometimes stay at his place when he was out of town. No, that didn't seem weird; she had always liked the lake. Yes, he could think of a good reason someone would drive across the ice: the cheese curds and cheap pitchers at the 12-Point Grille and Buckshot Room. No, he was not interested in meeting with an investigator to go over a few things. Yes, everyone should fuck off back to their offices.

The evidence that Heidi Hill had perished in the truck that went through the ice was inconclusive, since the cameras hadn't seen a body down there, but it was a big lake, and everybody but Darth was satisfied with any explanation that made their lives easier. Dragging the lake in the spring would be cost-prohibitive, plus it was the sort of thing that upset people like the Petersons and the brewery investors.

It was easier still when it turned out that Heidi had secured her will in a safe deposit box at the local community bank, naming me as the guardian for her son, now that I was conveniently and coincidently

Of ThE aGe Of LeGal MAjOriTy, aka a real adult. Many people don't plan ahead like that, the social worker told us. We were lucky, she said.

We offered to pay restitution of the unlawfully collected Social Security payments if the SSA would forgo any penalties. Selling the Rover would just about cover it. Darth argued against it, sure that Heidi was still out there somewhere, sure that Carna and I were her accomplices. But it turned out that Darth didn't quite have the clout in the department that he thought he did, which is why his colleagues were making headlines busting million-dollar phone-scam rings, while he was surveilling casino buffets and trying to entrap children. (Carna keeps checking his LinkedIn page, sure that any day his employment status will change to "Founder + CEO, KDB Private Investigations." I hope so. He'd feel so important.)

In the end, his department caved to the pressure of dozens of social media accounts (mostly ours) and their followers (also us) posting to close the case and let those poor kids get on with their lives. The nationwide network of BestU distributors got in on it, too, recommending their own stress-relieving and energy supplements while advocating to #DesignateDrewGuardian and #standWIththem.

The sale of the house plus a very generous financial aid offer from St. Dismas meant we could drop our fake reviewing, except for the ones that were fun or interesting **(personal trimmer, ★★★★★, goes through unwanted growth like the mower at Lambeau; Stabilizer sports bra, ★★★★★, excellent support if you suddenly have to jump out of a tree)**. A lawyer found us on Instagram and offered to represent us to get military benefits for Lachlan, which we declined, but we did accept a very generous scholarship fund set up for Lachlan from a local orthodontist.

"He's still a douchebag," Carna complained. "He's buying his way out of parenting."

"At least he pays well," I said, adjusting the investment choices in Lock's college savings account. He was on track to go anywhere he wanted someday, even Juilliard, and never worry about the money. Someday Lock would get curious, and the orthodontist would find an angry young man that looked vaguely like him in the waiting room, but all that would wait.

Aunt Krystal and Lisa-in-Phoenix came to Larch for graduation. Stephanya tried to talk Krystal into being a BestU distributor, plying her with samples from their CBD line, but Krystal said she had some other things in the works, which we thought it best not to ask about. Lisa stayed late, telling us stories about Heidi in high school, which were even more wildly irresponsible than I'd imagined. Bravo for staying true to yourself, Mom.

Malcolm asked a lot of good questions before he agreed to let Carna come to St. Dismas with me and Lock. He even looked into the local high school, which was full of smart, jaded professors' kids, had a huge makerspace wing, and offered a class called "Wilderness Survival Practicum." It was perfect place for her to start over. To me he said, "I know what Carna wants, but I can't tell what you want. You don't need to do this, Drew. Steph and I will make sure she's okay here."

I patted him on the arm. "I'll send her back if she gets too bitchy."

He still doesn't know exactly what happened. He will never ask. Not because he doesn't care or he's not curious. But because he trusts us. He doesn't trust us not to lie to him (or anybody else), but he trusts that we're doing it for honest reasons. And that, from Malcolm Krause, is the same as love.

# CHAPTER SEVENTY-FIVE

t took us most of a weekend to take down the shed. The new owners didn't want it, and we didn't like the idea of it standing there till it fell apart someday. The undoing felt good.

Carna and I tossed the siding in a dumpster at one of the new construction sites while Lock kept lookout in a ninja costume, which was really a black hoodie and Carna's old leggings. We stacked the two-by-fours of the frame for Malcolm, who had been hired by the Petersons to build a new ice house that "looked rustic but not quite as rustic as yours."

Lock worked hard without complaining, the baby already melting out of his cheeks. He liked feeling useful. "Whoa, he's a little worker bee," Audrey said when she stopped to say goodbye before heading to St. Paul for freshman orientation.

"Sometimes."

Darden was already gone, loving his daily workouts with the new team. He had quietly returned the infinity heart necklace he'd gotten me for my birthday when he found out I was now the head of a small household and moving to upstate New York. He bought me a new coffee maker (doesn't need a review but it's actually really nice) instead. "It seems like you're going to need it," he'd said, and I almost loved him for it. Maybe we'd stay in touch.

When Lock noticed Audrey, he dropped the end of a board on Carna's foot. "Audrey, you *have* to see the skull we found. It looks like a alien baby. Carna says it's only a possum but I don't think so. It was really smelly so I put it in the dishwasher."

"Wait. What?" I said.

When the ground was clear, and the pill bugs had busied out of our way, we dug a hole a few feet deep. The soil was rich and black and healthy under the surface.

Carna had wanted a hazelnut tree. She said Mom would think it was funny. Lock wanted a clementine tree and was disappointed when I said they wouldn't grow here. We got a willow instead.

"Because it's flexible," I said.

"Because it looks like Mom's hair," Lock said, holding the tag from the branch.

"Because it's shady," Carna said.

We untangled the root ball so it could spread out. I held the tree upright in the hole while Lock and Carna packed loose dirt around it. We mixed ashes among the roots.

Lachlan dragged the hose over, watering his shoes along the way. "Let's plant one of these at the new place, too," he said, running the water up and down the narrow trunk.

"I don't think you can plant a tree in student housing."

"We could find a spot," he said, confident. "We'll do it in secret." I laughed, but knew we would. "Except if that one could be clementines that would be good."

We watched the water sink into the ground while Carna ticked off

all the 5-star products we'd put in our epic garage sale. I noticed Lock
looking back and forth between Carn's arm and mine.

This again.

"How 'bout when I'm twelve?" he suggested.

"Nope."

"Thirteen?"

"How about eighteen, like I told you a million times."

"Carna was only fifteen!"

"Carna wasn't *supposed* to. They're permanent, Lock."

"I *know* they're permnanant." His stomp flecked mud on the new
tree.

"What would you wanna get, bud?" Carn asked, in her new role
as mediator.

He looked at her, shocked, then at me. I shrugged my shoulders,
wondering the same thing. Groot? Alien baby skull and crossbones?
A heart with "Ms. Emily" inside? What tattoo would an almost third
grader think he'd want forever? Lock focused on the water, looking
suddenly like he might cry.

"Lachlan?"

Finally he said softly, "Same as you guys."

My hand went to my wrist, to the healing black lines. To anyone
else, the shape looked abstract, like the logo of some company that
made yoga tights. But that's not it, not us.

Carna had worked it out on my whiteboard while she was supposed to be writing our packing list. She'd disappeared for the
afternoon and come back with her arm wrapped, the empty set trans-
formed into a knot of initials: DH CH LH. It looked as though they had
been there together all along.

I turned her right around and went back for mine.

I wrapped my arms around Lock and lifted him from the ground, the hose trailing cold water over our legs. Carn closed herself tight around us both.

"Sixteen," I said. "On your birthday, if you still want to."

"I will," he said. "I always will."

God, I hope it's true.

# Some Major Gratitude and a Minor Anecdote

In this book, Drew does nearly everything herself, without much help. I am not Drew. I am lucky to have a lot of help. I'm especially thankful to the following for theirs:

Tina Dubois (★★★★★, **would 100 percent hide a body for her authors**) is who you want in an agent—smart, practical, and kind in the right measures. She heard this story at the "but what if those children were hiding their parents in the boxcar all along" stage and said, "Tell me more."

Andrew Karre (★★★★★, **would drive his car over a frozen river to Wisconsin for "research"**) is like an editorial Captain Chad West, asking all the right (at times confounding, always confoundingly spot-on) questions a book needs answers to.

Julie Strauss-Gabel, Anna Booth, Natalie Vielkind, Melissa Faulner, Rob Farren, Anne Heausler, Kristin Boyle, Liz Montoya Vaughn, and their colleagues at Dutton and Penguin Random House (★★★★★, **publishing mic-droppers**) are simultaneously scrupulous readers and expansive thinkers, and are committed to filling libraries with the wildest and most wonderful ideas, which if you think about it, is the best side hustle there is.

From CAA, Abby Okin, Claire Nozieres, Zoe Willis, and Randie Adler (★★★★★, **agents extraordinaire**) expertly look out for me in all sorts of ways in all sorts of places, and ensure the Undersigned Always Understands What She Is Undersigning.

Bruce Manning carefully answered all my legal questions about guardianship, and in return I took enormous liberties with his advice such that he may hold me in contempt. E. K. Johnston shared insights into human decomposition, including stuff about exploding eyeballs that did not make it into this book because I'm not that kind of writer; and rodents eating frozen people, which did, because I am. Nicole Kronzer was a thoughtful and speedy reader and lent her Wisconsin bona fides to ensure all the cheese curds were in a squeaky row. (★★★★, with friends like these, who needs Wikipedia)

Kris Causton reads for me, cheers for me, inspires me, and is my first, best example of sisterhood. I am lucky to have added some brothers along the way. Among their other gifts, Jeff, Mark, and Phil taught me to drive a side-by-side and shoot crockery, sketched tattoos for me, and forged documents, respectively. (★★★★, put the bling in siblings)

Lee Zukor just does one thing for me over and over and over again, and will always be my top celebrity crush. Eli and Davie are my favorite whiteboarders of all, and deserve all the stars in the sky. (★★★★★★★★★★★★★★★★★★★★★)

## THE MINOR ANECDOTE

The day we brought my daughter home from the hospital, newly hatched, we snapped in the bucket-carrier holding the baby, then helped her brother buckle into his car seat. Once everyone was settled, Eli looked to Davie, satisfied, and announced, "Now we're da family."

He was barely three, and really didn't know that girl from a hole in the wall, but still, there it was, a declaration of interdependence: Now we're da family. We have rehashed and remixed his statement over nearly eighteen years, and it pops up every time we find ourselves together after time apart. It felt hopeful then; it feels like the very ground we stand on now.

I don't mean to suggest that a "family" requires any particular number of children or that the way people define their families should be one way or another. Only that there is something peculiar about the way siblings shape our worlds that's interesting and important and invaluable to me.

So lad and lass, remember this someday: The very best thing we can ever leave you is each other.

And if you get matching tattoos, I'd like to approve them first.